RECKLESS TOMORROW

Since the death of her husband whilst on their honeymoon three years ago, Karen Westbury had existed in a living nightmare. Nothing, and nobody, had been able to make her forget the horrific moment which had henceforth made her life seem worthless. It was not unusual then to see Karen on her own, walking across the moors, but to Chris Halliday it was like a dream. Staying together for safety when the fog set in made Chris want to stay with Karen forever and to forget the pain which he too had suffered in the past. But would he ever be able to convince Karen that tomorrow did matter, and that there was a future for her, and him . . .

RECKLESS TOMORROW

Kay Winchester

ATLANTIC LARGE PRINT

Chivers Press, Bath, England.
Curley Publishing, Inc.,
South Yarmouth, Mass., USA.

Library of Congress Cataloging-in-Publication Data

Winchester, Kay.
  Reckless tomorrow / Kay Winchester.
    p. cm.—(Atlantic large print)
  ISBN 0–7927–0408–8 (lg. print)
  1. Large type books. I. Title.
[PR6073.I476R4 1991]
823′.914—dc20

90–42455
CIP

British Library Cataloguing in Publication Data

Winchester, Kay *1913–*
  Reckless tomorrow.
  Rn: Emily Kathleen Walker   I. Title
  823.914 [F]

  ISBN 0–7451–9945–3
  ISBN 0–7451–9957–7 pbk

This Large Print edition is published by Chivers Press, England, and
Curley Publishing, Inc, U.S.A. 1991

Published by arrangement with the author

U.K. Hardback ISBN 0 7451 9945 3
U.K. Softback ISBN 0 7451 9957 7
U.S.A. Softback ISBN 0 7927 0408 8

RECKLESS TOMORROW

CHAPTER ONE

'We're lost!'

Her lips closed over the words, and her companion slid a quick sideways glance at her. Her voice had shaken a little and he knew she was nearly at the end of her tether.

'Oh, well, I wouldn't say that,' he began, and tried to manage a laugh. Through the little tendrils of mist swirling round her face, her blue-grey eyes sought his, and again his heart lurched.

'Why are you looking at me like that?' she gasped.

'I've known you just half an hour,' he said, soberly, 'and I'm still a bit shaken, because you know, you're quite incredibly beautiful. That, and being lost on this damned moor, and running into you, and the fog on top of it, makes a chap wonder if it is real after all, or whether he's fallen and knocked himself out, or got drunk or something.'

'Oh, that!' she said. 'I'm used to being told that. I thought perhaps you'd suddenly realized some other danger we were in, and were afraid to tell me. We really *are* lost, aren't we?'

'Yes, I'm afraid we are,' he admitted, reluctantly. 'Still, other people have been lost, hiking, and got found again.'

1

'How?'

'Well, look here, I can't find an answer to that one right away. I tell you what, though. We ought to introduce ourselves. We're going to be together quite a bit, and it's silly not to even know each other's names, isn't it?'

She agreed.

'I'm Chris Halliday.' He grinned encouragingly at her, and waited.

'Oh, why not? I'm Karen Westbury.'

'*Miss* Karen Westbury?'

Her smile vanished. It was an entrancing smile, and he was sorry that it went. It had begun in her eyes, and travelled, slowly, luxuriously over her creamy-white face, with its delicate rose-tinted cheeks, and fled across the full red mouth, making deep clefts appear on either side. A lovely face, a face to be studied untiringly.

'What did I say?' he demanded.

They trudged forward into the mist, occasionally stumbling over tufts in the rough moorland, now peering into thick mist, now looking about freely in a patch where the mist had thinned out to almost nothing. But always, there was that sense of aloneness, accentuated by the far-off cries of moorland sheep, cries so far away and so faint that they were like ghost voices in the distance.

Karen lifted her little round chin, as though making a decision. 'Don't repeat your question, Chris. Let's just be Chris and

2

Karen for this day, and when it ends, well, we'll see.'

'Oh, the brush-off,' he said, grinning. 'Now, lady, don't get ideas...'

Then she did smile. 'Oh, you understood better than I thought! Then that's all right!'

She came a little closer to him, as if deciding to accept without question the companionship he offered her, because of their predicament, and because his half-laughing protest had convinced her that she need have no fear of him.

'What's all right?' he thrust.

'Look, Chris, don't mind me,' she said, in a new voice, a voice warm and full of confidences. 'I'm the sort of girl who dashes away from what looks like being a very close friendship. I've learnt, by bitter experience, that you can't let yourself be misled into thinking there's something rather nice round the corner when someone starts getting interested in you.'

'And you think I'm not?'

'Well, not now,' she said, still smiling. 'I think you just want us to be matey for this day, because we're likely to be in further trouble before long, and then we can forget all about each other. Right?'

'Well, I don't know about that,' he protested slowly, yet he knew that was just what he had been wanting a moment ago. 'Well, all right, then,' he capitulated,

3

accepting the olive branch, but trying to see, at the same time, if there were any sort of ring on her fourth finger. 'Let's clinch it, then, by having some grub. Perhaps this mist'll lift, by the time we've finished.'

'I haven't got any more left,' Karen said.

'Share mine.'

He got out of his knapsack a large packet of sandwiches and a package of biscuits. 'Jolly good thing I had lunch at the "Bull and Bear" after all,' he said, happily, as she squatted beside him on a large flat stone. 'I often do that. How many times have you been over the moors before?'

'Never.'

'What, d'you mean to say you came on your own for the first time?'

'I always go about on my own,' she said quietly.

He screwed up his eyes and regarded her, munching all the while. 'Look, I've already been told it's none of my business but if *I* were one of the men in your family, I wouldn't allow you about alone, unprotected. Look at you now! I might be a wolf!'

'But you're not,' she said calmly.

'Have you any family?' he pressed.

'There are people,' Karen said, evasively, 'who would be quite annoyed to know that I was lost on the moors through my own silly fault, but I like to feel I'm really grown-up, and not just over twenty-one and not doing anything about it.'

'That tells me nothing,' Chris grinned.

'Well, if you want a matey conversation, how about letting up about yourself?' she retorted. 'I'm not inquisitive, but after all, it's a point of view, isn't it?'

'All right. I'm twenty-six. No family. No ties. No job. No fixed address. A happy, healthy wanderer.'

'I don't believe it.'

'It's true!' he grinned, yet she could see he was telling the truth. There was an element about him which warned her off asking any further questions, too, that left her in no doubt.

'Then, Chris, I envy you. That's what I've always wanted but never been able to get.'

'Freedom?' He shrugged. 'It isn't so easy for a girl as a man, admittedly, but if you want it that badly, all you have to do is take it, that is if you really haven't any ties.'

'I've one tie,' she said, quietly. 'My need for money. I can't live without money, and lots of it. Just don't seem to be able to get along otherwise.'

He silently agreed. While he wore the oldest and shabbiest slacks over his long, tanned limbs, and a faded and rather worn shirt and lumber jacket, she had the most beautiful tweeds he had seen for a long time. Superbly cut, with an expensive silk shirt, fine woollen stockings and near-new brogues.

Over her reddish-brown hair was a smart felt pull-on, and her raincoat was new and good.

'I'd like to see you in a cotton skirt—gypsy clothes—with your hair all loose,' he said, suddenly. 'Karen, for heaven's sake, hasn't an artist seen you yet? You'd make a wonderful picture!'

Again the smile faded. She looked round, nervously, at the engulfing mist. 'We'd better get along,' she said, with an air of finality.

'H'm, the brush-off again,' he grinned. 'Oh, Lord, I suppose you're an artist's model, or something. I hadn't thought of that!'

Her eyes glinted angrily for a moment, then she softened. 'You hadn't thought of that? Hadn't you? Why hadn't you, Chris?'

'Because you don't look like a model, in yourself, I mean,' he said, slowly, packing up their sandwich wrappings and strapping on his knapsack again. 'Come on, let's go.'

They trudged in silence, always with the mist around them, and never getting anywhere.

'How did we ever meet in this?' Chris said, once, and Karen said, softly, and in a preoccupied voice, 'I'm glad we did, Chris. I'd have hated being alone.'

He didn't answer. As the hours slowly passed, she got tired, and then they both sat down, for it occurred to both that it was a wasted effort. They were getting nowhere. They found a bit of rag clinging to a fence,

6

and it looked like a piece they had seen on a fence an hour ago. Chris shouted at intervals. Karen sat, taut and still, saying nothing, and he wanted to pierce her closed look, and find out who was waiting for her at home, and he knew he had no right to. The light faded, and at last he stopped pacing and shouting, and sat by her, defeated.

'What happens to people who stay out on the moors all night?' she asked, in a small, little-girl voice.

'They catch a nasty cold and have to stay in bed for three days,' he grinned, trying to be cheerful and failing dismally. 'I suppose you want to die in a blaze of glory and get your name in the papers?'

'You know, I wouldn't care much,' she said, suddenly.

He stared. 'Oh, come off your foot, Karen!'

'It's true, Chris. Oh, I don't say I'd like the *dying* bit. I meant I wouldn't mind if my life had to come to an end now, to-night. I've had everything. It would be tidier, I suppose, if I did die now. I mean, I know that nothing'll happen to me to improve on what has happened.'

'Good grief, what utter rot! How do you know what nice things'll happen to you in the future?'

'No one can expect to have it all the time Chris. I've had just about as much packed

7

into my life as anyone can hope to have. In the slang, I've had it! Now I'm just marking time, and I don't care.'

He was shocked beyond words. She was serious, of that he had no doubt. Yet there was no hardness in her face, no bitterness in her voice. There was, indeed, a soft look in her eyes—a remembering look—which added to the loveliness, if that were possible. He felt a lump come into his throat.

'It's the moor that does it, of course,' he growled, and got up, digging his hands deep into his trouser pockets. 'I almost started saying the same thing. I could say it, come to think of it. I don't belong to anyone. No one'd care a damn if I never appeared again, and someone found my skeleton years hence. I wonder how many blokes there are in my position? Just think, no one even knows I came out for the day. No one'd miss me because I don't work for anyone. I say, I wish you hadn't started this, Karen. It's a frightening thought.'

He started shouting again. 'Shout with me, old girl. Life may not hold overmuch at this moment, but I'm bothered if I'm going to be a corpse out here in this rotten mist. Come on, now, expand your lungs and let go!'

She sat and watched him in silence. 'Why fight, Chris, if there's nothing left to fight for?'

He stopped shouting and stared down at

her. 'Because I'm *me*, that's why. There was once a girl ... well, it's not a very original, nor a very pretty story. It's just that she meant, well, just about everything to me. And I meant a lot to her. Why not? I was lousy with money just then. Wouldn't think it, to look at me, would you? Well, I lost it, never mind how.' His lean, good-humoured face hardened beyond recognition. 'And I lost her. All right, fellows have lost girls before, but to me, the sky fell in. The world stopped. It's still like that. I don't like family firesides nor steady jobs because they remind me of what might have been. I spend all my energy and brains (and believe me it needs energy and brains) to avoid civilization and exist on nothing. *But*, Karen Westbury, that doesn't mean I'm going to die of exposure on this damned moor to-night. Hallooo!'

'Halloo! Where are you?'

His expression was ludicrous. Into the startled silence that followed the strange voice, Karen scrambled to her feet, and hung on to his arm.

The voice called again, nearer this time. They both shouted, and in less than no time, a stocky, heavily-built man with a great, lumbering dog, appeared out of the mist and shadows, and was taking them back to his farm.

'Heard voices, and Jack here was off like a shot,' the man said. 'Lucky I found you both.

9

Mist won't lift to-night.'

Karen started to giggle.

'Shut up,' Chris said, fiercely, and shook her a little. 'She's overwrought,' he explained.

The farmer nodded. 'Best come back with me for the night and have some food. A night's rest and you'll be all right.'

'We thought we were going to die out there,' Karen gasped.

'Aye, it has been known,' the farmer said, without a flicker of emotion, and that sobered her.

'Where's the nearest railway station?' she wanted to know. 'We must get back to-night.'

'Close on six miles the other way,' the farmer said. 'Need a conveyance, and I can't spare one to-night. Best wait 'till morning. We've plenty of room, and plenty of food.'

It was pitch dark before they descended into the tree-filled hollow where the farm lay. Its brightly lit windows looked inviting. The farmer took them into a big, stone-flagged kitchen where an inviting hot meal was being dished up.

'Got two more for supper, Martha,' he said, to a buxom woman bending over the fire.

There were other people already sitting at table. Farm hands, women servants, and a young man about twenty-two whom the farmer said was his only son. He goggled at

10

Karen as she took her hat off and patted her glorious hair. It was piled high in complicated waves and curls, and pressed into position by three large black combs. Chris thought it unusual and becoming; a style that frankly suited her.

'Come and sit by the fire, my dear,' the farmer's wife said. 'You and your husband'll know better'n to stay too long on the moor next time, I'll be bound. Mists are treacherous, this time o' year.'

Karen glanced at Chris. He stood staring at her, like a man transfixed. He began to say something, something about their not being married, when he saw she wore a wedding-ring after all.

Karen's glance wavered uncertainly between Chris and the goggling young man at the table, then she turned to the farmer's wife and said, 'Yes, my husband and I won't go on the moors again in a hurry.'

CHAPTER TWO

The farmer and his wife did most of the talking, which was as well. Chris was scared out of his life that the women—the farmer's wife and her sister, the equally garrulous woman who had helped her serve the food—would start asking how long they had

11

been married, whether they had any children, and where they lived. He had no idea what had prompted Karen to tell that outrageous lie, or how she proposed to get out of it when bedtime came, and they were shown to their room. Chris was conscious of being deadly tired. He studied Karen and decided she was beginning to droop too.

Karen quietly ate her food, nodding at the farmer and his womenfolk as if she hung on their words, and each time a lull looked like occurring in the conversation, she sleepily put another cogent question which started them off on another flood of reminiscences and gossip. They liked talking, and had friendly natures.

There had been fifteen births and deaths in as many years, it seemed. There had been more bad crops than good. The farmland was poor and the labour question disturbing. The prospects were bad, and they considered it hardly worth while going on. Chris, with brief and embracing glances round the kitchen, and from what little he had seen of the farm buildings as they passed through to the house, was inclined to think that this was a wicked fabrication, that the whole outfit struck him as being extremely prosperous, and that the womenfolk probably did a lot in their innocent way to hide the true state of affairs from the not-so-shrewd, and the merely inquisitive.

12

After supper, the farmer's wife said, 'Well, now, we've got no mending to do to-night. What do you say to a bit of a set in the parlour and a mite of music? D'you feel like singing to-night, Emma? (My sister sings in the village concerts, you know).'

Chris's heart sank, but Karen, quite unconcernedly, stepped in and saved the situation.

'I do hope you won't think me ill-mannered or anything,' she said, with a pretty air of apology, 'but we've had a tiring and rather upsetting day on the moor, and I would so like to go to bed. If you're sure it won't upset the household arrangements, putting us up for the night and all that, then I would like to go upstairs.'

Chris fancied the farmer's wife looked a trifle put out. He caught a glimpse, too, of the son; the half-boy, half-man, who had been ogling Karen so disgustingly ever since they had arrived. There was an almost eager expression on his face and he listened eagerly when the subject of the rooms were discussed by his mother and aunt. It seemed to be a question of the third back bedroom or one of the attics.

'Oh, the attic, if you please,' Karen murmured. 'I would like that best. How about you, Chris?'

Chris didn't follow, and stared blankly at her.

'It's none so comfortable,' the farmer's wife said. 'Best have the third back.'

But Karen stuck firmly to the attic idea. 'I've got claustrophobia,' she said.

'My wife means she doesn't like to feel hemmed in,' Chris explained hurriedly. 'I'd be grateful if you'd pander to her whim about the attics. I shan't get any sleep if you don't.'

They were taken up to the first floor, and then through a door and up a steep and extremely narrow staircase which creaked. Another door opened at the top, revealing in the lamplight a small bare bedroom, and a door which led into another and smaller apartment. The farmer's wife locked the inner door, and took the key away, explaining that the apples were kept in there, and not to be afeared of spiders and such which sometimes crawled under the door from the apple barrels. Karen shuddered, but thanked her nevertheless, and produced her shut look, which should have told the farmer's wife that she wanted to be left for the night, but which didn't and it was ten minutes before they were finally left alone.

Chris said, in exasperation. 'What's the idea of picking the attics and saying we're married? Now look where we are! Stuck at the top of the house, with no hope whatever of my getting out. Don't tell me you want me to spend the night in your room?'

'Oh, no,' Karen said, calmly. She went to

14

the door, and looked down the stairs. The bottom door closed softly. 'It's that son of theirs. I think he's going to be a nuisance.'

'Yes, I noticed the little blighter staring, but I'll take care of him.' Chris said. 'Just the same, you didn't have to say we were married, did you?'

'I'm sorry you find the idea so obnoxious,' she grinned. 'Yes, I did have to say just that, or we'd have been put in separate rooms, probably quite a long way apart, and there'd have been no sleep for me.'

Chris shrugged elaborately. 'I just don't follow you. How you think you're going to manage to get any sleep up here beats me.' He sat on the edge of the bed and tested it. 'Flock!' he said, disgustedly.

'It's good of you to be so concerned about my bed, Chris, but I can attend to that myself. You're going to sleep in there.'

'In where?' he demanded.

'In there. Among the apples. That's why I chose the attic. They said "attics"— plural—so I decided that was the only way out. Come on, you can have some of my bed spread on the floor in there, so you won't be so badly off. And keep an ear cocked in case sonny-boy comes up to see if we're all right.'

'Well, what's wrong with fastening that door? And how are we to get the apple loft open, since madame took the key away with her! Cheek, thinking we're going to pinch

15

their apples!'

'Well, I bet you would; you look the type,' Karen smiled.

He grinned. 'I might have, at that. I love russets.'

Karen took a pin out of her hair and tinkered with the lock, while Chris leaned against the door and watched her.

'I don't want to discourage you,' he said, some minutes later, 'but it's my belief—only my belief, mind you—that the lock's unpickable, on account of its being a trifle rusty. Still, you have fun, and meanwhile I'll lie on the bed and get some rest.'

'You're not to go to sleep, Chris. Come and help me, here.'

He tried, and succeeded only in breaking the hairpin.

'It isn't any use, Karen. We look like being stuck here for the night,' he said at last.

'Well, you'll have to sit on the stairs, and I'll bolt my door on you,' Karen said, with finality.

'I'm damned if I'm going to spend the night on those wooden stairs!' he exploded.

There was a taut little silence. Then he said, wearily, 'Oh, no, don't say you're going to burst into tears! That I couldn't stand—I'm just too tired. All right, I tell you what I'll do. I'll creep downstairs and see if I can find a tool to get that lock off. Serve 'em right for not trusting us with their blinking

16

apples. Bolt the door on the inside, and don't open it until I knock softly. See?'

She nodded.

'You know, I think you're more beautiful up here in this lamplight than out on the moor,' he breathed. Then, struck by a sudden thought, 'Karen, where's your husband? How comes it you've got a wedding ring on, and you're careering about like this all on your own?'

'I'm a widow,' she said, quietly. 'Hadn't you better go and find that tool, Chris?'

She bolted the door behind him, and after his quiet movements on the stairs had died away, she wandered round the bare little room, almost unseeingly. There was a faded rose and holly wallpaper on the walls, and in some places it was peeling. One of the spiders they had been warned about, scuttled under a crack under the wainscot. Karen shuddered. Not so much because of the spider, but because in situations like these she was so conscious of her aloneness. She used that word to herself rather than loneliness, because there was a distinct difference. She didn't feel lonely. It wasn't company—any company—that she wanted. It was just Blaize. It was three years now. Three years of being frozen, outside and in. Never letting up for one minute. Not exactly preventing herself from thinking of him, but thinking of him dispassionately, as if it were someone else's husband who had lain there, all broken and bleeding, among the wreckage of that train. Someone else's husband she had lain there staring at, physically dead while her mind worked. Physically dead for that short time, because although she had wanted to move, she couldn't.

'Give me a cigarette, sweetheart,' he had murmured, his face curiously still, although he must have been wracked with pain. 'A cigarette.'

She found herself in the farmhouse attic, shaking her head in distress, as she had then, because she couldn't make her hands move to get a cigarette out for him, though she could see her handbag lying only a short way away.

Her throat ached. 'Blaize! Blaize!' she heard herself murmuring, through stiff lips. Then, by custom, the old feeling surged over her. I mustn't give way. I mustn't think. I mustn't feel, not anything. Just shut down a curtain. Forget. Forget...

There was a sound at the door. Without thinking, she went over and drew the bolt.

'Chris!' she said, and was conscious of thankfulness in her tone.

It wasn't Chris who stood there, smiling foolishly at her. It was the farmer's son. It struck her that he wasn't very mature; a little simple, though not exactly wanting.

'He ain't here, is he?' the young man murmured. 'I see him go down-away.'

He had a thick, rather purring voice, sly. Triumphant at his own cleverness, as a schoolboy might be, after prolonged thinking effort, and having reached the conclusion he had hoped for.

Nausea overcame her. There had been so many similar situations, in different settings perhaps, but essentially just like this, since Blaize had died. She felt she didn't want to have to fight another single battle for herself. Rage surged up in her for a second, at the thought that she couldn't go through life without having to fight, and that the only solution—acquiring a permanent protector—was as obnoxious to her as the thought of facing these situations alone. There could never be another Blaize. She wasn't going to insult his memory by half-measures for selfish reasons. She glanced behind her to the window. It was small, high up. The young man gradually edging in the doorway followed her glance, and chuckled. ''Tis no way of getting out,' he told her, grinning. ''Tis too high. And I won't let you, neether.'

He put out a big clumsy hand, and grabbed her arm, jerking her towards him, and insinuating himself further in the doorway with one movement. Gradually he pushed the door to behind him, slowly, tantalizingly, and still holding her, easily, despite her struggles to get away.

Suddenly Karen stopped struggling, and

smiled. 'All right,' she said, shrugging.

The young man was at once sullen, suspicious, caught off his guard. He let her arm go, and came towards her, just as she doubled her fist and caught him in the eye. It wasn't a heavy blow. He had seen it coming, and moved back a little, but it enraged him. He let out an animal roar, and lunged towards her.

Then he swung round, or so it seemed to her, and Chris was there, punching out and ducking. In a matter of minutes, Chris was down, and dodging to avoid the young man's boot savagely kicking out at him, and then the young man was down, and Chris picked up the other's feet, and lugged him down the attic stairs. Karen heard Chris grunt as he shut the bottom door on him, and fasten it. Then he came back again, and bolted the top door.

As he stooped to pick up the tools he had dropped, Karen saw the blood, now smeared over his face. She cried out. He looked up at her from the floor, and said, curtly, 'Get me a cigarette, I need one.'

Something snapped in her. She was on the bed, sobbing, her whole body shaking. Chris stood up and went over to her. 'What's all that about? Blood upset you? Pull yourself together, Karen, for heaven's sake. D'you want to wake the whole house up?'

'It's Blaize! Blaize! Oh, I can't bear it! I

20

can't reach them! My hands won't work, darling! I can't get them. They're too far away! I can't move!'

Chris frowned and lay the tools down again. In the mirror he searched his face, and wiped it clean with his handkerchief dipped in the water jug. There was an abrasion that wouldn't stop bleeding. He held the handkerchief to his forehead, and went and sat down beside her. Shaking her shoulder a little, he said, 'Look, Karen, look, you'll make yourself ill. Here, have a good cry on my shoulder if you must, but not like that! Listen to me!'

She made the required effort, and was presently quiet, exhausted, against him. She peered at up him, and saw that the blood was gone.

'Better?' he asked, compassion in his tone.

She nodded.

'Was it that swine? What did he do to frighten you like that?'

'He didn't do anything. It wasn't him at all. He'd only just got in the doorway when you came. I tried to hit out at him but he stepped back. It made him mad. No, it wasn't him.'

'What was it, then?' He was insistent.

'Oh, please, Chris, I don't want to talk now. I just want to be alone. I want to go to bed. Get the door open, can you? Did you find any tools?'

'Yes. Right, I'll do that,' he said, and got up and left her. She lay flat on her back, listening to him unscrewing the lock. In what seemed a very short time, the door swung open, and he turned round to her with satisfaction. 'Put your chair against this side of the door, and don't unbolt the other one, Karen.'

'You'd better have some bedding,' she said, exhaustedly. 'Is it very awful in there?'

'Not very inviting,' he told her. 'But it doesn't matter.'

She helped him spread a few blankets on the ground. They were threadbare and none too clean, and she wrinkled her nose in distaste. She was deathly pale, and her eyes were pink-rimmed. There was a defenceless air about her now, which alarmed and touched him.

'You going to be all right now, Karen?' he asked, awkwardly.

She nodded.

'Karen, what did you mean by your hands not working?'

'Please, Chris!' she protested.

'All right,' he shrugged. 'Good night.'

He pulled the door to, on his side, and waited to hear her arrange the chair on her side. She took her jacket off, and shook down her glorious hair. It was waist length, and ought to have been brushed, but she had nothing beyond a small handbag comb with her. She shook it back tiredly, and put out the light. With difficulty she got the window open, and leaned out. All around were the sloping leaded roofs of the farmhouse. Beyond was nothing but the pearly mist. It seemed to creep up to the windows and poke out long, writhing fingers to try and touch her. She felt trapped. She fought back the feeling and told herself that the sensible thing to do would be to take her skirt and shoes off and get into bed. Sleep would soon come. But the farmer's son was still at the foot of the stairs, on the other side of the door below. Suppose he came up again? That thought drove sleep far off. She felt suddenly more wide awake than she had been for hours. An urge to get away from this place came over her, and it took all her strength to keep her from giving way to it.

She could not judge what time it was. Hours later, it seemed, a clock downstairs chimed three, and then the half hour. She fancied she heard a train whistle, and when she was deciding she couldn't bear the silence and loneliness any longer, she heard Chris struggling with the window in the apple loft, and a tinkle of broken glass as it shot up too quickly and jammed.

'Chris,' she called, softly, and went and took the chair away from the door.

'What's up, Karen? Anything wrong?' He was at the door at once.

'Chris, I—Oh, I can't sleep. I want to talk. D'you mind? I—I think I want to talk about—about Blaize.'

.

CHAPTER THREE

Dawn found Chris standing at the window of the apple loft. The door was again closed between the two rooms. Karen was sleeping at last. But the night was over for him. On thinking over what had passed in the room next to his, he found himself deciding that he had been no help whatever, and that he was, in fact, all sorts of a fool. The only consolation he had was that he was perhaps the best sort of listener she had needed, to talk to just then. All she had wanted was to get out of her system the reactions of that old and ghastly accident; reactions she should have got out of her system long ago. He couldn't imagine what the doctors had been doing, to let her get out of hospital in that state. She had been, in his opinion, steadily killing herself for three years. He hoped this night would help her to get on her feet again.

'We were on honeymoon,' she had started off. Her voice, normally husky-sweet, had taken on a quality which reminded him of a lost child. A lost and frightened child. 'We were coming back. We'd been away three

24

weeks. Three perfect weeks. To St. Miriam's Bay. D'you know St. Miriam's Bay, Chris?'

He had said, watching her queerly in the lamplight, that he didn't know St. Miriam's Bay, but he felt dimly that she didn't really want to know if he knew the place, and wouldn't have cared if he had. She was curled up on the bed, not at ease, but tautly, her hands clasping her knees, the knuckles of her hands white through the tanned skin. Only the backs of her hands were tanned, through constant exposure on weekend hikes, he supposed. It was queer. Her face wasn't tanned, but freckled, he noticed, over the bridge of her nose. And her hair, her glorious hair, swung down to her waist, a cloak of flame behind her.

'Blaize was talking to me when it happened. The train smash, I mean. Did I tell you it was a train smash, Chris? I think I did. When I was talking about the cigarettes, I mean?'

He assured her that she hadn't mentioned it.

'Our train ran through an oncoming one. Telescoped, I think they call it. Blaize was lying there, half lying, half kneeling, like you were to-night, and he kept asking for cigarettes. He had blood all over his face...'

She rocked herself, with her head in her hands, while he stood by helplessly. The reason for that curious outburst earlier to-night was clear to him now, as he watched her. 'I couldn't move to get them,' she moaned. 'I couldn't move. My hands wouldn't work.'

He moved over and lifted her into his arms, rocking her softly, and not saying anything. She clung to him, without knowing, he thought, to whom she was clinging. 'I couldn't ever get them. I never gave him a cigarette, and he *wanted* one.'

He remembered a similar time in his own life, when he had badly wanted a cigarette and had only a crushed and empty packet in his pocket. The shops were closed, the burnt-out shell of his factory was staring at him from across the way, like a creature with blind eyes, and Barbara's telegram—her farewell telegram—was in his pocket.

'One does need a cigarette, under such circumstances,' he found himself murmuring. 'But when the need goes, it doesn't matter.'

'He didn't die,' she sobbed. 'He didn't die. They took him to hospital, and I went to another hospital. There were so many people needing treatment. No one knew who was who. It was awful. And he didn't die.'

'D'you really want to go over all that again, Karen?' he was moved to ask her, with infinite tenderness.

'Yes, let me tell you! He didn't die. He lay there in awful pain and I couldn't find him and he kept asking for me. Then I found him

26

and they said he was going to live, and get better. He never believed them. He didn't want to live, he kept saying. We'd been so happy. For two years we'd been engaged, and then we were married three weeks. I can stretch those weeks to mean a lifetime, then I can make them dwindle so they only feel like three hours. That's when I feel cheated and bitter. But when they stretch and stretch, I feel rich. As if I've had everything, and it's pointless to go on living. Like last night on the moor. Like to-night, when that boy came up and was going to be a nuisance, and I didn't want to fight any more. He thought I was going to escape out of the window, but I wasn't meaning to. I was going to jump out of the window. Only I can see now that it wouldn't have worked. There are sloping roofs beneath. It's no use.'

He let her ramble and cry, and he hoped she'd cry herself to sleep, but she didn't. She rallied a little and said surprisingly, 'Have you any idea what fiends doctors and nurses can be? They try to hang on to the last little flicker of life, when someone's *praying* to die. Praying to die!'

'No, Karen, no, you mustn't talk like that!' he said, sharply, his own throat aching. 'No, I say. You've got to try and sleep.'

'What for?' she jeered, in a savage whisper. 'To dream? To have nightmares? Do you know that Blaize hung on to life for months,

months after the accident, because they wanted him to live. To be a surgical miracle. He would have been a cripple. *If* you had seen my Blaize, you would have known what I mean. He was perfect. Perfect. He was big and strong and fine. He swam and dived and ... he was so handsome. And good. And kind.'

She was crying again. And so it went on, for the best part of three hours. Chris left her at last, worn out and asleep, and felt that he had looked into a section of two people's lives and had had no right to. He felt he knew the dead Blaize, from the picture she had painted of him, and the things she had told him they did, and thought and said. Blaize Westbury should never have died. Chris himself didn't believe in perfection, and he thought privately that the fact that Karen and Blaize had never quarrelled was just a bit of luck, especially for her to look back on now. Still he had seemed the perfect partner for Karen, and a good chap in himself. But it was the waste, the utter waste of young life and perfect health that Chris deplored. That, and the stemming of what appeared to be a perfection of love and devotion between Karen and Blaize. He thought of Barbara. Barbara couldn't really love anyone. He saw that now. She hadn't got it in her. The love had been all on his side, and come to think of it, it couldn't have been the real thing, or it wouldn't have died when she left him, leaving him a wastrel. No good to anyone. An adventurer so deeply bitten with the wanderlust that he couldn't rest for longer than a night.

But what of Karen? What would she do now? What could she do? Jumbled details of her life had slipped out while she was telling him of the accident. There was some sort of estate, which had belonged to Blaize Westbury's parents. They were to have lived there. Karen had been spending freely, too freely, in these years she had been alone, and had got a mortgage on the place. A big mortgage.

She had mentioned a girl called Sally, who appeared to be her best friend. Sally seemed to have a lot of money and nothing much to do. Then Karen had mentioned two people called Mick and Dolly (or had she called them Rick and Molly?) and there was a man called Matthew Pevensey, who seemed to be in the picture quite a lot, but Chris had got no sense out of her as to just where this Matthew Pevensey did fit. He had let it go for the time being.

The time being ... Those words jumbled themselves about a bit in his mind, and suddenly it came to him with a jolt that he was making a new tie. He was not meaning to let Karen slip out of his life. He was going to follow this thing up, meet her again, care

29

what became of her, make an ass of himself as he had done before...

He revolted. All the unhappiness of the past came flooding back. He had sworn to himself he would make no new ties, and he hadn't. Barbara had left him four years ago. Somewhere about the time that Blaize Westbury had been pinned under the flaming wreckage of a train bound for the south, he, Chris Halliday, had been standing staring at the shell of his factory, and facing the fact that he hadn't a penny in the world, and that his fiancée had walked out of his life.

His lips twisted with scorn for himself and for Barbara, as he remembered just what he had done next. Without a word to anyone, he had walked out just as he was, without even a bag. A little mad, he thought, with a grim smile. I couldn't take a blow. I went a little mad, and walked out.

He had walked until he was hungry, and pawned his watch to get food. The next time he got hungry, he had worked for his food. He had worked at manual jobs which included chopping wood and serving behind a fish and chip bar. He had been a potman in a country pub, and a commissionaire for a week outside a small back street cinema in a manufacturing town. He had fished, and given swimming lessons on the coast; he had been a barker in a fair. He had fought by the wayside with other wanderers, and he had

30

spent his day's earnings on hiring a dress suit and gate-crashed a famous banquet. That, he recalled, had been a meal to remember, and was worth being thrown out at the end.

There had been good patches, including the time a man had taken a fancy to him and offered him a partnership in a back street greengrocer's. There had been bad patches, like the time he had run into Barbara, and known a lurching of his heart, which he took to mean that he was still in love with her. And now he wanted to hitch his wagon to Karen's star . . .

For a moment he was ashamed. What right had he to presume she would want to know him after last night? What had he got to offer her, anyway? Either she left her life for his, or he left his wanderings, and his old pledge to himself, and joined her world. Either way, he told himself savagely, it wouldn't work. As he visualized it, he felt the old itch to get moving again. Four years of being alone with nothing but his own bitter memories had done that for him. Supposing he settled down and worked again. What proof had he that it would be worth while? Supposing he offered to protect Karen? How would he ever know that, even if she did decide to turn to him for always, as she had last night in her need, she would stay faithful to him? Feeling as she did about the dead Blaize? And, his wild thoughts ran on, how would I know I'd still feel about her as I

31

do now?

This, he told himself, is the perilous hour between dawn and daylight. At the moment, I'm intoxicated with her beauty. But he knew in his heart that it was more than that. He remembered how she looked at him on the moor last night, when they thought they were lost; when she said she wanted to die, and he had passionately fought back the idea that any such fate could come to them.

He strode up and down the small garret, kicking the apples out of his path, and found to his amazement that he was remembering a shack he had seen, on a strategic section of the highway, by crossroads—a shack that could be turned into a filling station and café and would probably turn out to be a goldmine. He savagely dismissed it from his mind, and fixed his thoughts on the place he had been in before he started that fateful walk over the moor. It had been a small but prosperous country town. He couldn't, at this stage, remember the name. What was very much to the fore in his mind was the factory, on the outskirts, where he had begged a job. There were only five men in it. The principal and his four neighbours, running it as best they could.

'I could make this place pay,' Chris had heard himself saying and they had taken him up on it. He had left them without saying he was going; running, eternally, from a life of stability, because he was afraid of getting caught and tied down again.

And now Karen...

The farm began to come to life. Muffled voices shouted below. Animals awoke. The mist began to lift as the daylight grew stronger. The chair wasn't under the door as he had left Karen asleep. He decided to have another look at her, and to leave her there while he went downstairs in search of breakfast. She ought to have several hours sleep, but he didn't see how it could be arranged. After all, they were only there for the night. Further hospitality would need payment and he had no money.

If Karen had insisted on being taken to the station last night, and presuming they could have got a conveyance to get them there safely, she would have had to pay his fare for him. His idea of the railway station was merely to jump a train, and to disembark as it was slowing past the points near his destination. He wondered if she would have been shocked or amused at that? He didn't know enough about her yet to assess how far that curious sense of amusement would take her. A girl who could shrug at death from exposure on a moor was no ordinary person.

He cautiously opened the door. The room was empty. The bed was ruffled, as it had been when she lay sleeping on it. Puzzled, he hurried to the door and listened. She had been remarkably quiet, that he hadn't heard her.

The door at the bottom was ajar. He bounded downstairs, and almost fell over the body of the farmer's son. He stooped and examined him, and decided that he was still alive, though unconscious. There was not a sound anywhere.

Chris stood irresolute. If he dashed downstairs and found Karen in the act of leaving the farm, it would surely excite comment, since they were supposed to be married. Better, perhaps, for him to quietly leave himself, without looking for her. She might be lucky enough to get some sort of lift, and buy her ticket at the station but if he caught up with her, he'd have to admit he had no money.

All his instincts fought within him to leave without trying to find her. To cut clear and go on with his wandering life. Remember her only as a beautiful memory. Yet he didn't want her to go out of his life.

Then he heard her voice, asking someone if they'd let her get up beside them. A cart began to rumble. Horses were whipped up. Karen herself wanted it that way, evidently, to slip quietly out of his life. Why not let it be that way? Perhaps she regretted giving him those very personal confidences last night. Perhaps she'd just used him, because she felt lonely and bad, and didn't really want to know him at all.

The cart was rumbling out of the stackyard. Suddenly he made up his mind. He couldn't let her go. He'd run and catch her. He moved forward, meaning to take the stairs two at a time, when a heavy blow descended on the back of his head.

The stairs lurched up to meet him, and beyond was a void of blackness.

CHAPTER FOUR

Sally Sark said, 'Here she is!' and ran to open the door. The others stopped their noisy chatter and waited, cocktail glasses in hand, cigarettes drooping from lips. It was a small room, and very hot, and as Karen came in she wrinkled her nose in the familiar gesture.

'Ghastly stuffy in here,' she said, and waved a vague hand at them all by way of greeting. There was some laughter, laughter without umbrage. Karen's tastes were well known.

Sally complained, 'Well, darling, if you must have fresh air all the time, you'd better go back to your beastly moor. If it's your friends you want, you'll just have to take the atmosphere with us, because we like it that way.'

'No, thanks, I had enough of the moor to

last me a lifetime,' Karen grumbled, taking a drink from Nick Borden, and a lighted cigarette from someone else. 'Gosh, I could do with a bit of bright life, though.'

'What happened, darling? We're dying to hear the news!'

Karen shrugged as they clamoured round her. 'There's no news. That's just it. The whole idea's out—flat—dead as mutton. The plain facts (and how I loathe plain facts) are that I haven't a bean, and I can't raise any more on the house. The solicitors, damn them, are absolutely certain on that point.'

'But you only had one mortgage on it,' Molly Borden screamed. 'People take out second and third ones, I'm positive.'

Nick said gently to his mop-headed little wife, 'Darling, I've already explained about that. You have to have a little thing called "Security".'

'Well, hasn't Karen got any security?' Molly pouted, but it was a question.

Karen answered it. 'I have nothing, angel, n-o-t-h-i-n-g. See?'

'But what about those smashing clothes of yours? Darling, you must have trunk loads of them, and all practically new and up to the minute.'

'Oh, yes, I forgot about them,' Karen mused, laughing and pulling a face. 'I have yet to meet the bills for most of 'em, and they're becoming rather pressing.'

Sally said, 'Been to see Matthew, Karen?'

'Um.' Karen pulled off the bit of fur and veil that did duty for a hat on top of her glorious hair, and threw it down on a nearby settee. 'Matt is a beast. He dangles gold ... and wants to marry me.'

'Oh, he *is* the limit!' the others agreed, in unison and disgust. 'Why can't he finance you, just for this once. Darling, why don't you sit for him?'

'At model rates?' Karen laughed. 'What good would that do? A pebble in the pond. No, the only thing is the races, I suppose.'

'I wouldn't, old girl,' Nick Borden said, seriously. His wife stared. Nick wasn't given to seriousness. 'What happens if you lose? You do sometimes, you know, and bookies are stinkers who want paying on the nail.'

'I just can't see,' Molly objected, frowning in terrific concentration, 'why she can't make oodles of money with those looks. Why, if I were a beauty like you, Karen, I'd—'

Karen smiled affectionately at little Molly Borden. 'What would you do, darling?'

'Well, I'd—I don't exactly know, but people with looks are always in the news—'

'Mostly as corpses found on commons,' Karen said, tartly. 'Oh, I know I could get film work, but that, I'm afraid, means having a friend, male for preference. In fact, everything connected with making money by my face means that I've got to have a male

37

friend, and you all know how I feel about that! So, it's the poorhouse for me, unless someone's got a bright idea.'

'Well, let's forget it to-night,' Sally said, soothingly. 'We're going to a party. I don't know whose party it is but Wilfred said he wanted a gang along because these people like a crowd, so we're going to oblige. Wilfred's sister says they always have a lot to eat and drink and ask no questions.'

'Well, at least we eat and drink,' Karen said. 'What do we wear?'

'Oh, not evening dress,' Sally said. 'These togs'll do.' She stared with frank envy at Karen's cinnamon brown dress, with its knife-pleated skirt, and fluted basque trimmed with brown fur to match the hat.

Karen said, 'What sort of party is this?' and with a grin at Sally's expression, 'Might as well air this outfit for the last time, because it's on the list to go back ... unpaid for.'

Nick attached himself to Karen, as they piled into Roddy's car. 'Karen, about the money, I could lend you some. No strings and all that.'

'Why would you want to do that, Nick?' she asked quickly.

'I said no strings,' he insisted, and then, because she was pressing for an answer, he shrugged. 'Oh, well, then, because I knew Blaize and because I was damned cut up when...'

38

Karen swallowed, and hastily looked out of the car window. She couldn't answer, so she squeezed his hand.

'What's wrong with Matthew Pevensey?' someone asked, above the usual hub-bub. 'He's known Karen all her life. Why can't he cough up something on account to settle her debts?'

Karen said, with her nice smile, 'No one's a philanthropist, darling. I'll find a way. If it's only the gees.'

'Tell you what,' Nick murmured, as they all started arguing about something else, as they usually did with lightning speed. 'You pick a nag, and I'll put up the money, and we'll split the winnings.'

Karen answered, 'What if I lose?'

Before he could answer they had arrived. The party was in a large house in a quiet square. Wilfred was waiting for them at the door, with two servants. Karen said, staring at the red carpet, 'Someone got his facts wrong, or the address. Hadn't we better go back and change?'

'Never mind,' Wilfred said. 'Come on in, all of you. I explained about you all.'

'I'd like to know what he explained,' Sally said, with her throaty laugh. She was a mousy blonde, rather plain, who used very little make-up, and yet managed to look terribly smart and up to the minute. The others said it was a deliberate stunt to foster her personality. However she managed it, she achieved a terrific effect, and kept Wilfred dangling longer than any other woman had kept him dangling. Karen liked her for her disarming frankness, and because, whether her friendship was sincere or not, she certainly had the quality of sticking. They had been friends for eight years now, and though Blaize hadn't been over-enthusiastic, he had had nothing against Sally, and that in itself was to Karen a recommendation.

They were all swept in on the tide of the crowd. Although, at first glance, outside, it had looked like an orthodox party, inside they found it very mixed. No names were being called out, and Karen couldn't see who was the hostess. They were swept on to the dance floor, and Karen danced with Nick, who still talked about the money he was going to put on the horse. Then he surrendered her to Wilfred, who said there was a man he wanted her to meet, who had an idea for raising some money.

'No, thanks, Wilfred. I don't think Sally would care for the idea. Anyway, remember what happened the last time you found a man with an idea?'

'There was a spectacular fight, and the party finished in disorder,' Wilfred told her, seriously. 'Why bring that up?'

'Wilfred, I think you've had too much to drink already,' Karen said, the smile still on her lips but not in her eyes.

Two hours later, after hearing the proposition, Karen slipped out. It had been raining, and had stopped. The air smelt sweet and fresh. The square had a few trees in the middle, and a patch of grass enclosed in railings, with a locked gate for the use of the people who lived round it. Karen felt lonely.

The light was fading, and for no reason at all, she began to think of the night on the moor, now two months ago, when the light had faded and she had had a companion with her. She wondered what Chris had done when he found she had gone. Her cheeks flamed again when she thought of the idiotic way she had broken down, and showered on him gratuitous information about herself, which, she believed, he hadn't wanted. She seemed to remember him talking about a girl called Barbara, which had seemed to affect him a great deal. She was glad she had run out on him. It was the only thing to do.

She realized she was hungry. She had not eaten when the others did. The food was the messy, party type. She had never liked the buffet idea. Grabbing where you could, and getting things spilt all over you. She had had several drinks since lunch. She wanted plain, sensible food, and rarely got it these days.

She stopped at a coffee stall. There were one or two men standing around, caps on heads, drinking strong tea in mugs. One whistled as she went to the counter and asked for tea and a cheese roll. She searched in her bag, ignoring the comments around her, and said, suddenly: 'Oh, forget the cheese roll. I'll just have the tea.' She hadn't realized she was running so short of cash.

A familiar voice said over her shoulder, 'Have a cheese roll on me, Karen,' and she looked up into Chris's face.

'What are you doing here?' she breathed.

'Drinking tea,' he told her, solemnly. He waited for her to eat two cheese rolls, and a hunk of sponge cake, and then he took her arm and led her away.

'Don't look like that,' he said. 'It wasn't coincidence, my being here. I followed you, shamelessly.'

'Why?'

'Because I wanted to see you again.'

She frowned. 'Did I say anything about where I lived, that idiotic night at the farmhouse? I said a good many things, but I didn't think I gave my address away.'

He looked sharply at her. 'I'm sorry you feel like that about it. Personally I thought it was a pretty sensible thing to do, unloading your troubles on a complete stranger. Better than on one's friends. As to the address, no, you were pretty astute there. Your trouble was, you told me where the accident occurred, and when. I shamelessly looked up the newspaper accounts, to find you. Even then, it was rough going.'

'Haven't you anything better to do than pry into other people's lives?'

'I like you best on the moor, you know,' he told her. 'You were a nicer person than when you get back among these raffish friends of yours.'

'Let's leave my friends out of this,' she retorted.

'I can't very well. I've come to know one of them pretty thoroughly. Name of Wilfred.'

She swung round. 'You know Wilfred?' Incredulity flooded over her face, and she started laughing. 'That just shows you. I thought I'd keep a memory of you, as a nice, clean, adventuring type, the sort to meet for a day and remember for ever with gratitude, a sort of assurance that every man isn't a Wilfred or a Nick. And now you tell me you know Wilfred well. What a joke.'

'It's no joke,' Chris assured her. 'Any more than it's a joke to find the lovely person I met on the moor, all mixed up with this racy gang, and apparently enjoying herself with them very much. Karen, why do you?'

'If you've found me the way I think you have, you've got your answer, Chris.'

'Don't be cryptic,' he begged her. 'I found your district in the newspaper cutting. I came down south and found a wonderful old house, empty. I contacted the neighbours, and they told me, as neighbours will, that your present address is care of your solicitors. I got on to the solicitors, and they, in their usual and admirable way gave me quite a lot of information by merely saying nothing. That nice little question "What is your interest", tells a heck of a lot. I gave them to understand that I was thinking about buying just such a house. That's what this wandering life does for you, Karen. Makes you slick at handling even solicitors. I dare say you might call me a rogue, without running any risk of defamation of character.'

'Damn!' Karen said, under her breath. 'You might as well know there's a heck of a mortgage!'

'Oh, don't mind me knowing about that,' he said, cheerily. 'I'd have found out, anyway. Like I found out, by way of a word here and there, that the solicitor blokes were expecting to see you pretty soon. Well, I just hung around till you came. Then I followed you. By the way, you're pretty well known in a notorious sort of way. Racing, drinking, wild parties, and things.'

'What a lot of time you waste over someone as worthless as me, Chris!'

He laughed, shortly. 'Waste time—me? I've nothing else to do with it. Oh, by the way, while I was hanging about, waiting, I made quite a bit by collecting betting slips. There's a horse in the three o'clock—'

She looked sharply at him, then they both

burst out laughing.

'Oh, Chris, Chris! Just the same, in spite of it all, I'm so glad to see you. So very glad to see you!'

CHAPTER FIVE

They hung over the cement parapet for an hour, watching the river craft, and the lights on the water. Talking, covering the years in brief, almost terse comments, and under it all revelling in the warmth of their companionship.

'I got a devil of a clout on the back of the head, at the farm,' Chris said, laughing. 'That little swine I knocked out. He must have been lying there watching me, waiting to get his own back.'

'The farmer's son?' Karen frowned. She had almost forgotten him, in the hectic weeks that had followed, since her return to town.

'Um. When I came to, I gave him a thrashing. Had to take the old man on, too, for pitching into his precious boy. The woman came out and stopped it.'

'Did they discover the broken lock?' Karen asked, without much concern for his own bad luck.

'Didn't wait to see,' Chris laughed. 'It all came about because I heard you going, and

45

couldn't make up my mind whether I wanted to see you again or not.'

'And did you?'

He was too cautious to admit that he did. Instead he said, 'Well, that little blighter didn't give me much chance of prolonged thought on the matter. Get 'em from the rear is his motto. Now, having found you after so much trouble, I suppose you'll go off again with another unsuspected bunch of no-goods.'

'If you don't go off first, Chris,' she said, being prophetic without realizing it. 'I wonder you could let yourself stay in the one place for so long.'

'Oh, I stay put sometimes. A few weeks is my limit though.'

'Wonderful!' she approved, laughing. 'Aren't you afraid of running into your girl-friend?'

Chris frowned. 'That was a kick below the belt, Karen.'

'I know it,' she agreed. 'I wanted to find out.'

'Well, if you must know, I do catch sight of her sometimes, and if you want to probe further beneath the troubled surface, it still hurts like hell. Satisfied?'

'I'm sorry, Chris. I don't know why I did that, except that I've—well, I've been a bit of a fool in letting out so much of my own private and personal feelings that I sort of

46

wanted to see a bit of the real you in return. Is that horrid?'

'Quite horrid. You must have been a little beast when you were young. By the way, have you got any relations?'

'No. Why?' She was at once on the defensive.

'No old family friend or one-time guardian?' he persisted. 'Who's this Matthew chap you spoke about, that night at the farm?'

'Did I mention him?' she murmured, in a shocked voice. 'Oh, well, if I did, I did. It can't be helped. He's quite old, one of those frightful friends and hangers-on that families seem to collect, the sort the poor kids have to call "uncle" from the cradle upwards. I don't call him uncle now I'm grown up, but I always see him in that light. It's difficult.'

'Why is it?' Chris said, without noticing the belligerent note that had crept into his voice.

She shrugged. 'Well, I go and see him sometimes, and it annoys me because he wants to know everything about what I'm doing.'

'You don't like him, Karen?'

'Oh, I don't know. He's Matthew. One accepts him. I don't think it's possible to actually dislike him, though I just can't whip up any real liking for him.'

'What's he like? How old is he, I mean?'

She laughed a little. 'He's sixty and looks a

lot older. A bachelor. He's the sort of man who just hasn't any use for a wife. Never wanted children, and gets looked after quite admirably by his housekeeper.'

'Pretty dull,' Chris commented.

'No,' she said, surprisingly. 'Whatever you might say about Matthew, it isn't that he's dull. Far from it. Curiously and upsettingly exciting, sometimes. He's an artist. Quite amateur, but he's been hung—several times, I believe.'

'An artist! Oh, that makes it rather different.'

'How different, Chris?'

'Well, I'd thought of him as a safe sort of old bloke. Now, I don't know.'

'He's safe, all right,' she said, with an almost rueful note in her voice. 'Look, do you know how he sees me? Not as a person, but as a living model, one that—in his own words—has been denied him. Denied him! It all started when I was a kid, and he wanted to paint me. My people wouldn't let him, till I was older. He still wanted to, then I wouldn't have it. Blaize frankly revolted at the idea. I don't know why he minded so terribly, because Matthew only wants to paint my head. That's the part that makes me wild. He just sees me as a head. It's . . . eerie.'

She shivered a little.

'He's cuckoo,' Chris pronounced, with disgust. 'Why d'you have to see him?'

'No, he isn't crazy,' she insisted. 'He says my colouring is superb, and you only get it all combined once in a lifetime. I suppose if there's a model you want and can't get, it is enough to make you wild. I have to see him, anyway, because ... well, on the strength of the family friendship and all that, he helps me out.'

'What d'you mean, "helps you out"?' Chris demanded, savagely.

'With money, darling. We have to have it to eat and live.'

He shifted restlessly, 'I don't know why I should get all steamed up about you, Karen, really, I don't. I've tried to dissect my feelings, but I can't. You're none of my business—I know you don't want to be any more than I want you to be—yet I can't get this feeling out of my system that you'll come to some sticky end if I don't take you up and look after you. Hell!' he exploded.

'Am I a nuisance?' She was gently laughing at him. 'Chris, you ought to do something to take your mind off all your spare time, then you wouldn't bother about girls like me.'

'I don't bother about girls like you,' he corrected her, angrily. 'And before I met you, I didn't bother about girls at all. It's not just your beauty,' he said, as if mentally taking himself apart, to look at his own works. 'Although heaven knows, that's disturbing enough. It's the real you. There's so much in

49

you that I want to know more about, that I've never met in any girl before. Look,' he said, turning to her, and leaning his back against the parapet, 'honestly, I've never once wanted to kiss you, since I first saw you, and I don't think I ever will. But I'm dreadfully fed-up when you're not with me, and when you are with me, I'm all sort of contented, satisfied. Now what d'you make of that?'

She stared wide-eyed. 'How funny, Chris,' she breathed. 'I wouldn't have admitted it, if you hadn't said it first—probably wouldn't even have thought it out for myself—but that's the way I feel about you.'

'I don't believe in platonic friendships,' he said, fiercely.

'Neither do I,' she retorted. 'There are no such things.'

'And I believe that no good will come of my seeing you,' he went on, like a small boy arguing in the hope that he will be put right, sorted out, clarified, so that he can dismiss the subject for ever.

She stiffened a little, and didn't answer.

'What are we going to do, Karen?' he asked, in bewilderment.

She still stared, then her lovely face relaxed, and her beautiful smile chased itself fanwise, from her eyes outwards. 'Oh, come on, Chris!' she rallied him. 'Where's the big I-Am, the big fixer of everything, the big bloke who goes storming across the countryside, knocking little blokes about on farms, because they dare to look at your temporary companion? What's happened to him? Don't tell me he's stuck for an answer?' She started to laugh, softly, and relieved, he joined in her laughter.

'My girl, you've a positive talent for taking something out of the target space and putting it into mid-air for it to blow away all by itself. Come on, let's find something (and somewhere) to eat.'

'Ah, Problem No. 2,' she mocked. 'Got any money?'

'No. But I've got an old aunt!' and they both laughed again.

Mrs. Heath turned out to be very different to Karen's imagined picture of Chris's old aunt. She was a tall woman in her late fifties, extremely modern in dress, make up and manner, with beautifully dressed grey hair and a pair of shrewd grey eyes that swept assizingly over Karen before she realized it was Chris beside the girl.

'Well, if it isn't my wanderer, descending on me in search of food, I know!' she said, in a calm, well-bred voice, at the same time putting her cheek forward for a kiss. Karen noticed that Chris restrained himself as he bent to kiss her, and any boisterousness he might have been feeling, and which was indicated in the warm grin on his face, was duly tempered by the need of care for Mrs.

51

Heath's make-up. Chris, Karen decided, was—in spite of his joyous way of introducing his relative—well trained where 'old aunts' were concerned.

'Aunt Margaret,' Chris said, 'I'd like to present Karen Westbury, a great friend of mine, and,' he concluded mockingly, 'we really are very hungry.'

'Oh, Chris,' Karen protested, as she smiled nicely at the older woman, 'that isn't nice of you. I truly don't go cadging meals, Mrs. Heath!'

'No, my dear?' Aunt Margaret said, with a faint upward note in her voice.

Karen flushed, and followed Chris and his aunt into the sitting-room. A maid followed them in, and Mrs. Heath said to Karen, 'Of course, we've already dined,' and Karen wondered whom the 'we' comprised. 'But I expect we can rustle up a scratch meal, can't we, James?'

James, Karen decided, didn't look too pleased, though she agreed with her mistress that something could be rustled up.

'Gosh, it's nine o'clock!' Chris said, as if he didn't already know.

'Where's the watch I gave you, Chris?'

'Oh, well, Aunt Margaret, you see, there was a little fellow with three brass balls outside his shop, and I was hungry, and—'

'I see.' Mrs. Heath turned to Karen. 'Has your watch suffered a similar fate, Miss

52

Westbury?' but she was smiling good-humouredly enough.

'Please call me Karen,' the girl smiled, 'and although I have my watch at the moment, I really can't guarantee that I shall still have it to-morrow.'

'Um,' Chris said, running a finger round the top of his collar, 'I don't like this conversation. Come on, Aunt Margaret, you mad at us charging in at this late hour, or what is it? Out with it.'

'I am rather cross at you, Chris,' his aunt admitted, smiling. 'I confess I don't like all this dashing off, and then descending on me without proper warning. I hadn't guests to-night, but that was sheer good luck. Please let me know when you're coming, Chris, and if you're bringing anyone with you. Now that you're both here, you're both welcome. How've you been, Chris?'

'Fine.' James brought in a trolley with a plate of chicken sandwiches, a bowl of ice-cold fruit in syrup, some fruit cake and fragrant coffee. 'Now, this is food—eh, Karen? Tuck in!'

Mrs. Heath watched them with a faint, amused smile. 'You seem hungry, both of you.'

Karen admitted she hadn't eaten since lunch.

'I went to a party, and there was a buffet and rather a crush. I didn't like the party so I came away, and ran into Chris.'

Mrs. Heath looked politely puzzled.

'Chris and I were at a coffee stall,' Karen explained, with a quick glance at Chris. He was grinning. His aunt glanced at him; then back to Karen.

'You've both descended on me for larder purposes, I see,' she said, at last. 'Do I take it that you both have beds somewhere to-night, or am I expected to put you up as well?'

'Oh, I still have a roof over my head,' Karen said, and without actually taking a dislike to Mrs. Heath, she lapsed into her frivolous mood, which was, for the purposes of dealing with strangers, purely defensive. 'It's the roof of a friend of a friend of mine, and I won a package on a horse yesterday, so I'm not actually more in debt than usual, but to-morrow, well, I just can't see that far.'

Chris said, 'Don't be pessimistic, old girl,' but he was frowning. 'I'd like to stay here, Aunt Margaret, if you don't mind, and although Karen's position isn't quite so spectacular as she paints it, I would be grateful if you'd put her up too.'

'No!' Karen said sharply. 'I'm living with Sally. It's all right, Chris. There's plenty of room there. I happen, Mrs. Heath, to own a house larger than this. I just don't live in it. It's lonely.'

54

CHAPTER SIX

But Karen did stay the night in Mrs. Heath's house. A sudden revulsion for going back to Sally and the crowd, probably drunk and certainly in a belligerent mood after the party, came over her. Mrs. Heath, too, capitulated, and showed how charming she could really be. Chris, watching the two women, felt the tension ease.

'Look, my dear, you must forgive an old woman being scratchy about invasions of this kind. Now I've had a chance to look you over, I find you not so bad. I hope you'll come to feel the same about me,' Mrs. Heath said, smiling winningly.

Karen realized she was very tired. She stopped being frivolous and smiled nicely. 'Thank you. I quite appreciate how you feel. I would like to stay if I may.'

Chris growled, 'Well, now you two women have stopped leaping at each other's throats, perhaps we can go to bed and get some sleep.'

It was then ten o'clock. Margaret Heath usually went to bed early when she wasn't entertaining. To-night, however, she altered a rule of a lifetime. She took Karen up to one of the guest rooms, and left her in the care of the now amicable James, who was turning down the bed. 'Find Miss Westbury a nightdress,'

Mrs. Heath said. 'Luckily we're about the same size, my dear.'

Downstairs, she said to Chris, 'Now, young man, stop drinking my whisky and come and sit down and talk.'

'Oh, not now, Aunt Margaret, I'm tired, too,' he complained.

She patted the settee beside her. 'No, Chris. Now!'

'All right, but questions such as "What about Barbara?" and "What about my settling down in a steady job?" are barred.'

'Naturally,' she agreed. 'The question that isn't going to be barred, however, is "What about Karen Westbury?"'

'What about her?' He was at once belligerent, his aunt noticed, thoughtfully.

'Well, is she Miss Westbury, or is she married? I wasn't made quite clear on that point, though I left it nicely open.'

'She's a widow,' Chris growled, restively.

'Oh?' Polite interrogation was all over his aunt's face.

'Look, what have you got against her, Aunt Margaret? You've never asked searching questions about any other young women I've been interested in.'

'No, because until Barbara, your interests in that line were obvious and—er—transient, shall we say? Barbara we all know about. But this Karen, well—'

'Well, it isn't like that at all,' he retorted.

'We're just friends.'

'Rubbish!' She selected a cigarette, waited for him to light it, and when no such courtesy was forthcoming, because he was obviously too preoccupied with his own thoughts, she shrugged, and found a match herself and lit it.

'All right, you win!' Chris exploded. 'We're taking your hospitality, so we pay for it by pandering to your insatiable curiosity! But I'd like to say here and now, Aunt Margaret, that you're an inquisitive old woman!'

'I think you're in love with Karen Westbury,' she said, calmly.

'Oh, for goodness sake, you women are all alike. Can't a fellow take up with a girl because he likes her mind, without someone wanting to marry him off to her five minutes later?'

'No. No man that I've ever met has taken up with a ravishing beauty like that girl, with nothing further in his thoughts than the state of her mind, and you're no exception to the general run of young men, my lad! I know you too well!'

Chris stared at her, worriedly, hoping against hope that she wasn't right.

'About her widowhood,' he said, slowly looking down at his hands, 'she was coming back from her honeymoon when their train telescoped another. She was pinned down, and suffered delayed shock. Her husband, however (and this isn't going to make pretty listening) was so badly mutilated that there wasn't much that could be done with him, yet he was still conscious and talking to her.'

Margaret Heath stared, aghast. 'Oh, no, Chris!'

'Yes. I thought you'd change your mind when you heard the gory details. What's more, she couldn't find his hospital at first. She was taken to another. When she did find him, he was praying to be allowed to die, and they were doing their damnedest to keep him alive. He died in the end.'

'When did all this happen?' his aunt asked, after a short silence.

'About three years ago, as far as I can make out. I ran into Karen hiking on a moor. She does that, and other mad things, to try and forget. We got lost, in a mist, and when she thought we were going to die of exposure, she was glad. Glad, d'you hear? I'd forgive that girl anything.'

'Well, if that's what happened to her, I think I would, too.'

'No, you wouldn't, Aunt Margaret, because, nice as you are, you're a woman, and there's something about a woman's attitude to another woman that absolutely beats me. They tear each other's eyes out, yet they're different creatures when it comes to dealing with men. I don't know, I don't understand it at all.'

Mrs. Heath chuckled. 'Well, you'd grumble if it were otherwise. It all makes variety, doesn't it? Now, where does Karen live at the moment? (I'm confused on that point). Something about the friend of a friend, I think.'

'She lives with a most unsuitable blonde in a stagey flat, and there are most unsuitable people sharing her life with her. That's what I found out by emulating my favourite aunt, and being damned nosey.'

Mrs. Heath raised her eyebrows at this piece of information but said nothing.

'There's a dago called Nick Borden whose name stinks with the punters. A fellow called Wilfred, whose milk-bar is as good a cover as any for the other rackets he runs. And there's an old chap, a sort of family friend, I can't quite place him at all, but it seems he's harmless and on the strength of his association with the family, Karen occasionally visits him and touches him for a few quid. I confess I don't like the set-up, but there's little I can do without getting involved. After all,' he added, hurriedly, 'it's hardly my business.'

His aunt let that pass, and asked about Karen's house.

'Don't know much about it, except,' Chris began, and then suddenly decided to dry up. 'I think we'll leave the question of the house out of it, Aunt Margaret,' he said. 'After all, it belonged to her dead husband, and naturally she has memories about it. If she doesn't want to live in it, that's nothing to do with us.'

'Except that she might be persuaded to let it, and raise quite a bit of money to live decently on, instead of careering around with this mouldy crowd, and borrowing from them,' his aunt said, with asperity.

'Afraid of what will be said about us for knowing her?' he asked, slyly.

'Among other things, yes,' Mrs. Heath said. 'Look here, Chris, you're a grown man, and you form what friendships you like. But if they're going to be shady, don't bring them to my house, please. Oh, I found the girl pleasant enough, but there's a lot about her that I don't understand, and which is apparently not to be forthcoming. How, for instance, does she dress so well, if she's heavily in debt and has no income?' As soon as she said it, she realized she had gone too far.

'I think,' Chris said standing up, 'that if Karen isn't in bed, she'd better come along. We won't stay here the night if that's how you feel.'

'Oh, don't be an ass, Chris. You mustn't mind my saying such things, if you're going to be difficult, too. Put yourself in my position. James is a good girl, and she's already looking peculiarly at Karen. It's her

60

hair, and her colouring, oh, and that rakish air of smartness about her. Altogether, she's enough to make people talk, taking the looks of her alone. Besides, she doesn't care! You can see that!'

Next morning Karen came down looking radiant. Mrs. Heath stared.

'D'you know,' she said, to Karen and Chris, 'I believe you haven't a shred of make-up on!'

Chris frowned and hoped there wouldn't be any more nonsense between them, but Karen said levelly enough, 'That's right. I don't use it.'

'Oh, no, it's too much! Much too much for this time of the morning,' Chris's aunt protested, passing a hand over her forehead.

They were better friends after that. In the general laughter, Karen made a graceful little speech of thanks for her night's rest, and for Mrs. Heath's hospitality, and said that she wouldn't impose on her any longer, but would go after breakfast.

'Well, if that's the way you feel about it, you might do something for me, to prove it,' Mrs. Heath said, briskly. 'Come shopping with me. Both of you!'

Chris stared. 'Who, me?' he gasped.

'Yes. Both of you, I said.'

Somehow, Chris never found out how, they got from the subject of kippers for breakfast, to oysters for dinner, and then by easy stages to the problem of entertaining in a small house, the need for a larger one, and from thence by a small jump to Karen's house, which, Karen said, she half hoped to be able to sell.

Chris said, wearily, 'I knew it! There never was a house for sale which Aunt Margaret didn't immediately want to look over.'

Karen's face took on its closed look. 'I don't feel I want to go over it this morning,' she said, 'and in any case, I hardly think it's suitable.'

But they went, just the same. Mrs. Heath ruthlessly held the night's hospitality as a gun at their heads, and Chris found himself at the wheel of his aunt's car.

'Why don't you drive the thing yourself, Aunt Margaret?'

'Stop grumbling, Chris. You know I like a man to squire me, particularly a young man. Don't you agree, Karen?'

'No, I prefer an older man,' Karen said, perversely.

'But I don't suppose you have the luck to know any,' Aunt Margaret probed, with a sweet smile.

Karen answered with an equally sweet though vague smile and the subject dropped. Chris found himself grinning at the road ahead. Aunt Margaret was an ass if she thought that Karen was going to give buckshee information about Matthew

Pevensey like that!

Chris, who had already gathered from the solicitors the sort of house to expect, was still rather surprised when Karen said: 'Sharp turn left, and up the drive through those trees,' and the house came to their view. It was quite a large house and, as Karen explained in a dead sort of voice, it had been built to the mutual tastes of both of them. It had a white stucco frontage, with a steep and gabled roof of old, mellow red tiles, and there were green shutters to the windows. Around it ran a verandah on the first floor, with a sun porch beneath. The ends of the sun porch were glassed in. Yet, with all the additions which had been the inspiration of two people crazily in love, the house had (perhaps by the skill of the architect) preserved some sort of quaint dignity and evenness. It had none of the negative quality that amateur-designed houses usually finish up with. Chris liked it and said so. Aunt Margaret said nothing. She was a follower of the Georgian and William and Mary traditions and no doubt privately thought the house a monstrosity. Yet she, too, was interested.

The gardens, now badly neglected, had at one time been beautiful as well as unusual. Over all was the sad brooding spirit of the two young people who had never had the chance to dwell in the Eden they had designed.

Chris felt lumpish in the throat, and

avoided Karen's eye. He got out, and helped the ladies out, and took the shallow steps to the sun porch at a bound. 'Is it locked?' he asked.

Karen nodded, and silently passed him the key from her handbag.

It was Karen who unfastened the shutters to the hall windows and let in a flood of autumn sunshine. Thoughtfully, she ran a finger over the dust on the glass, and as she turned round to Chris, her face was wet.

He followed his aunt, who was already doing a tour of the rooms. They left Karen to follow, as she wanted to.

'How funny,' Mrs. Heath murmured. 'I got the impression that it would still be furnished, left in fact as it had been.'

Karen, suddenly behind her, said, 'Oh, it was, you know. I've sold the furniture bit by bit, to live on.'

Mrs. Heath turned and stared at her. 'Sold it?'

'Yes. And the carpets,' Karen said, with a twisted smile. 'Why not? I'd never mind selling the house, but surely no one would expect me to let it go furnished, just as we'd planned it?' Her young face was suddenly hard.

'Well, it would have brought quite a bit of money,' Mrs. Heath said.

'Don't be obtuse, Aunt Margaret,' Chris snapped, and taking Karen's arm, led her through to the kitchen quarters.

'Pretty big place,' he said, for want of something to say.

'Yes. We had three servants, waiting for us. It wasn't nice, that sort of home-coming from honeymoon.'

Chris tried to picture the place, and Karen said, as if divining his thoughts: 'We had the whole place carpeted in green; green with red leaves. Very warm and gay. Went nicely with the cream walls. You see, the curtains are green and crimson, too. I left them—who cares about curtains, anyway?'

'And mahogany furniture, I suppose?' Chris murmured, and without noticing, had slipped his arm round her shoulders, in a funny little protective gesture. She made no attempt to break away, and even leaned slightly on him.

'Three servants,' mused Mrs. Heath. 'But my dear child, forgive an old woman's stupidity, but surely, a man who could afford three servants to start off with, would have some sort of financial standing? You shouldn't be like this—' She broke off, knowing she had gone too far, yet wanting desperately to assess, and possibly help Karen in assessing her precarious financial position.

'Oh, yes,' Karen said, calmly. 'Blaize had a half partnership in a firm. He was doing very well.'

There was a little silence, in which Mrs.

Heath waited, politely inquiring.

'I sold it, his share of the partnership, to pay my debts,' Karen said, bleakly. 'There's nothing left. Nothing whatever, but the house.'

'I don't want to appear any more obtuse than my nephew asserts I am,' Mrs. Heath began, when Karen broke in fiercely.

'All right, they were some debts! They were debts that your silly little mind couldn't rise to, because I don't believe you've an ounce of warmth or feeling in you! You can't imagine what it's like to lose someone you're so madly in love with that—Oh, what's the use? When I lost Blaize the world stopped. The sun went out. Nothing made sense. Where's the sense of being in love and waiting to be married, and then only having three weeks? Where's the sense of a young and perfect life being taken away, and taken away so horribly? So vile a death?'

'Steady, old girl,' Chris murmured, staring distractedly into her white face.

'Steady! What do you know either, about it. You think you were in love with your Barbara! If you'd loved her, you'd never have let her go—taking your pride in your hands like that, and wandering like a tramp. What sort of man are you? I tell you both, you just can't realize! Me—I went a little mad. Debts? What do I care about debts? I drank, I smoked, I slept for days, and went without

66

sleep for days, and I live at such a fierce pace that I can't think, I can't remember. Any new stunt I find, I take it up, because it keeps my mind off ... things. And I go on living because I've got too much self respect to take my life. Now, if you've both seen everything, after tearing aside all the veils I've decently drawn across my grief and my private life, perhaps we can leave my house.'

CHAPTER SEVEN

Sally Sark found out about Chris almost before Karen realized it. Sally, besides being coarse and good-natured, was at once broad-minded and inquisitive. She studied Karen after the girl had run out from the party, and decided at once that they must all know what was going on. She put it to Karen.

'Rather nice, eh, honey? The lean type. I like 'em that way.' She laughed slyly, and to Karen, seemed to suggest that there was no good in her friendship with Chris.

'How did you find out about him?' Karen demanded.

'Oh, news gets around fast in our set. You know that. I don't like anyone holding out on me. I'm a good friend, and you ought to know that. Why don't you tell me all about it, honey, and let's chew the whole thing over, nice and cosy.'

'There's nothing to chew over,' Karen said, nettled as always when she felt she wanted to keep something to herself, yet forced out of justice alone to admit that Sally had indeed stuck by her, and that she supposed it was her due to know things.

'Well, that doesn't go with that special secret look in your eyes, nor your way of moping around in corners, a way I've only just noticed. Funny thing, it all seems to date from that day you got lost on the moors and didn't come home that night.'

'Oh, don't be beastly, Sally. You're making it sound as if I had spent the night with Chris.'

'And didn't you?' Sally asked, laughing. 'If not, then you're a silly girl. From what I've seen of him, and that isn't much, he looks a pretty nice fellow. Exciting, too.'

'Look, Sally, for heaven's sake, I suppose I'd better tell you all about him, so that you don't put the wrong story around.' She slid into her green housecoat, and squatted on the end of her divan, polishing her nails. 'I ran into him on the moor, we got caught in a mist, and a farmer rescued us. We stayed at the farm all night.'

'Huh-huh!' Sally said, with an insinuating smile which to Karen suggested that they stayed in the same room.

'Don't do that, Sally!' Karen snapped. 'We

68

didn't share a room, whatever your nasty mind might think.'

'Oh, well,' Sally shrugged, 'so you had separate rooms. How near were they?'

'Next door,' Karen said, scowling, 'with my door bolted on the inside.'

'More fool you.'

'No,' Karen said. 'He's a good pal. He didn't expect anything like that, and what's more, he didn't want it. He's a woman-hater, if you must know.'

'There's no such thing,' said the worldly Sally.

'He's been frightfully hurt by the girl who was going to marry him, and he doesn't want to be tied down to anyone else.'

'Who said anything about being tied down?' Sally laughed.

'You'll believe me, or I'll slap your silly face,' Karen said, angrily. Her face was flaming, her eyes glinting.

Sally laughed again. 'Red-head, sorehead, gingerbread,' she teased. 'All right, I'll believe you, though a good many wouldn't. Oh, it's no use your being indignant and all that. You know what our crowd's like, and from one friend to another, there happens to be a fellow in our bunch who's got ideas about you. If he thinks you're making a special of some bloke, after all you've said about being the grief-stricken and faithful widow, well, I warn you, it won't go so well for you.'

Karen flinched at Sally's description of her, but said nothing. Sometimes she wished she wasn't friends with her. Sally was a pal, and stuck by a pal, but she wasn't the type that Karen always wanted to be with. Her outlook was crude, and no one had any special virtues, in her view. You were either a sport or a drip. A drip, Sally held, was all virtue and nothing else, and as such, a very dreary person. A sport, in her view, and in the view of most of the crowd, was a person who went with the gang, and refused to do nothing that they wouldn't do. Karen hardly qualified for sportsmanship on their lines, as it was, for she rarely drank much with others; but they knew she had drunk quite a bit on her own, when she was first widowed, and that, to the rest of them, constituted hopes for her becoming as they were. She smoked heavily, too, and had their rakish, almost flashy way of dressing. Yet sometimes they looked queerly at her, and wondered what she was doing in their set at all.

'I think I'll go away for a bit, Sally,' Karen said, that night. She spoke through the darkness, after they had smoked a packet of cigarettes apiece, and talked till well after midnight.

'With Auntie?' Sally chuckled. 'Oh, yes, we know all about that, too. Auntie's been making inquiries about us. She's got an idea or two about you, or I'm a Dutchman.'

'She can have as many ideas as she likes,' Karen retorted, 'and though I haven't said this before, I wish you'd all mind your own business. I hate to feel I'm being discussed.'

'Pooh, you'll have to put up with it,' Sally said. 'If you're not going with Auntie, I suppose it's the boy-friend.'

'No, it isn't. I want to go away on my own.'

'Where?' asked the practical Sally. 'You haven't a bean, and Nick seems to think you owe him something on that last cert.'

'I might get a job, and make some money I won't have to look over my shoulder about,' Karen said, bitterly.

'What, with hair that colour? What sort of a job would *you* get?'

'An usherette, in a cinema, so no one can see me and get ideas,' Karen retorted, bitterly.

'Oh, don't get up on your high horse, old girl. Have a break by all means. Come to think of it, I could do with a break myself. Tell you what! I know a fellow who knows a girl who's got a real grandmother. Lives in the country. The old girl'll let us have a room in her cottage, I know!'

Karen sat up. 'You, Sally, in the *country*?'

'Oh, don't get ideas about me, old girl. The cottage's near a village, where there's a decent pub, the sort that cars come to, and there's a holiday camp not far away, so there's plenty of sport going. We shouldn't be dull, and we'd get our room and board free, on account of our all being friends, see?'

'No, thanks,' Karen said. But she altered her mind the next day. Nick came over, and wasn't so friendly, and talked about repaying kindnesses. The weather changed to sticky heat. An Indian summer, everyone said, and although it was getting late in the year, Sally was all for going down to the cottage of which she had spoken, to be in at the end of season fun with the holiday camp people.

'Besides, I'm getting a bit fed-up with the gang myself, to tell you the truth,' she confided to Karen.

Karen said to Nick, 'I've got a bit of cash. Put it on Black Brother for me, and if it doesn't come off, I'll hock some of my things and pay you right up.'

Nick said nothing, but went quietly.

Sally raised her eyebrows, and looked thoughtfully at Karen. 'You know, Molly's awful stuck on him,' she murmured.

'I know Molly's still in love with Nick,' Karen agreed. 'What about it?'

Sally shrugged. 'You know, Karen, I think it's a good thing for us all that you and I are clearing out of town for a bit. We'll meet all the others again fresh after a few weeks.'

The cottage was quite attractive, and set a little apart from the rest of the village. It had whitewashed walls, a pretty garden, and a few fowls, and there was a river running at the end of the garden, with a small jetty where Sally said it was possible to swim or push a boat out. Karen, who didn't know much about boats, but who swam a great deal, was attracted, and against all her instincts, she was inclined from the first view to look forward to their impromptu holiday.

The old woman in the cottage was not so old nor so dopey as Sally had made out. She eyed them both, and said smartly how much she wanted from them by way of board.

Sally smiled disarmingly and said that as they weren't sure how long they'd be there, might they leave the question of the board over for the time being? Meantime, they had not come empty-handed, and Sally made the woman a gift of a small bedroom clock she carried with her, and looked at Karen.

Karen, who carried most of her belongings about with her if she was away from the flat for longer than a week, said swiftly, 'I'm sure you'll love a small bedside lamp, run by a battery.'

Up in their room, a pretty room under the eaves, with a view of the river, Karen said to Sally, 'I thought you said we wouldn't have to pay anything?'

'That's what I said, and that's what I thought,' Sally said, sourly. 'The old girl was sharper than I expected. Still, she needn't expect anything else now she's got the clock and lamp.'

Sally made acquaintances quickly and easily. She and Karen went out for an evening walk that finished up in the private bar of the pub with two crowds from huge saloon cars buying them drinks and taking bets with them on a darts match against the locals. The locals started betting for drinks, and finished by betting for half-crown stakes, until the landlord discovered it and stopped the game. Sally and her new friends were satisfied, but Karen felt a little sick. She had wanted so much to get away alone, but always the need for money pressed her into the companionship of people whom she hardly knew if she liked.

The people in the cars took them with them. Sally in one car, Karen in the other. They went to a roadhouse, and then on to a big country house, where the people started a radiogram and had dancing. Finally they ran the two girls back to the end of the village, leaving them, at Sally's request, to step the last few yards to the cottage on their own. Karen was dropping, but Sally seemed quite bright and fresh.

The old woman was waiting up for them, and looked grim.

'Maybe I didn't mention it,' she said, 'but our Olive has to keep good hours when she's down here, and the same goes for any of her friends. Eleven o'clock, and I bolt the doors, and I'll have no climbing in the windows.'

Sally disarmingly agreed, though neither she nor Karen had the faintest idea whom Olive was. That night they went to a dance at the holiday camp, and got back at 11.30 and found that the woman was as good as her word, and had locked them out. Their windows were fastened, and the dog snarled at them from the kennel in the back yard.

'We'll knock her up,' Sally said, with determination.

They knocked for twenty minutes, but they couldn't wake her, and Sally, at last, with her usual belligerence when she had tried the peaceful way and failed, picked up a stone from the garden and broke one of the windows of the parlour, at a point near the catch. It was easy work to put her hand through, open the window and climb in.

The woman was waiting for them at the door of their bedroom. 'I heard the glass break,' she said. 'You'll pay for the new pane to be put in to-morrow, miss, and you'll both get out. I didn't like the looks of you from the start, neither of you, but being as our Olive asked me, I said yes.'

'You can't put us out,' Sally shouted.

'Can't I? You've paid nothing, neither of you. As for the clock, it don't go. As for the lamp, there's no battery, and no one around here knows where I can get one. Worthless, them things, like you two.'

Karen felt sick and ashamed. 'What did you have to break her beastly window for, Sally?'

'To get in and get my pinching shoes off,' Sally said, between her teeth, 'and to get to bed. Even I have to get some sleep sometimes.'

'Where are you going to get the money to pay for the window?' Karen asked, worriedly.

'Oh, something'll turn up,' Sally yawned. 'If the worst comes to the worst, I'll do a cabaret turn in the pub for coppers. Come to think of it, we might do a double turn at the concert the holiday camp's doing.'

'That's amateur, and the pub's out,' Karen said, with finality.

Just the same, next morning Sally approached the secretary of the camp's entertainment committee, and put up some preposterous story about their being stage artistes 'resting', and extracted from him the promise of a fee. At the same time, the first post brought a letter from Nick. Black Brother had come in first, and he had enclosed the full amount for Karen, and some for Sally, who had backed it and said nothing.

'Now we'll collect the clock and lamp, pay the old devil for her window and clear out,' Sally jubilated.

'I don't want to see that lamp again,' Karen said, miserably. 'I knew it was empty, but I did think she might be able to get a battery.'

'Oh, don't be such a misery,' Sally protested. 'We'll keep those two items to serve for gifts in the next tight corner. Meantime, we've money in the kitty, and there's our engagement to-morrow at the camp. We'd better rehearse.'

'Rehearse what?' Karen gasped. She hadn't taken the idea seriously.

'An act,' Sally said, and though her manner was nonchalant, there was a glint in her eye.

'But I can't do a thing. Can you?'

'Of course,' Sally said. 'My mother was in a touring company most of her life. I was in pantos as a kid. Easy as blinking.'

'Perhaps so, for you, but the most I've ever done is to sing at parties, and that's asking for trouble.'

'Oh, stop nagging, and wait till I've got a chance to put you through your paces,' Sally snapped, thankful that as yet Karen hadn't put her foot down on the concert party as she had on the pub idea.

Once away from the cottage, and installed in the guestrooms over the pub, Sally said, 'The landlord's a good sort. I told him what we're going to do, and he's lent us the piano in the bar. Come on, let's see what you can do.'

It seemed that despite Karen's misgivings, a decent double act was got up, with the landlord and his family as an interested and appreciative audience. Sally, a trouper to her finger-tips, despite her absence from the stage (through laziness, Karen suspected, in some surprise) did a bit of dancing, a bit of singing, a bit of saucy patter, and led the act. Karen could play the piano well enough, and sang in a pleasant little voice. Her superb style and colouring did the rest.

Sally was jubilant. But Karen couldn't resist adding what Sally called her 'damp squib' touch.

'What,' she asked Sally, worriedly, 'did Nick mean by sending me the full money for my winnings?'

'What am I supposed to say to that?' Sally demanded, genuinely puzzled, and caught off her stroke.

Karen stared at her. 'If I can remember I owe Nick quite a lot of money, what does Nick mean by forgetting it?'

CHAPTER EIGHT

There were two more weeks of the season to go, at the holiday camp. It had been a good season, and right to the end they were fairly full. The manager, a go-ahead man, watched Karen and Sally do their act, and was thoughtful. When they came off there was such applause that they had to go back again twice. Professionals, even small-timers and

78

unknown, were a big draw. Besides, these two had something else. The blonde one, he considered, was a madam, and knew where she was going. Her smile, wide and friendly, 'got' the audience. The other, the red-head, was a beauty, and no mistake.

'Look girls,' he began, when they came off. 'The show's finishing early. The last turn isn't much good. What d'you say to going back on and leading some community singing or something. Finish the evening with a bang. Eh?'

Sally said, smartly, 'What's in it for us?'

He nodded appreciatively. He liked dealing with people with an eye to business. 'I'll make it worth your while.' He named a figure, which, though not large, Sally approved. He said, 'I've got more ideas. It might be a good thing for all three of us, this last two weeks. See, what I want is good-will, make 'em want to come back next year. Get me?'

He looked at Karen's figure, in her white model gown, and at Sally, whose gown wasn't quite so expensive, but brought out the best points of her figure, and was brown and yellow striped and of a daring cut. 'Got style, you two. Swim?'

They nodded. 'And dive, fancy stunts,' Sally added.

'Might arrange a contest, in our own baths here,' he mused, and watched them with a good deal of eagerness as they took the audience with them, singing and shouting, till the end of the evening.

There were dancing contests, and a fancy dress ball, all the usual stunts, plus a little extra, from the manager's ingenuity, and Sally's stage directions. She and Karen caught the imagination of everyone, and were tremendously popular.

Too popular, Karen thought, busying herself with plans of how to keep in with this new venture and Sally, while she staved off the unwelcome attentions of the manager.

And then one day Chris came down.

'Great snakes, you always turn up as if your entrance were timed,' Karen said, with a mixture of relief and displeasure. She was in a white swimsuit which was very, very brief, and her flaming hair was hidden beneath a white diving helmet.

Chris eyed it with a curious expression, and said nothing.

Sally, joining them, said, 'Ah, the boy-friend. Now perhaps I can be introduced.'

Chris permitted Karen to introduce him in an abstracted way. Sally chattered, while Karen ripped off her rubber cap and shook her hair free. 'It's hot,' Karen complained.

'You *got* to go?' Chris said, turning to Sally.

'No,' she said, in surprise, walking with

them. Then: 'Oh, marching orders! I get it,' and went off, laughing.

Karen turned on him at once. 'Chris, how did you find me here?'

He shrugged. 'It wasn't so difficult after all. You know I was in with Wilfred. Well, 'in' is perhaps not quite the word. Skimming round his outskirts, shall we say, while I thought over the deal. Well, before I decided he was too dirty a business associate for even me to mix with, he mentioned casually that Nick had got some money for you and was sending it on.'

'Oh, so you found out about that, did you?'

'I did,' Chris answered, composedly. 'Furthermore, I got a fair idea of how you two girls came on the woman in the cottage, and when I came down here, I got an even better idea of the way some young women go on in a strange place.'

Karen's manner changed. 'Oh, Chris, that was beastly. Beastly! I'm so ashamed.' She told him rapidly what really happened, with no frills.

He nodded. 'That's what I made it, when I put two and two together, knowing you,' he smiled. 'Well, it wasn't difficult to get news of you over the bar, while I was having a pint—it was hot, and I was thirsty.'

'So with your usual timidity you came charging out to the holiday camp and crashed through the main gate, regardless? Nice

81

going, Chris.'

'Oh, no, not quite like that,' he protested, pulling up before an ice-cream counter and buying her a mixed ice with a wafer sticking in the top. 'Let's find a table, and talk.'

'You know me,' he said, with a funny mixture of an engaging grin, and a rueful look because she also happened to know the worst about him. 'Rolling stone and all that. But if there's a chance of making a bit in an interesting way—Well, I had a chat with the manager here. The P.T. instructor seems to have had a fight with him and sheered off. It isn't worth his while to engage a new one at the end of season.'

He waited, with a twinkle in his eye.

'You're not a P.T. instructor,' Karen accused.

'No, but I'm going to be one, plus!' he chuckled. 'Just as you two aren't real troupers, but—'

'That's blackmail,' Sally said, coming up behind him. 'I just had a word with O'Leary and he told me what you're doing. I must say you've got a nerve, crashing in on our show like that.'

'Why, were *you* going to conduct the P.T.?' Chris asked with an impudent grin as he ran his eye over her figure. Sally flushed.

'We're giving dancing lessons,' she said, sullenly.

'And diving lessons,' Karen said, but she

looked worried.

Later, after lunch (to which Chris had got himself invited by O'Leary the manager, who seemed to have taken a fancy to him), Karen and Chris went for a walk together.

'I suppose I'm not wanted,' Sally said, grinning.

'You can come if you like,' Karen said.

Sally shrugged. 'Oh, if it's going to be that sort of party, never mind.' She sauntered off, and her fair hair blew out like a pennant behind her.

'That girl gives me the creeps,' Chris complained, with a frown of distaste.

'How odd,' Karen mused. 'Everyone likes her straight off.'

'Doesn't it rather depend on whom you mean by "everyone"?' Chris argued. 'If it means your crowd at home, I'm not surprised. She's their sort.'

'No, I didn't mean that, Chris. I mean the people down here, in the camp, in the village—'

'With the exception of the old dear in the cottage,' Chris chuckled. 'She was vitriolic.' He sobered, immediately. 'Unfortunately she was the same about you, and obviously classed you with Sally. That's what I don't like about the whole show.'

'Neither do I,' Karen agreed.

'Karen,' Chris began, hesitatingly, 'I know it's none of my business, and you can snub me if you like, but I do feel most strongly about the way you're going on. I know what it feels like to be without money, and I know, too, that a fellow can scrape along, more or less easily, where a girl can't.'

Karen said nothing, and permitted him to pull her down beside him on the grass, in the shelter of a haystack. It was hot—the difficult, dry, suffocating heat of a late summer day, when after a too-long dry spell the whole earth is panting for rain. Insects alighted and stung, and the grass—too long and almost white—had a harsh pricking touch to bare limbs.

Chris eyed Karen speculatively. The heat was taking it out of her already, and the job in the camp was no easy one.

'I appreciate only too well what you felt, when you chucked your money about like that, just at first. I did the same sort of apparently silly things for much the same reason. And while we're on the subject, I want to apologize for my aunt. She doesn't mean to be inquisitive or censorious. She doesn't think she has been. It's just that her generation simply can't make allowances for young people with different standards.'

'I know,' Karen said. 'I liked her well enough, but I had to flare out at her to stop her probing further. She's rather inclined to . . . goad.'

'Yes,' Chris agreed. 'I know. We've had

84

rows about it before, she and I, but we manage to stay good friends. I hope you'll be on the same basis with her. She could be a great help, you know.'

'I don't want anyone's help!' Karen flashed, angrily.

'I meant in the way of supplying a supper and bed sometimes,' Chris said, mildly. 'Like you accepted before from her, that night we went there.'

'I didn't like it,' Karen said.

'Yet you stay with this rackety crowd whom you like a great deal less,' he said, shrewdly.

She had nothing to say to that.

'You accept charity from them, Karen. It's no good denying it. You owe them money, and even if you do repay it, until you make money to repay it, you're in their debt.'

He had her there, and she knew it.

'Karen, if you must owe some fellow money, let it be me. At least I've no interest in women, and I wouldn't take it out of them as your crowd will.'

'That's just it,' Karen exploded. 'Just because they look cheap and act cheap sometimes, it doesn't mean to say they haven't any morals. I've only owed Nick money, and he's happily married to Molly and as decent as they come. He'd help anyone, so would Molly. I wouldn't owe Wilfred money.'

'Well, I'm glad you've sense enough for that,' Chris allowed, 'but from what I've seen of this Nick fellow, I wouldn't trust him an inch. Don't be deceived because he's got a nice little wife.'

'I think you're wrong about Nick,' Karen said, knowing in her heart that she was doubtful herself about him, but not wanting to give in to Chris too far. 'Don't let's talk about it any more. It's too hot.'

'You needn't talk, but I'm going to,' Chris said, blandly. 'I have a great idea. Of course, you may not be the girl I'm looking for to come into it with me, but on the other hand, you may. You'll just have to see what you think about it.'

He was looking into the middle distance, a curiously eager expression in his eyes.

Karen yawned. 'If you must be energetic and talk in this heat, go ahead. But don't be surprised if I go to sleep.'

'Thank you, ma'am,' he said, gravely, not looking at her. 'The thing is, Karen, you and I could make money, decently, on our own, without backing horses, without cadging meals or a bed, without anyone else's help—all we want is a brainwave.'

'That,' Karen said, rolling over on to her back and stretching like a puppy, 'is what many others have said, and found no answer.'

'Ah,' Chris said, lying down beside her and staring up at the shimmering, angry blue of the sky. 'That is where they were unfortunate and we are fortunate. I have found the answer.'

Karen's eyelids dropped. She thought what a nice voice he had. So pleasant, so full of merriment and warmth. So different from the hard voices of the others she knew and went around with. They were smart and clipped and often laughing, they turned on the charm when it suited them, but they weren't the possessors of a genuine voice. Genuine. That was the word that described Chris.

She was happy about having found the right word. She muttered it beneath her breath, and hearing her say something, he stopped. She was scarcely conscious of what he had been talking about, beyond a hazy recollection of finding a primary need of the general public, and playing up to it in an interesting, attractive way. That much she had absorbed without knowing it, when she murmured the word 'Genuine', and having found the right word, gave up the mental struggle and allowed herself to slide rapidly into deep slumber.

It was cooler when she woke up. Chris was sleeping gently beside her, his light-brown, tousled head buried in the crook of his arm. She studied him. He was not so slightly built as she had at first thought. There was strength in his muscles, even in the relaxed attitude of deep sleep, she could see that. And there was an air of fitness about him, which she remembered was sadly lacking in the men of her crowd. He was clean, in mind as well as body. She warmed to him, and was glad she knew him.

She settled herself back and was aware of Sally, leaning on a nearby fence with a fag drooping from her mouth, grinning a little. She had a meaning smile on her face, and Karen, seeing it, blushed hotly and struggled up. Chris didn't wake, and Sally moved off before Karen could reach her.

Karen stood fuming. Sally's being there had ruined everything. Karen stooped and picked up her wide shady straw hat, and quietly left the sleeping Chris beneath the haystack, and went back a different way to that Sally had taken. She was angry with Sally, and with Chris, but angrier still with herself. She had no right to put herself into positions like that. A wild desire came over her to go away, right away from the whole lot of them, so that no one knew her, or anything about her. Change her name, dye her hair black, or bleach it. Anything, anything, for peace, and a respite.

But custom dies hard. She was used to the gang, and she liked Chris's friendship. She effected a compromise with herself and decided to try and keep both.

O'Leary stopped her, and talked. Aimless talk, with his shifty little eyes darting all over her, and at the same time darting here and there, watching the people in his camp as they drifted by, seeing they were happy, while he himself was happy talking to Karen. She fascinated him, both by her superb colouring and good looks and also by that vague, smiling, stand-off-ish air, which to O'Leary, had the effect of urging him on rather than repelling him.

She got away at last, and found Sally again at her elbow. Sally smiled and chattered, and said she was sorry she had stumbled on them like that, and that Karen should know that she, Sally, was no spoil-sport, and that was why she had got away so quickly. She was sure Karen understood. All the while she chattered, Sally watched Karen, and Karen noticed her eyes had a new hardness.

Chris came back and couldn't find Karen anywhere, but Sally was hanging about. There was a dance, and O'Leary had worked wonders with the place. He had had fairy lanterns strung across the dancing space, and little tables and chairs put around in a wide ring, where soft drinks and ices were served. A radiogram, with loudspeakers suspended (and hidden in) nearby trees, fed the dancers with appropriate music. The harvest moon rose in a sky still very blue, and the fierce heat of the day abated to a pleasant warmth.

There was a nostalgic quality about the whole thing. Chris mooned around trying to find Karen, and when she appeared—in a foaming frock of sprigged blue muslin, her white shoulders gleaming bare above the low, frilled corsage—he forgot to grumble at her, as he had intended, for going off and leaving him. Her beauty, as on that former occasion, knocked him speechless.

She was in a strange mood to-night. She smiled a lot up into his eyes and told him she was very happy, but when he wanted to talk she wouldn't let him. 'I just want to dance, Chris,' she said. Her hair, scent-fresh from a shampoo, was close to his face, and she seemed not to mind him holding her close, which surprised him.

'Karen, what did you think of the plan I told you of, this afternoon?' he pressed, wanting her opinion, eager for it.

'Oh, not now, Chris,' she said, not liking to dampen his enthusiasm by saying she had (as she had threatened) gone to sleep after all, and hadn't heard a word. 'I've got to give an exhibition soon. Maybe after that, we can slip away quietly somewhere and talk.' She had in mind that with a little time, she could encourage him to go all over it again, for the sake of clarity, and in that way get the story after all, without his knowing she hadn't heard it the first time.

He was staggered, and pleased. Intoxicated a little by her dancing and her nearness, and by the artificial magic of the night and the atmosphere, an atmosphere fostered by the bemused look on the faces of the other dancers, and the careful choice of the gramophone music.

He stood on the fringe of them all and watched her dancing with a tall, insipid young man, whose main claim for breathing, it seemed to Chris, was the fact that he not only danced superbly, but communicated a deceptive air of easiness about it which convinced everyone else that with a little practice they could do the same.

Sally strolled up to him. She looked nice, in a limpid green, a sort of taffeta stuff that rustled coolly as she walked. She exuded the 'I'm not a woman, but just a pal' air, which she guessed appealed to a man like Chris. Although he didn't like her, from instinctive reasons, he accepted her as someone to talk to, about Karen. 'She's—amazing,' he breathed. 'Isn't she?'

'Amazing,' Sally agreed, with nothing beyond good-nature in her voice. 'I'm awfully sorry for her.'

'Why?' Chris wanted to know. 'Because of her tragedy?'

'Oh, no,' Sally repudiated, in a surprised voice. 'No, that business is all over. She never thinks of it now. No, what bothers her is the loneliness. Mind, I don't blame her. I suppose when once you've been married, it's just hell being single.'

Chris frowned. 'I think you're very much mistaken. As I understand things, Karen simply revolts at the idea of a second marriage. The memory of the first was too perfect to be spoilt by any other.'

Sally looked pityingly up at him. 'If she said that, well, we women have a little pride. But you can take it from me, she's not that way at all. And I don't blame her. In fact, I've often said to her, "Get around and meet more men, old girl, there's no one left in our crowd who wants to get married". That's true. You know Wilfred. You know the others, too, I suppose, and Nick's all tied up.'

Chris was silent. Sally pressed on, with a pretty unwilling air, as if torn between giving away Karen's inner feelings, and furthering her friend's interests.

'Of course, there's O'Leary, here. He's pretty gone on her. But I suppose you know as well as I do, that you're the big bug as far as Karen's concerned.'

'Rot!' Chris exploded, his face flaming.

'Oh, don't be modest,' Sally smiled. 'Why (and this is in confidence, mark you) only this afternoon I happened along while you were asleep, and she was *yearning* over you. Positively adoring, she looked. Good old Karen, she'd make you a splendid wife, Chris. Good luck to both of you!' and as if conscious of having done her day's good deed, Sally pressed his arm warmly and floated off.

Karen finished her exhibition, and returned to Chris. She was happy, tired, and inclined to lean a little on him, confident that with Chris, she had no need to worry. His lack of response assured her that her feelings were right, and she chattered gaily.

He danced with her, but was silent, preoccupied.

O'Leary came over to them, and said he deserved a dance, he did know. Jocund, red-faced and shining, he took Karen away from Chris, and Chris noticed that he held Karen closely and she didn't seem to mind. She talked and laughed a lot, too, as she had done with him. Chris scowled, and strolled out of the camp.

The roadway was quiet. Dark, still and restful under its roofing of trees, after the bright lights of the dancing square. The further he walked, the further the music receded, until it was so quiet that he could hear a cricket chirping, and pick out the faint rustlings of birds in the hedge. The night air soothed him, but he couldn't get out of his mind that old trapped feeling. He wasn't in love with Karen, he told himself; only half-mad with her beauty. He didn't want to have to rent some suburban villa and go to some office each day, for the sake of security—a security which would have to go on and on, because, from what he had seen, when there was little money, responsibilities piled up and invariably children came.

He didn't want children. He didn't want to wake up each morning and find Karen beside him; he had the odd fancy to know her only as she was, an exotic tropical flower. He had seen her dishevelled once, crying her heart out on the attic bed at the farm. He didn't want to see her like that again. If he were a wealthy man, and could rely on her only appearing in wonderful clothes, with other people to see to the drudgery of domestic life for her, then it would be different. But still the shackles remained, wealth or no.

He smartened his pace. The village pub was still open. Its lights, streaming across the dark lane, beckoned. He went in, and ordered a half pint, and taking it to a small corner table, wrote a brief note to Karen.

'My dear, I'm off again. My feet, curse them, have the itch to move. I wish you all the best of everything. Take care of yourself.—Chris,' he wrote, and folded it neatly. There was an envelope in his pocket addressed to himself care of his aunt, containing a bill. He scratched out the name and address, substituted Karen's name, and stuck it down. He swallowed his pint, gave the letter to the barman for Karen, and with a shrug of pure relief, he went out into the night.

CHAPTER NINE

Matthew Pevensey smiled whimsically at Karen. She looked as lovely to him to-day as she had ever done, and yet, he tantalized himself with the thought, there was something new about her.

'My dear,' he murmured, fixing an expensive cigarette into an ivory and onyx striped holder, 'don't tell me you've fallen in love again?' He leaned back comfortably in his favourite armchair and studied her, studied with pleasure the swift tide of red running up her fair skin, at his suggestion; studied with pleasure the flashing of her beautiful eyes, in swift anger, at any such idea.

'Don't be horrid, Matthew, or I'll go this minute!'

'Sit down again, Karen, pet, and don't rise so easily to the bait. You know old Matthew well enough by now.' He smiled at his suggestion that he was old, because he never thought of himself as old really. He had just seen his sixtieth birthday; seen it with very real regret and was vain enough to think that no one else could add up his age or remember how long he had occupied the big red-bricked house at the end of the avenue. He forgot that his housekeeper had been with him for close on forty years, and that he had already attained his majority then. He had long since left off counting the various charities to which he subscribed annually, and the number of cheques that had gone to each. He had forgotten everything that he didn't want to remember, and now, tall, lean and upright as ever, he went about his work, and took his daily exercise and promised himself that he would stop counting the years at all, and that everything should be given up to the pursuit of beauty.

'I came to see you, Matthew, because I thought you might have some constructive idea—other than the one you mentioned when I was last here—which might help me to scrape through.'

'Are you still with those fantastic friends of yours?' he wanted to know.

She hesitated ever so slightly. 'Well, sort of, but I'm hoping to get away from them, just as soon as I can.'

'My offer still holds good,' he murmured, watching the smoke from his cigarette curl in delicate tendrils, and comparing them to a woman's hair with a breeze blowing through it.

She shrugged impatiently. 'It's no good, Matthew. You know I won't ever marry again. Let's have done with that, please!'

'A woman's negative is never final,' he observed, mildly. 'Each time you come to see me, I shall always ask you. Not perhaps in so many words, for even I tire of reiteration. But I shall remind you of that offer I made not so long ago, and I trust you'll remember that I too, have no mind to acquire a wife, as such, but merely to hold you by matrimony, to me. I want to paint you, Karen.' In the last sentence only, did he come to life. There was a frightening amount of suppressed passion in those few simple words. 'I want to paint you Karen.'

Almost at once he recovered himself, and smiled blandly through the smoke at her. 'I don't believe I have any warmth in me for persons, so it would be foolish, and dishonourable, to mislead you. I could never bring myself to pet a woman, or to caressed or in any way suggest warmth of feeling. So don't be afraid. But,' he said, leaning forward, 'I have had a desire these many years, to run a hand through your hair, to let the light play on it, and bring out all the facets and colour-shades ...' The light of the fanatic played in his eyes, then died out.

'Sometimes, Matthew, you frighten me,' Karen said, in a low voice. 'I just wanted you to suggest somewhere where I might go and work, or something.'

He shrugged amiably. 'What can you do, my child?'

She scuffed her shoe off, and caress her slim foot. 'It pinches,' she said, in disgust.

'You know perfectly well what I can or can't do, Matthew. Good heavens, you've known me since I was in my cradle—what a silly question.'

'Yes, and if your parents had not been so pig-headed, you'd have had a private income of your own. I wanted you to sit for me at each year of your age, but they wouldn't let me.'

'Yes, I know. For your album of studies of heads of all ages,' she said, with the faintest trace of weariness.

'Do I bore you, Karen?'

'Oh, no, Matthew. Of course not. But sometimes I just wish you could like me a little for myself, and not just for my head.'

'It's a fantastically beautiful head,' he murmured, almost reverently.

She looked round the room with distaste. This room was perfect Regency in style. Each reception room represented an age in the history of furniture and interior decoration. Matthew, with his private fortune inherited from his vulgar pickle-manufacturing grandfather, had spared nothing in the pursuit of the beautiful, yet he had done it in his own peculiar way. Eccentric, Karen thought, with disgust. If she had had Matthew's money, she wouldn't have built a red-brick house with green cupolas at the end of a tree-lined avenue. She'd have bought a country house, built in a set period, a graceful gem of architecture, in a gracious setting. In a dip in the hills, or on the slope of a wood. Not in an avenue.

She got up to go. 'Never mind, Matthew, I suppose you try to help in your way. I'll just have to work it out for myself.'

'Would you like to see the conservatory before you go?' he said. 'The grapes are out.' He wanted to keep her there. He hated the time for her to go, because he was convinced that one of these days she wouldn't come back, and he'd have to admit to himself that he'd lost her for ever. 'What will you do for a living, Karen?'

'Matthew, you know very well how limited the market is. I don't know what I'll do till I try.'

'You can't do anything. You'll never get a job. Why don't you sit for me. No strings. I promise you. Just promise to sit for me regularly, say for five years. I want to do a series . . .'

She lifted her shoulders impatiently. 'I can't tie myself down to five years, Matthew. How do I know that I can keep my promise?'

'I'll pay you well, Karen. You don't like charity from me, and this will be a regular salary. A retainer fee. What do you say?'

She was sadly tempted, but something warned her that he wouldn't let it rest at that. The more he saw of her, the more he'd press the point of tying her there for ever. He hated to let go of anything he got his hands on. It wasn't that he was dishonest. It was just that he had a boyish way of persuading himself that what he was doing was right, even if it was right from his own advantage.

'Well, I won't say now,' she compromised. 'Let me think it over. I expect,' she grinned, 'I shall have to come and take advantage of your offer. I don't suppose there'll be anything else.'

'Going back to that Sark woman?' he murmured.

'Sally Sark has known me for eight years,' Karen said, defensive immediately. Then, because she was honest, 'No, I'm not going back to her. At the moment, we don't quite see eye to eye about such things as men, personal belongings, money and the gay life. Damn it!'

Her next port of call was the office of the solicitors. They were equally unhelpful. They told her there was nothing left; just the house and the mortgage on it.

'I didn't really want to let it go,' she objected, thrusting her lower lip out. 'I really hoped I could raise enough money to...'

'Live in it?' The solicitor smiled. 'Oh, come now, Mrs. Westbury, surely, now,' and he waved his hand in a vague way which suggested that the idea was fantastic, now and for ever.

When Karen broached the subject of work,

he was equally unhelpful. 'Can you type or take shorthand? No? Well, that narrows the field, rather. You could, I suppose, take a housekeeper's job, but without references, and you'd have, of course, to live in, and be on the go from morning till night...'

Again he left it in the air, and leapt to another subject. 'Have you thought of any of the more spectacular forms of employment, such as—ahem—photographer's modelling, and so on? And I believe if you can get a contact, a certain type of film work is not badly paid.'

Karen told him brusquely she had no taste for such things, and that although she was well aware that he knew of the sort of people she was living with, that had nothing to do with what she hoped to do. 'Expediency, as you have often reminded me, Mr. Charles, accounts for our doing many things we wouldn't otherwise do.'

She didn't want to be bad friends with him. She realized that it was definitely to her advantage to keep him as a good friend. He could help her, or do the very minimum of what he was required to do, and where he thought he was going to get his fees, eventually, she hadn't an idea.

Nostalgia took her back to the house, and to her precious prized memories of Blaize. Blaize and the irritating Mr. Charles had gone there together when it had been built, and

Mr. Charles had had many suggestions to make by way of improvement. Blaize had been a very good client of his. They had also belonged to the same club.

Karen shrugged in annoyance. She was allowing the solicitor's bland common sense to spoil her memories. She didn't go in the house, but roamed around the grounds, not getting as much pleasure as usual, and she finally went away in a hurry. Quite suddenly she had called to mind that distressing last visit of hers, with Chris and his aunt. Chris was a disturbing person to know, and of late she had found he had a tendency to pop up in her thoughts when she least expected or wanted him there.

She went into a teashop and ordered a cup of tea and a bath bun. She lit a cigarette and drew hard on it, and thought over where she stood. She and Sally had made quite a bit of spare cash out of their holiday camp adventure, but she herself had gone off without collecting hers, because she could see that the manager was going to be tiresome. She had left it to Sally to see to it for her. Sally, when she came back to the flat, was flabbergasted. She had, she said, no idea that Karen had been referring to her share of the money. O'Leary had said nothing to her about it when he paid her what was due to her.

'What did you think I meant when I asked

you to see to things for me, then,' Karen had demanded, acidly.

'Oh, I thought you just wanted me to explain to O'Leary why you had gone off in such a hurry. You know, give you an alibi and all that, because, as you can guess, he was pretty fed-up with your not saying good-bye personally to him. He was counting on it.'

'I'm sure he was—to the tune of the money he owed me,' Karen retorted. But she was angry and put out. Angry because she was so tired of this shilly-shally, hole-and-corner business of getting money on which to exist, a hole-and-corner business that permitted of no outside help. It was all verbal arrangement, a nod here, a wink there. Suggested fees which could not be pinned down in terms of actual figures, and usually relied on the amount of friendliness one was prepared to show.

'I wonder,' she mused, 'what it feels like to go to an agency and state your qualifications, get a job all drawn up by contract and apply for wage increases every so often? I wonder,' she went on, with an amused smile, 'what it feels like to be a union member, with a body of people behind you, protecting you?'

But as always the old yearning for freedom overtook her. She didn't really want anyone else to fight her battles for her, because experience showed her that whatever the protecting body were like, you always owed it to them, and had to toe the line in some measure or other. In that, both she and Chris were deplorably alike. They wanted to be free as birds of the air; free to work to-day and be gone to-morrow. 'I suppose,' she finished, as she popped a tip beneath the plate and got up to go, 'I suppose I shall just have to take what comes and be philosophical.'

She bought an evening paper outside the café, and sat on a park bench to read it. The evenings were getting chilly now. A lot of the heat was fast leaving the glorious late summer they had had, and nothing but a memory remained of the shining, brassily hot days of the holiday camp period.

Hopefully at first, she scanned the advertisements for staff, and it was only when she was deciding to put the paper down in disgust that she caught sight of an advertisement in the personal column. It required a young woman of good education and good background, with tact and the quality of handling people rather than a commercial training, to assist a charity organizer. Would applicants please apply by telephone, before 6 o'clock.

Karen made an appointment by telephone, to call at 6 o'clock, and was given the address. She went there at once, to see what sort of place it was, and found a quiet block of flats, in a quiet, sedate street. Her heart sank. She knew that her appearance alone would go against her. Her dark-green corduroy suit, with its narrow edging of fur all round the jacket, was too smart of cut, too expensive of material. Her hat, with its sweeping black feather which curled under her chin, was not conducive to her receiving an organizer's assistant's post. She went back frowning to Sally's flat.

Sally was out. Karen got out all her own things, and found at last an extremely plain dark brown dress, and a fine wool scarf, which she bound round her head turban-fashion, and completely hid the offending hair. With the dress she wore hogskin gloves, and got out a plain brown bag and shoes; things she seldom wore because of their very plainness.

The girl who stared back at her from the mirror was a stranger, and not a very exciting stranger. To complete it all, after she had had a quick bath, and got into what she now mentally referred to as her 'fancy-dress costume', she also omitted lipstick.

Mrs. Lawrence, the person interviewing, was a busy little woman in an austere suit and man's shirt. She said she had no time for dawdlers, or persons not prepared to be extremely interested in the work. She preferred someone with experience, but if that couldn't be, then she wished for someone who would succumb to her training. How, she wanted to know, did Karen feel she fitted into this? She sat back, her tubby little figure straining at what were obviously expensive fitted corsets and brassiere and glared aggressively through pince-nez at Karen, who was very glad her red hair was out of sight.

Karen drew a breath, and leaned forward slightly. 'Mrs. Lawrence, I must tell you first of all that I am a widow. I came from a very good family, but I am too proud to return to them for sustenance. I've always had a secret yearning (of which I dare not tell my family) to have the opportunity of studying organizing at close quarters. Whether I shall be of any use to you I cannot say, but it would be, for me, an opportunity of which I have dreamed, just to be given a short trial, in which I can, shall we say—show my paces?'

The little woman's face flushed with pleasure. Karen's sentiments, she said, were the right ones. It would be her privilege and pleasure to personally train her into being her assistant.

Karen, she felt, had spoken from the heart, and as such, was the right material. Did Karen, she asked, know that she was the founder and governing body of the Saint Letitia's Circle for Improving the Mental Outlook of Destitute Girls? The destitute girls came to her for a job, which she invariably found, and then stayed with her in their time off to have ideas instilled in them for improving their ways of spending their leisure, and their thinking hours. She was immensely wrapped up in her idea. A sincere and talkative little woman whom it was, while impossible to like her for herself, equally impossible to dislike her, owing to the depth of her sincerity and purpose.

Karen left the flat a little dazed. She wanted to talk to someone, tell someone all about it. But there was no one. Chris was off, heaven knew where, and it was certain that he wanted nothing more to do with her. His aunt was one of those unpredictable women, evidently, whose sympathies were swayed according to circumstances and appearances. Sally Sark was out of the question, because Karen had already made up her mind to collect her few belongings from Sally's flat and just leave a brief note explaining that she had made other arrangements, and would be writing. A vague and in this case, extremely satisfactory way of leaving things.

The fact that she had got a job, in such a short space of time, and so apparently easily, too, was not the prime factor just now. It had surprised Karen, but only in the way that fate did surprise her. You just couldn't plan, nor rely on anything it seemed. Sometimes luck evaded you; sometimes it dropped into your lap, with no particular reason. No, the job, after the first breathless feeling about it had gone, left Karen rather cold. What did weigh heavily on her, as she put the key in the door of Sally's flat, was why Chris had gone off like that, with nothing beyond that poor, brief note.

CHAPTER TEN

Mrs. Lawrence, Karen found in the weeks that followed, had bought the house that was now the hostel. It was her own energy and the vast circle of friends she had, that accounted for the jobs that were found for the girls.

Mrs. Lawrence personally roped in people to give charity concerts to raise money for her schemes, and also to give entertainment to the girls; she also had them taught the useful arts and crafts. Any latent talent anyone was found to have, was brought out and trained. Their doubtful backgrounds were wiped away as far as possible, by pleasant surroundings and companionship. In all, any destitute girl who found her way to Mrs. Lawrence, Karen felt (thinking of herself not so long ago and the way she had scraped an existence) would have a friend and adviser for life. Well, an adviser, anyway.

As for herself, most of the misgivings she harboured about the possibility of success in this job were swept away in a matter of days. Although she couldn't type or take down shorthand, she had a pleasant voice on the telephone, and a great deal of common sense.

She found she could cope with Mrs. Lawrence's appointment pad, and could keep away from that busy person those tiresome people who are to be found in most offices, who will bother the heads of such organizations. Karen had a bland yet firm method of dealing with the beggar, the crank and the pest, and could tell unerringly after a very short while, who had something to offer in the way of ideas, who had time or money to spend, and who was, in fact, gong to be of any use at all to Mrs. Lawrence.

In many other ways she made herself if not indispensable, yet so very useful and likeable that Mrs. Lawrence decided to raise her wages as a token of her belief in Karen and the future. Although the wages weren't large to begin with, there was enough to pay her rent and food bills, and to buy the simple clothes she had found Mrs. Lawrence approved of.

Karen had a tiny office off Mrs. Lawrence's big one, in a building kept for such organizations as this. Mr. Lawrence had a lot of money, a lot of spare time and very few ideas. He kept his cashbook handy it seemed, for Mrs. Lawrence's many needs, and he tried, rather unsuccessfully, it appeared to Karen, to run one or two organizations for himself, but these usually flopped after a year or two. Mrs. Lawrence told her that poor Quested had the heart but not the head for such things.

Every so often Mrs. Lawrence, who was generally on the Board of one of her husband's companies, would take time off from her own busy day or night, to go over things with him and try and see what was going wrong. Usually she said it was staff, and they would have a clean sweep. Then advertisements had to be sent out for more staff, and time had to be made to interview them, and to take up their references. Then once again things would settle down. But Mr. Lawrence looked no happier, and Mrs. Lawrence's help didn't seem to be so wide-sweeping as it was when applied to her own organization.

Karen couldn't decide whether she looked on her husband with good-natured contempt, as a complete fool and a buffoon or whether she just hadn't the time to give to really help him to any large extent. She certainly didn't worry about the way in which he squandered money, or where he spent his time after he left the office building. She herself, and Karen, often worked until quite late at night. Karen enjoyed it all. She liked the busy days and she was grateful for being so tired at night that she hadn't time to think before she dropped off to sleep.

Karen stayed there until Christmas. It was, in fact, the getting together of a company of entertainers for the Christmas holiday, that caused Karen indirectly to leave a job in which she was daily growing more interested.

She was now right away from the gang. She had staggered them by the news that she had got a job, and offended them by not giving them details of her new address. She had moved her few belongings from Sally's, to a small and decent bed-sitting-room she had rented within walking distance of the office, with the object of saving fares. She hadn't even told Matthew what she was doing, and because she knew that the gang weren't above calling up the solicitor to find out about her, she had not acquainted him with the details of her new life either.

She now wore excessively plain clothes, and kept her hair in the turban as part of her new 'style'. Mrs. Lawrence, who had firm ideas of how a young woman should dress, especially a young working woman, approved her plain frocks but was darkly suspicious of the turban. She felt it was ultra-fashionable, and in some way not quite ladylike to hide the hair completely. By hints and innuendos, she tried to draw Karen out. Was she suffering from some skin disease, Mrs. Lawrence asked, in an infinitely sympathetic voice, because if so, she knew just the man to cure it. He would do it solely because he was a friend of hers and she had asked him. No? Was it, then, that her hair was not tidy, because surely, then, a net would be better.

No? Just a habit of dress? That, she felt, was worse than ever. But it was hardly a big enough point on which to quarrel with someone who was becoming so useful to her, so Mrs. Lawrence wisely let it go.

But with Christmas near, even Karen thought that she might make an effort to abandon the now objectionable headpiece. Surely now, Mrs. Lawrence was too used to her, and too satisfied with her quiet ways, to feel any of the usual reactions which most older women seem to experience, when Karen was dressed in her usual smart way? She thought it over, and decided to take a chance.

There was to be a party given for the 'girls' at Mrs. Lawrence's own house, just out of town. It was a big old-fashioned house, and Mrs. Lawrence prided herself on her idea of a big, old-fashioned Christmas to go with it. 'The girls,' she told Karen, 'had never experienced any such thing in their lives, and at Christmas, one must make an effort.'

Mrs. Lawrence had a dozen women helpers congregated to carry out her directions for the festivities. To Karen she said, 'You know, my dear, your features are pleasing, and you have fine eyes. I think if you tried you could really *make* something of yourself. Now I want you to wear your prettiest dress, and let your hair down—don't be shy. Let us see what sort of hair you've got, just for this once.'

Karen wore the sprigged muslin dance

frock she had last worn at the holiday camp. It was pretty, and the least sophisticated thing she had, and in any case, she couldn't afford to buy a new evening dress of the kind she had been used to. She wore her rich red-brown hair bunched in great curls at the back of her head, and allowed small curls to escape in a fringe across her forehead. Small blue and white flower earclips and a necklace to match, and the merest trace of lipstick, and she felt she was an altered creature from the quiet brown-clad figure who sat in the office with a turban on.

Someone else agreed she was different. Quested Lawrence was looking for his sister, so he said. He looked for her in Karen's bedroom. He had been drinking, and was very merry, a completely unfamiliar figure from the rather lost individual who haunted his wife's office building.

Karen, with the rather cruel outlook of discerning youth saw him as a comical little figure with too much stomach, an oldish man trying to be young and devilish, impossibly gallant.

'My dear,' he said, thickly, 'I always knew you had hair that colour. Know how? Saw it, 'scaping one day from beneath that turban thing. Never wear that turban. Scrap it. Doesn't suit you. I wouldn't make a dog wear the thing. No, no, defin'te mistake.'

He had left the door open, and advanced

towards her with his eyes popping with pleasure, his hands held wide. 'S'Christmas, my dear, and I don't think even my dear wife would mind me stealing just li'l kiss. Do you?'

Karen was bored. As soon as she showed herself as herself, and not as some frightful frump, the trouble seemed to start again.

'Don't be absurd, Mr. Lawrence,' she said, wearily. Men were all the same. And it was the weariness and contempt in her young voice that stung Mrs. Lawrence most, as she passed the open door.

She hesitated for a moment only, then passing on, called to her husband. He came, trotting rather than hurrying, docile like a pet dog. She was angry with him, angry and rather sorry for him. Angry because no one had the right to be anything but respectful to him. Quested with all his money! If only he weren't such a comic figure, or if only she could persuade him to stay out of business, get someone really competent to run things for him.

She shrugged business off her shoulders. It was Christmas. Her highest success point of the year. There was to be a lot of gift-giving for the hundred or so 'girls' downstairs, there was to be an array of nice party food for them; there was a band and dancing, one or two concert turns (chiefly among her friends) and there were to be speeches. Speeches intended to show them what a lot had been done for them, and in quite a nice way, too. She was always happy about Christmas. But this year it was marred a little by that girl.

She couldn't take her eyes off Karen all the evening. She bore with hearing everyone say what a surprise packet Karen had turned out to be, heard them asking Karen why she had disguised herself for so long, hidden her lovely hair like that? She had put up with the 'girls'' eyes following—not herself, as usual, as the organizer and great lady of the proceedings—but Karen, the picture piece of all.

The photographers she had got in, instead of being keen and anxious to take her picture, with Quested, beside the enormous tree, wanted to take Karen by it, and when she had protested (in as nice a way as possible, of course), they had finally compromised by putting Karen in the picture with them. The 'girls' had all clapped and called for it, so she had to give in.

But all this was a mixture of small irritants, Mrs. Lawrence, with her curious philosophy and talent for turning everything to her own ends, might have forgotten the shock of Karen's beauty, and turned it to some useful purpose, had it not been for an unfortunate conversation she overheard, between two of the caterer's staff.

'Where did those two old frumps get *her*

from?' one said, looking at Karen on the improvised stage, as she led some community singing, not quite in the style of the holiday camp, but in a quieter, more appealing way which in other circumstances would have pleased Mrs. Lawrence very much. The girl might have been popular enough to use for the charity concerts and bazaars.

'The old lady's secretary, they say,' the other mused.

'*Her* secretary? *That* dish?' He had laughed, vulgarly. 'The old man's piece, I should say!'

'The old dog! Didn't think he'd got it in him,' was the remark which put the seal on to Karen's future.

Mrs. Lawrence looked across into one of the big mirrors and saw herself standing by her husband. Two squat little figures. Frumps, it was true. She had always known it, but hadn't minded very much. But she recalled Karen's weary bored tone, instead of anger or indignation. She despised them both. Mrs. Lawrence glanced down at her fat white arms, in her sleeveless black gown. She always wore the same style, in the hope that it gave her dignity, forcefulness. Now it looked all wrong, and slightly ridiculous. Quested looked ridiculous in his tails, yet it had been made by one of the best tailors in London.

She felt, in that moment, that she could have stood seeing Karen's beauty each day, and could even have borne the thought that Quested hankered for her. But the thought that others felt he wasn't able to attract such a beauty, Quested with all his wealth, was too much. Fat and little and old, and rather funny, the pair of them.

Tears stung her eyes, and she blinked them away fiercely as she was called upon for a speech. Karen was clapping and smiling up at her with the rest, but she felt that Karen wasn't smiling with her but at her. She faltered in her opening. In all, it was a bad speech, and everyone looked at each other, wondering what was the matter with her She, with all her confidence and sincerity, had never made such a bad speech in her life.

Somehow she got through that Christmas, hating it, hating herself and Quested, hating everybody. The mood of suspicion lasted afterwards. She found herself asking others of the staff how they found Karen, and whether she had been saying anything about Quested or about herself. Everyone noticed the change in her, and it ran like wildfire, that mood of suspicion and uneasiness, until everyone was affected by it, and it came back to Karen herself.

At the end of the week after Christmas, Mrs. Lawrence sent for her, and asked how she was getting on with the job.

'I think I'm getting into my stride,' Karen said. She had put on the turban again immediately Christmas was over, but because the old quiet atmosphere had not been resumed, she had felt something was wrong. 'Is there something you're displeased with me for?' she asked Mrs. Lawrence.

By way of answer, Mrs. Lawrence started asking searching questions about her former life.

Karen stiffened. 'I'm sorry, but I answered all the necessary questions at the interview. You took me on then, and said you were satisfied and that you were a good judge of character. My private life is my own, and I'm afraid I must refuse to answer questions about it now.'

'Were you ever on the stage?' Mrs. Lawrence insisted.

'Oh, my hair?' It was the first, and defensive question, with Karen. At times she hated it. At all times she played with the idea of having it dyed, but shrank from it as a distasteful one. 'I'm not a professional artiste, though I have sung in an amateurish way.'

Mrs. Lawrence wasn't satisfied. By hints and darting questions she tried to suggest that Karen came of stage people, or something similar, which would naturally make her unsuitable for her job.

At last Karen, smelling the signs, grew tired. 'Look, Mrs. Lawrence, this has all boiled up over Christmas, hasn't it? It seems to me that you and I will never get on, so I'd better leave and have done with it.'

Mrs. Lawrence didn't want her to leave, from the point of view of her ability, but from the point of view of her own feelings, and the devil of tormenting doubt inside her, she knew in her heart that it was the best thing. But she wanted Karen to stay, until she could find out all about her and feel justified in dispensing with her services because of her background. She was in an unknown and frightening mood which scared her. In all her life she had prided herself on being a judge of character, on having superb self-confidence, and in being a success. By chance, Karen had undermined all that, and the little woman found herself hating the girl. Repelled and yet fascinated by her.

Karen put her out of her misery by going quickly and cleanly. But for herself it was not the end, and as she walked along the pavement, carrying her one suitcase, on that cold December day, she felt unnerved and cold. Not that she had given up that job. It was just a job. Not that she had given up the room, because it was associated with that job. But because of the nagging fear that it would always be the same, wherever she went, whatever she did. There was no respite. No peace.

CHAPTER ELEVEN

And yet the getting of a new job wasn't difficult. Karen, in a beautifully tailored navy coat—a relic from the days when her wardrobe was more expensive—and a close-fitting felt over her glowing hair, spent a miserable January afternoon in a big cinema, and idly took in details of an advertisement flung on to the screen in the interval for usherettes. She had gone back to betting on horses, and was having a run of good luck. The wages of an usherette would supplement it.

It wasn't that she wanted any job that was going, so much as this particular type of job. She reasoned that for the most part she would be working in the dark. Her hair, that bane and troublemaker for her, would be mainly hidden under a dark beret which was part of the uniform adopted in this particular picture house, and during the short interval, she reasoned that she could keep out of the way. The manager, sadly under-staffed, accepted her right away, subject to references. These she got from the doctor and vicar near the old house, who had known her in Blaize's time. Both were reluctant, and only gave in when, in a telephone conversation with each, she intimated, without actually telling a lie, that she needed this particular job because of something she was working on. She said she didn't expect to be there long, and that was true too.

She didn't like the job. It was boring, tedious, and at times rather difficult. The other girls were inquisitive, and wanted to be friends too quickly. One was cantankerous, and inclined to be resentful of Karen, for no particular reason, as far as Karen could see. Instinctive, she told herself, with a grin. I don't like her, either.

One day she met Chris's aunt in the street. Mrs. Heath had been shopping in one of the big stores, and had stopped to look at the stills outside the cinema. She saw Karen come out, and asked if the film were good. Karen, who had seen it already some twelve times, could not bring herself to speak rationally about it. She said, 'I'm biased. I don't like pictures anyway.'

'My dear! Why go there, then?'

'I work there,' Karen said, with some pleasure, hoping to make Mrs. Heath look horrified.

She was disappointed. Mrs. Heath looked staggered for a moment, then quickly recovering herself, she said, 'Karen, I'm dying for a cup of tea. Come to my favourite restaurant with me.'

Karen found herself going without protest. Partly because she had nothing better to do, for it was her afternoon off, and because she felt it would be nice to talk to someone of her own acquaintance. She hadn't seen the gang for a long time, and wasn't particularly anxious to.

Snow fell while they were having tea. They watched it from the window of the restaurant, and Karen said suddenly: 'D'you know where Chris is? What on earth does he do with himself in this sort of weather?'

'I had hoped,' Mrs. Heath said, 'that you would be able to tell *me* that!' Into the little silence, she said, 'Karen, I didn't like you at first. I can't say for certain that I do now, mind you. But there's something about you—you *grow* on people.'

'How awful!' Karen said, flippantly. She was so surprised that she couldn't think of anything else to say.

'I'd like you, if you will, to develop the habit of droppng in to see me now and then. I know that you won't tell me what you've been doing, or why you had to take this fantastic job, or wear these simple clothes. I didn't like the flamboyant way you dressed before, but I can see now, that it suited you. I can't say I like you in that get-up.'

'I loathe it, too,' Karen said, without any ill-will. It struck her then that the two of them—neither having any great liking for the other—were being deliberately drawn together by the mischievous spirit of the

122

absent Chris. They both missed him and wanted to hear about him. To each, the other had seemed—and probably would go on seeming—the only link.

'When did you see Chris last?' Mrs. Heath wanted to know.

'At the end of September.' Karen played with her roll and butter. She didn't know whether she wanted to tell Mrs. Heath about that or not. Then a spirit of mischief entered her, and she did tell her. The whole episode, which of course, led in its turn to the way she had been living with Sally and her crowd. Horse racing, debts, drinking and parties, her restlessness and hatred of the whole thing, yet her not knowing where else she could go or what else she could do to forget Blaize.

She told it in a quiet matter-of-fact voice, as though she were telling a story she had told so many times before that it now had no meaning for her. At this stage, she really did shock Mrs. Heath. Not so much because of the things she had been doing, but her curiously impassive acceptance of her inability to do anything else.

'Oh, my dear, I'm so sorry,' Mrs. Heath said, impulsively. 'I didn't ... I just didn't know. Didn't realize.' She sounded helpless, as if she felt she ought to say something quite different, yet couldn't think what to say which would be really appropriate.

'What on earth for?' Karen asked, in surprise. 'Why should you be sorry?' She shrugged, lightly. With a grin, not at Mrs. Heath, but at herself, for succumbing to this curious delight in telling stories against herself, she entered into minute details of her job with the organizer, and how it had finished up.

At the end, she laughed, a little light gay laugh. 'There now, that's paid for my tea, hasn't it? And I really believe I've kept you amused solidly for close on two hours.'

Mrs. Heath looked ashamed and slightly angry. She had believed it all implicitly. 'It wasn't true, then, was it? You were just making it up in the mistaken idea that I needed amusing.'

'On the contrary,' Karen said, 'it was all true, painfully true. Down to the last detail. The joke, if there is any, is on me, Mrs. Heath. I've broken a rule of a life-time and told you about it. I broke the same rule when I told your nephew all about my ... widowhood.'

'I see. Then I can only thank you for the confidence,' Mrs. Heath said, doubtfully, then, recovering herself, she said, with asperity, 'but just the same, young woman, I think it's a disgraceful way to go on for a girl of your upbringing. What would your parents think about you?'

Karen looked blankly at her. 'I haven't the

faintest. Honestly. Mummy died when I was little. I don't remember her. My father? Oh, he didn't care what I did, so long as Matthew didn't get hold of me to paint his beastly heads.' She laughed, and murmured, 'And if you think you're going to pin me down to tell you about Matthew, you're mistaken. I've told you quite enough about myself for to-day.'

'You're a strange girl, Karen. Nevertheless, I do really mean that I'd like to see you. Come next week, at this time, will you? To tea.'

Karen gravely thanked her.

Before she got up to go, she said, 'Barbara, what's she like? Really, I mean?'

Mrs. Heath looked startled. 'Well, really, I don't know how to answer that. She's a very nice girl. She comes to see me sometimes. To tea. You might meet. Would you like to meet her?'

Karen thought about it. 'Not specially. I was just wondering ... you see, Chris isn't the sort of person a girl would leave, just like that, when he's in the lurch. And yet, well, he does such unaccountable things. I don't know. Look at the way he left me, at the holiday camp. Of course, I know there's no comparison. We're just friends, and all that. Just the same, if you look at it from the point of view of civilized persons, well, it was just plain rude. And ... Chris isn't rude.'

The two women stared at each other for a moment. 'Did that friend of yours meet him, on her own, I mean?'

'Sally? No, I don't think so. In any case, Sally and I don't interfere. Not that you can imagine Chris taking any notice if she did, that's if he didn't want to, I mean.'

They left each other at the door of the restaurant, Karen to walk to her new bed-sitting-room, Mrs. Heath to take a taxi back to her house. It had stopped snowing now, and was bitterly cold.

As they shook hands, Mrs. Heath said, 'Karen, about your job and money and everything, don't do anything foolish, will you? Not before you tell me about it, anyway.'

Karen smiled. 'That's rather nice of you. In fact it's very nice of you. And being me, I feel awful about it, because I can't promise. Just the same, it was nice. Good-bye.'

Karen went to tea the following week. Mrs. Heath was agreeably surprised to see her. 'I really didn't think you'd come, you know.'

'Neither did I,' Karen smiled. 'Then I thought I'd like to. You haven't heard from Chris, I suppose?'

'I was just going to ask you that,' his aunt said, with a troubled smile. 'Well, I don't think we'll be disturbed so let's sit down by the fire and have a nice long chat. I've got some pictures of Chris when he was small that

126

I thought you'd like to see. And some cuttings. I'm one of those queer people who keep a cuttings album, and mine is pretty comprehensive.'

'Will you tell me why you keep it?' Karen smiled. 'I've so often wanted to know why people do.' She didn't really but she had a sudden aversion to letting Mrs. Heath see how madly anxious she was to see Chris's early photographs. As she pored over them, she kept up a deceptive flow of bright chatter, and Chris's aunt, watching her, was disappointed.

The cuttings book was mainly about family and friends. There was something interesting to say about each of them, but the only one that had any interest for Karen was from a local paper, describing the sports day at Chris's college. It looked funny to see him described as Christopher James Halliday. He looked as if the name, and the importance of it, sat weightily on his shoulders; a tall, thin lad with a serious face, and an air of panting to get out of his prize-day clothes and into something really old and comfortable, to be off and away at swimming, fishing or football. Those, the cutting said, were his hobbies.

Karen said, 'Isn't it funny? Always, when you see pictures of people you know, when they are young, you wish you had known them then? I probably shouldn't have liked Chris very much when he was at school, and

I'm pretty sure he wouldn't have liked me at that age.'

Just as they were having tea, Barbara was announced. Karen wondered if Mrs. Heath had asked her specially, since she didn't seem surprised at her coming, and when she said she was, Barbara looked rather confused.

She was, as Mrs. Heath had said, a nice girl. Not very smart but smart enough. The sort of girl Mrs. Heath would have had as a daughter.

She looked at Karen with frank curiosity and with franker admiration. 'Are you engaged to Chris?' she asked, when they were finished tea.

'Good heavens, no,' Karen laughed, and caught Mrs. Heath's eye. 'Mrs. Heath wouldn't like me to be, either. Would you?'

'I find it a bit of a strain to keep up with your peculiar sense of humour, my dear,' she admitted, 'but if Chris has to bring some young woman home to me as his wife, it might as well be you, as Barbara here says it won't be her.'

'Oh, come now, Chris might find some girl you'd like better than either of us,' Karen teased, smiling at Barbara.

Barbara looked rather pained, and Karen couldn't understand why. She couldn't understand why she constantly came here, either, running into the danger of a meeting with Chris, since it was she who had thrown him over, and at a time when he had needed her.

Mrs. Heath said, with the corners of her mouth down a little, 'I don't think it likely that Chris would bring anyone home that I'd really like and I've got used to you now, Karen.'

At that, the two girls burst out laughing, and the tension eased. They went at the same time, and walked to the bus stop.

Karen said, 'Do you go out to work?'

Barbara said she did, and was a business man's secretary.

'Then you won't want to know me,' she said, with a hint of mischief. 'I'm only an usherette in a cinema.'

Barbara said, hesitantly, 'Mrs. Heath told me a bit about you. I've often found that when people have had a lot of trouble, it either makes them bitter and beastly, or makes them develop a sense of fun that recoils on other people. I wish you'd try to overcome it, Karen. It spoils you, you know.' And then, because she was just what Mrs. Heath said—a nice girl—she said, quickly, 'I say, I hope you don't mind my saying that. I'd like to see you again, really I would.'

'Well, let's meet then,' Karen said, making a date, without any hope of Barbara keeping it. But she did.

To Mrs. Heath's chagrin, they became quite good friends. She said to Karen once, when she was at her house on a day when Barbara couldn't come, 'Really, Karen, at times, despite all my trying to like you, I find you are exasperating me cruelly. Why are you going about with Barbara?'

'D'you mind, really, I mean?'

'Naturally I mind. I think it's grievous bad taste. Her one time connection with Chris, I mean, and so on. I don't think it's nice.'

'Have you told Barbara how you feel about it?'

'As a matter of fact, I have.' Mrs. Heath looked genuinely distressed. 'She didn't see why I should feel like it. I *do* think young women are tiresome.'

'Well, you brought us together,' Karen laughed.

Mrs. Heath laughed, too. A rueful laugh, at her own expense. 'I'm caught out, and I admit it. But,' she said looking nettled again, 'I didn't do it for you two to become friends. I did it because—well, I rather hoped you'd see what a nice girl she was, and realize I was trying to bring her and Chris together again.'

'And back out, obligingly?' Karen hazarded. 'But I thought you had reconciled yourself to Chris and I being friends—when we are friends, that is!' She was genuinely puzzled at Mrs. Heath's attitude.

Mrs. Heath shrugged. 'My nephew seems to get into touch with you and not with me. I hoped to hear from him through you.'

'Oh!' Karen said, in a small voice. 'What a funny thing. I began to think you were liking me a little for myself.'

'That's just the nuisance of it!' Chris's aunt exploded. 'I am!'

One day, Karen said to Mrs. Heath, 'Has Chris been here? He's in town.' She looked rather upset.

'No, he hasn't, Karen. Where—how did you get to know?'

'It wasn't—very nice. I was on a train. Only an underground. One of those stations where two trains come into the station. I was looking into the other one, and realized I was staring at Chris. We just stared. It was horrid. Then his train moved out. Mine did, too, a minute after.'

'Well, what happened? Did you go back to his station? Or wait for him at your own?' asked the practical Mrs. Heath.

'No, I just sat on in my train. I didn't think it would be any good getting out. I didn't even know if he'd come on my line, or if he'd want to see me. I do so hate those hit-and-miss affairs. And I just hate seeing someone I know in another vehicle. It's happened to me before.'

She was furious with herself for appearing distressed, but had to speak about it. Mrs. Heath thought about Chris, and wondered.

Karen didn't go to Mrs. Heath's house the following week, and didn't send a note or telephone any explanation. Barbara, who came expecting to see her, was disappointed, and showed it.

'Well, when did you see her last?' Mrs. Heath said, having now accepted their friendship with good grace.

'Only two days ago,' Barbara said.

There was an impatient knocking on the front door. 'There she is!' Barbara said, with pleasure. 'Shall I go?'

'No, let the maid go. I never believe in robbing them of their job.'

'I hate bringing her up from the kitchen when we know it's Karen,' said the kindly Barbara, settling back in her chair.

There was the subdued sound of voices, and one was a man's. Mrs. Heath got up, frowning, and made to go to the door. 'Who can it be?' she murmured half to herself.

Barbara, recognizing the voice, whitened. At that moment the door opened, and the maid, also looking distressed, with an eye on Barbara, said, 'It's Mr. Christopher, Madam.'

CHAPTER TWELVE

Mrs. Heath said, nervously, 'Well, well, where is he? Don't keep him at the door like a stranger!'

Barbara said, in embarrassment, 'Oh, no, I don't want to see him, please! How can I get out of this room?'

Mrs. Heath said, 'Well, really, Barbara, surely you take that risk every time you come to this house. What is it, May?'

'Mr. Christopher wouldn't stay, ma'am, when he heard that—' the maid looked apologetically at Barbara. 'You see, ma'am, he asked especially if anyone was here. He wanted to talk to you alone.'

'Oh, well, perhaps it's as well,' Mrs. Heath said. 'Really though, Barbara, I don't pretend to understand you. I thought it was all settled between you and that you wouldn't mind meeting my nephew again.'

'I'm sorry, Mrs. Heath,' Barbara said, vaguely, and went without disclosing anything that would satisfy Mrs. Heath's curiosity.

Chris didn't come back. He was furious with his aunt. The first thought that came into his mind when he heard a girl's voice talking to Mrs. Heath in the drawing-room, was that Karen was there. He had no great wish to see Karen after he had left her, but he did want to discuss with his aunt a matter that was becoming an increasing problem to him. It was while he was nosing around the shell of his old factory that the idea came to him for starting up again. It was winter, and the road had no longer any great attraction for him.

133

On that day, he ran into a man he had been in business with before he had started the factory. He had a little money. Chris would need some, too, and he hadn't a bean. The prospects looked good.

Mrs. Heath had always represented to Chris the rather out-of-the-ordinary kind of aunt who would give a fellow friendship and ask no questions; who would overlook his queer comings and goings, his moods, and his need for an occasional loan. He also thought of her as a sage woman of business, one who might be persuaded to take a chance in something new. Her income was safe and assured. She speculated in property. No one knew quite how much she had, but she certainly had no fear of poverty if she lost any. Chris had gone to her unhesitatingly.

Now he shrugged angrily, at the thought of what he might have run into if he hadn't had the forethought to ask May who was there with his aunt. He had never suspected her of matchmaking before, but there could only be one interpretation, as far as he could see, on Barbara's presence there. His aunt had disapproved of Karen. He had felt it, although he had not been able to pin her down to an admission. Now, he considered, this proved it. He didn't know that Barbara had formed the habit of visiting his aunt because she liked her, nor did he know that Barbara had met Karen and was friendly with her. He just looked on Barbara's visit with the gravest suspicions, and was proportionately angry.

He got on a bus, and rode unheeding, until he realized he had gone in the wrong direction. He got out, and walked moodily about the cold streets. He thought of Karen, and those friends of hers, and he went over and over again the shady deals which Wilfred had offered him. Wilfred had the wrong idea about him. He thought that because Chris hadn't a bean, or a place of his own, and led a wandering life, that he must be in some unorthodox way of business, and wanted to get in. So he tempted Chris with slick money.

Chris was sickened and angry. He didn't want Karen to be friends with that crowd, yet he was afraid of going back to her, in case it was true what Sally had hinted. He was perfectly happy to be friends with Karen. A girl like that for a friend was a treasure. If he had come to feel something rather special for her later on, well, that would have had to be. But he had always hated to feel that the girl he was interested in was driving up to an engagement.

That was one of the things that had made him angry about Barbara. She had engineered the whole thing, and then, when his business had failed and he was talking wildly about flinging everything up and going abroad, she had decided that her judgment had been wrong from the start, and thrown everything over. He didn't understand that Barbara was afraid of being jilted; that having brought things to a head herself in the first place, she had no idea of the depths of his feelings for her, and so couldn't assess whether he would stick to her despite his wild talk, or leave her. Barbara was not the type of girl who could have endured being jilted. She would rather do it herself, if only for face-saving. When she had first heard of the way he went about the country like a tramp, she was sure she had done the right thing, though she still couldn't bear to think of it. It grieved her that Chris had proved to be what his aunt called an 'unstable character', and though his aunt uttered the description in affectionate tones, it didn't lessen what Barbara considered to be a definite flaw in his character, which no woman could do anything about.

Chris smiled grimly to himself as he recalled that not so long ago he had been dreaming (in connection with Karen) of founding a business in one of the towns he had been through. What an ass he was! Much better to keep away from women altogether.

There was more snow on the way. He watched the lowering skies, and decided to go back up north and accept the temporary managership of the factory which he had been offered by a man he had made friends with in the last week. It was a badly paid job, in a mean little town, but the beauty of it for Chris was that there would be the familiar smell of a factory about him again, and yet the job was only temporary. There was no feeling of lurking chains, and there would be food and some sort of roof over his head. He didn't like the way of life he had come to take lately. It vaguely worried him, yet his panic at the thought of being tied down was in its way more worrying. He was prepared to accept the lesser of the two evils.

Karen watched the skies, too, with much the same feelings. She was in bed with a high temperature. One after another, the usherettes had contracted 'flu. It was about, and the extremes of temperature—stifling hot in the cinema, and sharply cold outside—did the rest. Most of them lived at home, so could be sure of someone being able to attend to them. Karen had a room in a house overflowing with tenants, yet no one knew she was ill, or cared.

A girl called Doris who had been working at the cinema just a week longer than Karen, looked in one day. She was a wizened little creature, dark and shifty of eyes, lank and greasy of hair. Karen loathed her, yet she seemed to want to be friends.

'Thought I'd look in and see if you wanted anything,' she said, not looking at Karen, but at the room itself; her little mean eyes darted all round, missing nothing. 'Not much of a dump you got here,' she observed.

Karen said, 'It was kind of you to come. I don't want anything, really, except a prescription making up, but I expect the chemists are closed now, aren't they?' Her eyes were heavy and her head ached intolerably.

Doris said, 'Yes, you're right there. Can't someone in the house do it?'

'Yes, I expect so,' Karen said, wearily, wishing she would go. 'Please don't worry about me. I'll be all right.'

'Haven't you got any folks?' Doris asked, curiously. 'Anyone I can take a message to?'

Karen thought of Sally, and revolted against getting drawn into the gang again. She hadn't backed a horse or drunk or smoked since she had been at the cinema. It was a new code with her, and though she ached for a cigarette at times, she took a vicious pleasure in denying herself. She felt that if she gave way over the cigarettes, she'd do the same over horses because she was hungry and often cold, and the money wouldn't stretch. She had never been used to economizing, and wondered more each day how the other girls lived on it.

'No,' she said, now. It was on the tip of her tongue to mention Matthew, but she knew that Doris was only waiting for the opportunity to get a sight of Karen's real background. She had always hinted that she

138

knew Karen was different to the rest of them. For this reason, Karen also ruled out the thought of Chris's aunt, and Barbara. Out of all her acquaintances, there was no one whom she could feel comfortable in calling on to help her, in this squalid room, where there wasn't even a stove on which to cook invalid food. She had managed up till now with a gas-ring.

Doris went at last, dissatisfied at having discovered nothing, and with a bitter parting shot. 'The manager says he hopes you'll be back to-morrow or he'll have to think about getting someone else.'

Karen lay with her eyes closed, feeling very, very ill. The doctor was coming again to-morrow. He would again press her to allow him to send her to hospital. The landlady, however, didn't want that. She was afraid that Karen would slip through her fingers, owing rent, and she knew very well that Karen hadn't enough of anything in her box to make it worth the landlady's while to keep it. The landlady herself had already been pressing for details of her friends.

'I know you got some, ducks,' she said. 'Seen you meself with a rare smart woman, once, in the High Street.'

Karen smiled involuntarily. She wondered what Mrs. Heath would have to say about that description of herself. 'If you want to be helpful,' Karen had said, 'for heaven's sake

139

make me a cup of tea.'

'Have you got any?' the landlady asked, suspiciously.

Karen shook her head.

'I thought not. Well, I'm not starting it. Tea costs money, and once started, I shall find myself with an invalid on me hands. No, I'll send for your friend, with pleasure; you just give me her address, now, and be a sensible girl. But starting tea-making, I won't do.'

The next day Karen was so much worse that the doctor said he would send her away on his own responsibility. And then Molly came.

'I'm Mrs. Borden,' she said, briskly, her little-girl manner for the moment forgotten. 'I was wondering what had become of Karen, and one day I saw her come out of the side entrance of the cinema in the High Street. I telephoned to them, and heard she was ill, so I made them give me her address.' She looked round the poor little room with surprise. 'She can't stay here.' The doctor agreed grimly. 'Don't take her to hospital. She must go back with me to my place,' Molly said decisively.

Molly had money, and new clothes. The landlady assessed the latter, and rapidly totted up what Karen owed, and what she could reasonably afford to ask Molly for, over and above that sum. She plumped for double the amount, and got it. Karen was too ill to

140

know or care.

Nick was out when the ambulance drew up at the door of the mews house in which they lived. Karen was taken up the iron staircase outside, and along the little runway to the flat door. Molly installed her in her own bed, and made up the divan for herself in the sitting-room. When Nick came in, he stared round the place—disordered in the way that a small household gets when there is sickness—and asked if Molly had gone mad.

'Shh! Karen's here,' Molly said, hurriedly. 'I found her in an awful little room, and she's ill. You didn't mind, did you, Nick?'

'Bit late to talk about that now, isn't it?' he grumbled. 'She owes me a packet anyway. Seems like my hand's going to be in my pocket all the time.' He thought for a minute. 'What sort of a place did you say she'd got?'

'Don't be horrid, Nick,' Molly pleaded, rubbing her face against his shoulder. 'It was a beastly place. Bare and cold and shabby, and the landlady was hateful. I had to give her Karen's back rent before she'd let her go, Nick! I think that old woman would have let her die there!'

'Oh, no, she wouldn't,' Nick said, callously. 'They don't like deaths on their hands. Bad for business.'

But he said no more about Karen being there, and Molly thought that he'd decided to accept it. Karen was past the crisis in a day or two and with good food and Molly's careful nursing, she soon began to pull round. But she was as uneasy as Molly, about her being there.

'What did Nick have to say about it?' she wanted to know.

Molly hedged. 'Oh, well, you know how men are embarrassed about illness in the house. I threw him out. Sent him to Wilfred's place.'

'What did Wilfred say about that?'

'Oh, well, I don't know. They're in business together just now. I don't think you'd better worry about it, Karen, till you're better.'

'How soon will I be up and about?' Karen wanted to know, her lovely face pale from the attack, and drawn with anxiety.

'Well, of course, in the ordinary way you can hope to get over 'flu in a week or two, but you've got very run down. Were you slimming or something?' she smiled, and tried to sound very bright and flippant.

'I was starving, and you know it,' Karen said, well aware how Molly had found her. She had caught Molly's eye on the day she had first seen her leaving the cinema, and had hoped that she had escaped into the crowd before Molly had noticed her.

'Well, let's forget about all that now,' Molly soothed. 'I brought all your things away with me,' she said, hoping to please

142

Karen, and realizing too late the implication of her remark.

'That means you paid my landlady up, or she'd never have let you bring them away.'

Molly flushed, and looked down.

'What did she ask you for?' Karen insisted.

Molly told her, reluctantly.

'She dunned you,' Karen said, tears of weakness starting to her eyes. 'It was bad enough wondering how I could repay her half that. Now I owe you for double the amount, and I'm in debt to Nick, too. You know about that, of course?'

Molly said she did, but she hadn't known about it. Nick kept his racing deals to himself. 'How much do you owe Nick altogether, Karen?' she asked, trying to sound casual.

Karen said, 'You'd better not ask, if you don't know. Oh, don't worry. I'll repay both of you, but I'll never be able to pay you back for your kindness in nursing me. It isn't everyone who cares to take an invalid on their hands, let alone upset their place, and their husband too.'

'That isn't true,' Molly protested, hurriedly.

Karen grinned. 'Molly, these walls are thin, and Nick's voice very often carries farther than you realize. Every night this week he's grumbled about it, before he cleared out to sleep.'

Molly was very distressed, and between the two of them, she was often near tears. Karen idly wondered what she could see in Nick and why she had married him in the first place. Outside, with the rest of the gang, Molly kept up a façade of drinking and smoking and bright remarks, but in the flat, and while Nick was out of it, Karen noticed she was not like that at all. She seemed a quiet, almost domesticated little thing, with little or no make-up and a simple house frock that completely transformed her. She had been almost unrecognizable to Karen, the first time she saw her, without make-up and with a serious look on her face.

'I'd like to get up to-day,' Karen said, one day towards the end of February. It was a bright, sunny day, and not so cold. There was a hard, glittering light outside, and the air was almost bitter in its cold crispness. Karen staggered out into the sitting-room in Molly's wrap, and Molly hurriedly jumped up and closed the window.

'You shouldn't have got up yet,' she said, helping Karen on to the divan. 'You know you're still awfully weak.'

'I'm going to get well just as quickly as I can,' Karen said, thankfully subsiding, and allowing her feet to be put up. 'I've got things to do.' She was working out whom she should go to for help, to pay back Molly and Nick; Mrs. Heath, or Matthew. It was difficult to make a choice. It would, at least, be merely another loan again, and she would need time, lots of it, to pay it back, for the money she could earn, when she was lucky enough to get a job, wasn't good. Unless she could get a secretarial job that needed no typing and shorthand, as at the organizer's office.

Karen smiled regretfully about that. She had been laboriously putting by a little each week from that job, to pay back her debts, but her small savings had all gone, to help out the poor wage she earned at the cinema.

'What are you smiling about?' Molly said.

'About how I'm going to raise money, quickly,' Karen grinned.

'You're not to worry about that,' Molly ordered, but there was that shade of uneasiness underlying her tone, which Karen had noticed before.

'I've got a couple of good ideas,' she laughed. 'Tell me, did you know Nick before you came to London, or have you always known him?'

Molly crimsoned. 'I met him on a holiday cruise,' she said. 'You know Nick. I never thought he'd marry me, but he's funny sometimes. He said he wanted to marry me because he thought a man ought to have a wife who was *different*. But I don't think he really meant that, because I found he always admired other girls when they made up a lot and dressed smartly, so I had to make up and

145

dress smartly too. I hate it. I'd much rather be comfortable.'

'Perhaps Nick didn't mean he wanted you to do the same as they did,' Karen countered, wondering why she had asked her, but having had to divert Molly from the subject of the money, she had had to think of something quickly.

'I think he did,' Molly said, anxiously. 'Because he always seems more pleased with me when I do manage to look smart.' Then, after a little pause, Molly ventured, 'I think Nick likes red-heads best.'

'Why d'you say that, Molly? He didn't sound like it when he was grumbling at my being here.'

'Oh, that's just because illness unsettles him,' Molly said, uncomfortable again. 'But I happen to know he thinks you're very good-looking.'

Karen thought nothing more of it. It irritated and amused her to hear that sort of remark from wives, and even in Molly's case, after her having been so good and kind, Karen felt no extenuating circumstances. In her code, it was faintly indecent for a wife to let another woman think that she couldn't please her husband by her looks, against the other woman's. It was an admission of failure. Karen thrust the thought from her.

But it came back in no small measure when, as she got stronger and about again,

Nick took to coming over and spending the evenings with them both, and managed to invent quite a lot of excuses for getting Molly out of the room, for longer and longer periods.

CHAPTER THIRTEEN

Nick Borden was tall and dark; handsome in a Spanish sort of way, and clever. It was his cleverness that Karen distrusted most of all. He had a disarming air when he was among his friends, almost an air of simplicity, which his slight lisp accentuated. But at home he was at once a petulant small boy and a calculating rogue. It was in the flat that Karen had first seen this side of him. It occurred to her now, that he might have married Molly because she was the only woman who bolstered up his ego and put up with his fretful complaints and grumbling, while other women—with sometimes no more than a glance—tore his ego to shreds.

Karen had been out and about once or twice before Nick openly tackled her about the money. He looked at her glorious hair, as she took her hat off, and ran an experienced eye over her, noticing the shabby and rather ordinary coat and frock she wore. Very unlike the Karen he had known, not so many months ago.

'Been out, I see,' he murmured. 'Feeling better now, Karen?'

'Yes, Nick, thanks to Molly's kindness and yours in letting me stay here, and thanks of course to Molly's super nursing and patience.'

'Yes, patience. She has that,' he allowed, thoughtfully. He half-pointed to her shoes. 'Not so smart as they used to be, Karen.'

'No, Nick,' she said, serenely. 'I am no longer smartly turned out, Nick. I can't afford it. But I will be, one day.'

'When?' he shot at her, suddenly.

She frowned. She had had no intention of telling him all her business, even though she owed him so much.

She had been making quiet visits, first to Mrs. Heath (who was shocked and appalled that she had been ill and not let her know about it) and to Barbara, who voiced the same protests, but had been equally unable to help her. Of both she had asked, by way of the first skirmish, if they knew of anything she could do in the way of untrained work. Mrs. Heath was all against Karen's working at all, and pressed her to sell the house or let it, and invest the money.

Barbara was horribly nervous about being approached at all, and held it against herself that she knew of nothing, nothing at all that would suit anyone as flamboyant and as untrained as Karen, but didn't like to say so.

148

Instead, she offered, in a distressed voice, to have Karen to stay with her. She didn't specify whether this meant at her own home, at which she stayed occasionally, or in her own tiny flat, which obviously wouldn't comfortably hold two people.

Karen turned the idea down, on the grounds that she could hardly foist herself on Barbara or her family, as she hadn't known them long enough, but in reality because she didn't want to share another small flat, and was uncomfortably aware that if she did, she would have to run the place while Barbara was out, as that was the least she could do.

'When my friends find something really suitable for me,' she answered Nick, adding, 'I've got them all looking for something, and anyway, there is still a small asset I have yet, which I can use to write off what I owe you.'

She fancied he looked disappointed.

'Oh, you don't want to realize bonds or anything like that,' he said, persuasively. 'Hang it all, we're old friends. 'Tisn't as if I were a bookie, or something, and had to press for the money.'

'I owe money to Molly, too,' she said.

'I know. Molly told me. I paid her up, so now you only owe me.' He was bland, suave. Karen stared at him, wondering what was in his mind, and wished he wouldn't look at her like that.

'I'm going to sell the house, Nick. I've

made up my mind.'

'Don't do it, Karen. I'm asking you not to. You may want it, some day. You never know. Anyway, it's always good for a loan.'

'I've made up my mind,' she repeated.

He shrugged. 'Oh, well, if that's the way you feel about it, there's nothing more to be said. When's the sale going through?'

'It'll take a month or two. The solicitors tell me they know someone who's interested in it.'

'Um.' He stood, staring down at the floor, somewhere in the region of her feet. It made her feel distinctly uncomfortable.

'You're not in that hurry, are you, Nick?'

'No, I'm not in that hurry,' he agreed.

Karen, having made up her mind, went to see the solicitors again. It was a very unsatisfactory interview. They had known her since she was a child, and took the same sort of paternal interest in her that Matthew did. They talked to her about Matthew, and about what had been happening to her. When she reluctantly admitted what she had not told them over the telephone in previous conversations—that she had been ill, destitute and alone, and was now in debt to the friends on whom she had been dependent—they had all sorts of unsuitable advice to give. Both the partners, father and son, considered she ought to marry again.

She owned it to Blaize, they told her, but

didn't explain how they considered she owed it to Blaize. As always, when mention was made of him without warning, she flared up, defensively, and a stormy half hour followed. During the half hour, her activities over the time since Blaize died, were brought to light again, and they pointed out to her that Blaize would hardly have been proud of the way she had been going on. Debts, horse-racing, bad investments—everything contrary to their advice. What, they inquired, had become of the filly she had bought, at great expense, and at direct variance to their advice in the matter?

'It died. There was funny business in the stables. I think the poor brute was jimmied, or something.'

'Does that mean,' asked the senior partner, idly, 'that certain low individuals injected a hypodermic syringe into its hind quarters, in order to ensure that it lost in the next race?'

'I said it was jimmied, and I mean jimmied,' Karen flared, although she meant pretty much what the senior partner had suggested, and had merely made up the word herself, in order to sound less to blame. 'Anyway, it was only half mine.'

They would like to know, they said, who had owed the other half. Karen said it was her business, and they pointed out with some heat that her business was necessarily theirs, since they acted for her. And so it went on,

151

until she brought them back to the question of the house, and whether they had a purchaser for it, as they had intimated.

They had, and what was more, there need be no delay in the sale, after the mortgage was paid off. There would be, needless to say, very little in it for her, after that was done, but at least there would be the casting off of yet another millstone round her neck.

Karen faced them with startled eyes. 'Not much in it after the mortgage is paid off? Well, who in the world will buy the thing, then, if there's nothing in it?' A sudden suspicion assailing her, she demanded: 'I hope that you two aren't going to buy it out of kindness! If that's the case, then the whole thing's off.'

They met each other's eyes. It was a delicate situation. 'Our client who is a private property investor, wishes to remain anonymous for personal reasons, and has given us a Power of Attorney to carry through the sale.'

Karen stormed that she didn't believe it, and they had difficulty in soothing her down, but they wouldn't divulge the name of the client.

The most they would admit, presumably to convince her that it wasn't either of themselves, was that the purchaser was a woman. Karen agreed after another tussle with them, and then asked belligerently what

152

she could hope to get out of it, after their fees, and anyone else's rake-off, had been settled.

The sum was larger than she had been led to think, but only just large enough to pay Nick off, and there'd be little left over. Karen and the solicitors parted company on frigid terms. She had infuriated them and they had infuriated her, and she vowed she wouldn't go near them again. Of late, she had stopped wondering what Blaize would say, if he knew. She had the secret shrinking fear that he wouldn't be very pleased with the way she had gone on. She had certainly got through a great deal of money, and mixed with people whom, she instinctively knew, he wouldn't have been intimate with, even though he knew them, and admitted them as his acquaintances. Blaize had had that rare gift of being able to be charming to people with whom he hadn't wished to be friends, and at the same time holding them off from becoming intimate without giving them cause to take offence. Karen felt she would never be able to do that, although she had often studied Blaize when he was doing that very thing. Even with Sally, Karen had made the rift too sharply, and Sally was bitter; yet Blaize had managed to keep her at a most comfortable distance without Sally's even being aware of it. She was, as far as Blaize was concerned, merely the intimate friend of a great friend of his, and whether his friend had made a transient or a permanent thing of that friendship, Blaize felt it was hardly for himself to care. He left it at that and kept in everyone's esteem.

Molly said that Karen was to stay on with them, and until the sale went through, she could do little else. Karen had hoped that Chris's aunt would again ask her to stay with her, and in that case, she would have accepted willingly. But no word came from her, and when Karen met Barbara one day, and asked how Mrs. Heath was, Barbara looked uncomfortable, and said she had been very busy conducting some business or other of hers, and hadn't been at home when Barbara called.

Nick said one night, 'I suppose you'll be in the money, then, Karen?'

She hurriedly repudiated it. 'Oh, don't be silly, Nick, I've got to pay off the wretched mortgage with what I get for the house.'

'Oh, pity,' he said, sitting gnawing his lip.

'Why?' Molly wanted to know. She was darning Nick's socks, and doing them as though she loved the job.

'Oh, I just thought Karen might like to help me out, for once.'

'Why, of course Karen will, won't you, dear?' Molly said at once, looking from one to the other.

Karen was distinctly suspicious. Nick

never mentioned business in front of Molly unless he had a very good reason. Usually he used her as a stage act uses his stooge. She supplied all the questions for him to make all the smart answers, only Molly did it unrehearsed, and it pleased Nick more that way.

'Well, it depends on what it is, and whether I've got the money for it,' Karen smiled. 'Suppose Nick tells me more about it.'

'Oh, I don't want *money*,' Nick said, quickly, waving a deprecating hand in Karen's direction. 'My dear girl, I know you're hanging on to the money to pay us back, and I wouldn't dream of interfering with that. I know how it bothers you to be in debt to us, or in fact, to anyone, and I wouldn't stand in your way at all. No, it isn't money I want.'

'Well, what is it?' Karen asked, patiently.

'I just want you to stand surety, that's all,' Nick said, studying his nails. He waited for both Karen and Molly to press him for further details and then embarked on a very involved story of a friend of a friend of a friend who had put him on to a very good tip in the way of French fillies, and to show how sincere he was, he had offered to put on the bet himself (and a big one at that), only wishing to take back his stake out of the winnings. Naturally, as this man didn't know

155

Nick personally, but was the friend of a friend of Nick's friend, he felt that he had to (just to safeguard himself, as you might say), ask for a surety, just in case the horse didn't romp home as they all expected.

'You know what fillies are,' Nick laughed. 'But of course, I know—I knew all the time—that it was asking too much of you, Karen. Still, it does seem a pity, all that money almost in my pocket, for the want of a backer.'

'Why can't you put the stake up yourself, Nick?' Karen asked.

Nick was hurt. Affronted, in fact. It wasn't, he assured her, like that at all. It was a matter of confidence. He could go, like a common little hack with his twopenny halfpenny bet at each bookie's stand, and violate the confidence placed in him by the gentleman, whom he hadn't the honour to have met yet, by the way, and make the poor man look a perfect fool, and as if Nick didn't trust him. There was a lot more in this strain, and unexpectedly Molly started to back him up. As of course, Nick had known all the time that she would. Karen thought bitterly that Molly would back him up in murder, if he could make it sound necessary enough.

'Oh, for heaven's sake, Molly, stop reminding me of how much I owe you both,' Karen said, impatiently. 'I'll do it.'

'No,' Molly moaned. 'I don't want you to

do it in that spirit at all. I didn't mean to remind you of what we'd done for you! It was precious little we did, when all was said and done, and if you can't nurse a friend when she's ill, well!' Molly, following time and custom immemorial, burst into a flood of tears and groped about the room for a hankie, which Nick discovered she had been sitting on all the time. Karen watched him in fascination, as he handed it to her with complete unconcern. He looked at Karen and smiled faintly, and both of them waited for Molly's storm of tears to abate before they took up the discussion again. But indirectly it had given Nick the pause he wanted, and lost Karen the ground she had gained.

'No, we'll think no more of it,' Nick said, in such a tone that it would have looked pretty poor of Karen to accept it.

'I said I'd do it,' she said, angrily, 'and I will.'

'Well,' Nick said, 'I'll tell you what I'll do. I want to prove to you that I'm not the heel you think I am—'

'Oh, of course Karen doesn't think you're a heel, do you, Karen?' Molly gasped, and afraid she would burst into another session of weeping, Karen hurriedly agreed that she didn't.

'Well, then, I'll tell you what I'll do. When the filly wins (as of course she will) I'll wipe out your debt without taking a penny from you. How's that? Just to show how grateful I am to you for standing behind me.'

Molly was in raptures. She thought Nick was too generous and didn't Karen agree. Karen scowled. 'What's the catch?' she asked.

Nick said he was as shocked as Molly was, and hadn't realized that Karen could be so ungracious. There was, he assured her frigidly, no catch. Just friendship. Friendliness and kindness and big-heartedness and decency, and other things if he could think of them. Karen listened cynically, and wondered what he would do with her debt if the filly lost. She put it to him.

'The filly isn't going to lose,' he snapped. 'I would have offered you a slice in the tip, but since you're so damned sceptical, I'll hold my tongue.'

It appeared that he wanted a written agreement from Karen, which he himself had already got typed out ready, against her anticipated acquiescence.

'I didn't have a chance, did I?' she grinned, sardonically, as she signed it.

The race was run on the day that the cheque for the balance of the house sale came through. Karen looked at the cheque in some amusement. She did really feel that she should have been given the satisfaction of holding on to the money a little longer, even though she was not deceived as to how much of it would really be hers eventually. It seemed a cruel streak of fate that the race had to be run so quickly, even on the very day of receiving the cheque.

Nick and Molly went to the races. Sally was to go with them, and of course, Wilfred. Sally hadn't seen Karen since the autumn before, and although she had no doubt heard from Nick and Molly about Karen's illness, she had made no move to get in touch with Karen, nor had she sent any message. Karen merely shrugged and let it go, with a curious mixture of surprise and gratitude. She was glad that that friendship had been terminated, though she hadn't liked the manner of the termination, and she still missed the friendship, for what it was worth. It was more a habit than a benefit, and Karen never liked parting with habits of long standing, whether they were good or bad. With that habit had gone the twin habits of drinking and betting, until this day. Karen hoped that—win or lose—she would now be done with it for always.

The filly lost.

It wasn't entirely a surprise to any of them, Karen perceived, and wondered what Nick had had in mind all the time. Molly was distressed and uncomfortable in Karen's presence. Molly was sensible that she had been instrumental in urging Karen to do as

159

Nick wished, and she also realized, at this late stage, that Nick had done a good deal of pressing himself, without Molly having noticed it at the time.

Sally, for no good reason, asked Molly to go back to her place with her, and Nick had another deal to put through, he said, and added that it had better not be as disastrous as the one had been that day. Karen went back to Molly's flat by herself, her head swimming. She had run into them at the station; Nick standing by himself, waiting with ill grace for Molly, who was in a telephone box. Molly gave no reason why she should have been telephoning to Sally on the way home from the races, unless, of course, Sally had known about the business and had wanted to hear of the result.

Karen thoughtfully made herself some cocoa. It was spring, and the weather, as if to make up for the severity of the winter months, had been delightful. Yet there was still a nip in the air, and Karen went over to the windows to shut them against the evening chill.

Nick, head bent and with something in his gait which suggested aggressiveness, was coming up the iron steps. He said, as she shut the casement: 'Open it. I'll come in this way. I've left my key behind.'

She opened it silently, and watched him fling his long legs over the sill. 'Good thing you haven't got window boxes,' she said, for want of something to say.

'I wouldn't have them,' he said. 'Can't stand flowers.'

He stood staring at her.

'Well, what made you come back?' she asked. 'I thought you'd another big deal to put through?'

He laughed. 'I had. I've done it. It didn't take long.'

She shifted uneasily, and he laughed again, and walked over to the one easy chair which had its spring intact. 'Gosh, I'm tired,' he said, flinging himself into it. 'I'll clear off soon, and get some sleep.'

She allowed a short breath of relief to escape her. She had thought for a minute that he was going to be difficult. 'You still living with Wilfred, Nick?'

He nodded. A sharp silence ensued, during which she thoughtfully sipped her cocoa, then he said, with his characteristic suddenness:

'About that loan of yours, Karen.'

'Well, what about it?'

'Well, now the filly's let us down so badly, it's considerably bigger, you know.'

'I worked that out for myself,' she said, smiling mirthlessly.

'Good girl. I knew you'd take it in the right spirit,' he said, nodding approvingly. 'Roughly twice the figure now, I'd say,' he went on, getting out a grubby scrap of paper

161

covered in figures, and adding more figures to it with a gold screwpencil.

Karen watched him without amusement. She was used to Nick now. 'Put that away, Nick, and never mind the arithmetic. Just come to the point, will you?'

He put the paper away with the air of being obliging and carefully clipped his gold pencil into his breast pocket. 'Of course, Karen, if you don't want exact details. I was just wondering how I could break it to you, the exact amount I mean, because I don't see how you can pay it.'

'Neither do I,' she snapped, 'and I'm too tired to think about it now. You'll just have to wait. Meantime, would you kindly clear out, because I'm not going to bed until you do.'

'Fair enough,' he said, getting up. 'Not going to be lonely, to-night, eh?'

'Isn't Molly coming back, then?' Karen asked, alarm and suspicion flaring up in the ready flush on her face.

'Well, you know what girls are,' he said. 'Sally, she wanted to go away for a week or two, and I thought it might be nice if Molly had a bit of a change and went with her. I haven't got time to take her, and Sally thought it'd be a great idea.'

'She would!' Karen snapped. 'So I suppose you want to close the flat up?'

'No,' Nick said. 'I can hardly do that, seeing as you have nowhere to go. Fact is, neither have I, because Wilfred—you know Wilfred, he fixed up some time ago for his mother to come and stay with him.'

'Sounds incredible,' Karen said, watching him, 'but if that's so, right! You come back here, and I'll move out. There's a newish friend of mine who's asked me to stay with her parents. I didn't want to, but now's as good a time as any,' she said, remembering Barbara's carefully worded invitation, and picturing her dismay when Karen took her up on it.

Nick said, 'Don't be hasty, old girl. I'm not a leper, you know.'

'What d'you mean?' she asked, in a low, furious voice.

'Well, if I must explain,' he smiled, 'here we are, you with somewhere to go, if you don't mind me being here too. A debt on your hands which you won't be able to pay in a month of Sundays, and here between us a very good, very easy and very satisfactory way of paying it.'

'I may be stupid, but I don't think I follow,' Karen said, mentally totting up the appalling figure which the filly's loss had now made the figure she had originally owed Nick.

'It's very simple,' Nick purred. 'Molly's away, so I shall want someone to cook and wash for me, darn my socks and be nice to me. In fact, I want someone to fill Molly's place, for just a couple of weeks. And here you are, just made for the part.'

CHAPTER FOURTEEN

Nick behaved with old world charm after that. He went into the bedroom—to get one or two of his own things, he said—and came out again in a very short while. Then with a bland smile, he said good night to Karen and went, by way of the flat door this time. Karen watched him go, with mixed feelings, then carefully latched all the windows and put the chain on the door.

She needn't have bothered. She knew he wasn't coming back that night when she went into the bedroom. He had carefully collected everything of hers except her nightwear, put them in the corner cupboard, locked it and taken the key away. What she had been intending to do—pack and clear out straight for Barbara's or Mrs. Heath's that very night—he had thought of and forestalled her. She thought of wrecking the lock or the door, but both were heavy and well-made. She was defeated and she knew it. She could still walk out, but it meant leaving her few things behind, including a rather nice leather case in which she kept her few treasures to remind her of Blaize and his photographs, and the leather dressing case he had given her, and

164

which she had kept, when she might well have sold it to buy food.

She was trapped. Whichever way she turned, she seemed unable to keep away from becoming indebted to people, and the people she knew were all the kind who pressed the debt home relentlessly. Not that she wanted to escape repayment. She just wanted time. Yet, in her present financial state, the time she required was infinite. She might not even live that long, she reflected, grimly—at the rate of her earnings, that was.

She thought of Chris, and wondered what he would suggest if he were there. She knew what he would do, whether it would help or not. He would punch Nick's big nose and take a lot of pleasure in kicking him down those iron steps. But, Karen reflected sadly, there was still the debt, and kicking Nick from here to Timbuctoo wouldn't wipe that out.

She lay flat on her back in the darkened room, staring out at the stars in a superb spring sky, and wondering where she could turn now.

She played with the idea of asking Mrs. Heath for a loan, and shrank from it. She knew instinctively that Mrs. Heath expected her to come and ask for money sooner or later, and she wouldn't give her the satisfaction of refusing.

She had already asked Barbara if there was

such a remote thing likely to be available, as a job which was at once well-paid and needed no qualifications. Barbara had stared back blankly, and it had not been difficult to read her thoughts. The two girls had sensed a mutual liking for each other, and Barbara wasn't the type to use the word 'cheek' yet Karen had felt she had come near to thinking it then. Karen herself, being miserably aware of this, had not felt equal to explaining that it had been done once, in the case of her job with Mrs. Lawrence. It is doubtful if she would have mentioned it, anyway, in that connection, because the result of the job would give Barbara the opening to say, 'Oh, well, what could you expect, with that sort of set of circumstances?' And so Karen had said nothing, and would say nothing now.

Having wiped out Mrs. Heath and Barbara as likely possibilities, there only remained Wilfred (whose offer to help might well be spontaneous but not much better than Nick's own way out), and of course, there was Matthew. There was always Matthew.

After a night of tossing and turning, Karen got up, hollow-eyed and feeling as dreary as she looked, and put on the clothes she had worn when she worked as an usherette. They were all she had, since Nick had thoughtfully locked away the one good suit she had hung on to, against emergencies. She looked dreadful and knew it.

Matthew's housekeeper stared, and would have shut the door in her face, if she hadn't said, 'Gosh, don't you recognize me, Mrs. Snowdon? It's Karen Westbury!'

Mrs. Snowdon, her black-rimmed reading glasses still perched on the bridge of her big nose, stared blankly over them, and her mouth dropped. She didn't say anything, but held the door wide, still staring.

'Is Mr. Pevensey in?' she asked, feeling rather irritable at the woman's surprise. She knew she looked awful, and didn't want to be reminded of it. She still felt, at times, far from well, after her illness, and weeks of going without proper food.

'Well, no, miss, the master's away for a few days.' Mrs. Snowdon looked infinitely regretful, but stood her ground. 'He wasn't expecting anyone, he said, and he's gone to Winchester where there's a sale of some old pictures.'

Karen's legs gave way and she sat down suddenly in a nearby chair. Of all things, the least she had expected was to find Matthew not in his own house. In all the years she had known him, his rare holidays were the subject of much planning, discussion and advertisement. He never dashed off quickly, and he never went anywhere without acquainting his many friends. He was a man who was morbidly afraid of missing anything by his absence, and liked to give due warning

167

against it.

'You wanted him special, miss?' The old woman, a dumpy little figure with iron-grey hair uncompromisingly drawn back, and a face above her severe black dress which was set in the lines which indicate an acceptance of life and people. Nothing surprised her now, after a lifetime of service in this house. Artists, she was convinced, were on quite a different plane from the rest of the human race (especially the artist she worked for), and as such, had to be forgiven, or at least made allowances for. She never set any store by them, and in that way you got no shocks or disappointments. Karen, it seemed, was not so prepared.

Karen slumped a little, and felt incredibly tired. She put a hand over her eyes, and started to cry. The helpless tears of a woman who has tried every way out, and is caught in the last one.

'Oh, now, I wouldn't do that, miss, if I was you,' Mrs. Snowdon advised. 'Very bad for you. Make yourself feel that ill, it do. Now you come into the drawing-room and ... No. I'll tell you what. You come to my sitting-room, where it's real cosy and I'll make you a nice hot cup of tea.'

Karen followed, hardly knowing where she was going or what she was doing. Mrs. Snowdon walked at a slow pace, because her dumpy little legs wouldn't go any faster, and in her slow gait, and slow manner of speech there was something rather comforting and secure. Karen knew that she wasn't really a 'Mrs.' and had heard the little woman say she couldn't ever abide the thought of a man of her own, but she had, in course of custom, taken the married state for the purposes of a housekeeper's dignity. Karen thought it a very odd idea, and reflected that Mrs. Snowdon might just as well have married, for she was the motherly type who was wasted in this house.

When the housekeeper had settled Karen in a comfortable chair by the fire, Karen said, 'Sorry to be such an ass. I've been ill and it's left me rather weak.'

Mrs. Snowdon said she was very sorry, and that she had known many cases where illness did just that. 'What was the illness, may I ask?' she said, in such a polite tone that Karen nearly laughed.

'Only 'flu, I'm afraid, but it's a beastly complaint. I felt rotten all the time.'

The old woman gave her a cup of tea and a digestive biscuit and observed that she had known many cases of 'flu which turned to a permanent depression. 'There was young Nelly, who worked in the kitchen here—couldn't speak to her for a long time afterwards, without she'd throw her apron over her head and cry her eyes out. And as for old Mrs. Lacey, who used to work for the vicar, not the present vicar but the one that died two years ago come Lady Day, she was never herself again after 'flu, never. And such a nice body she was.'

Karen felt that she, too, would never be herself again. She stirred the tea, and nibbled at the biscuit, and wondered what she would do afterwards. There was only one course, as far as she could see, and that was to go back to the flat. Molly wouldn't be there, and Nick undoubtedly would. She started to cry again, and spilled the tea.

Mrs. Snowdon hastily took the cup and saucer from her, and mopped her skirt, observing that tea never did material no good, ever.

'Oh, never mind the tea or the frock, Mrs. Snowdon,' Karen wept. 'I'm in such terrible trouble, and I don't know what to do, now Mr. Pevensey's away.'

'Perhaps I could help, miss,' Mrs. Snowdon said, accepting Karen's statement of being in trouble as the most natural thing in the world. She sat down in the chair opposite, and spread her hands on her knees, and stared at Karen down her long nose, in an expectant attitude.

'I don't think so,' Karen said, mopping her eyes. 'Only Mr. Pevensey can do that, and then only if he wanted to, which I doubt.'

'Perhaps it would help you to tell me about it, miss,' the old woman suggested. 'You know, you're looking far from well, and it's my belief you want nursing up, which you won't get if someone doesn't look after you soon, if you'll pardon the liberty.'

'Mr. Pevensey wants to. At least, he did. He's asked me lots of times, but I keep saying no. I've been pig-headed.'

'Yes, miss,' Mrs. Snowdon said.

'You know about Mr. Pevensey asking me?'

'Yes, miss. He often says, and a nicer gentleman never breathed, he often says, Snowy, he says, she's said no again. She'll come to no good, that girl.'

Karen doubted that he had used that exact phraseology, but she didn't doubt that he had told his housekeeper in disgust. She also guessed that Mrs. Snowdon also knew the reason why he wanted to marry her. You couldn't look after a man like Matthew for all those years without knowing pretty well everything about him.

'I've got in an awful mess, and I came to ask him to marry me and get me out of it. It's pretty selfish, I know, but he won't mind—at least, if he still feels the same as the last time I came, he won't mind.'

Mrs. Snowdon watched her anxiously and said nothing.

'I've been away from that nasty crowd that Mr. Pevensey didn't like, you know,' Karen said, hesitantly.

171

'I'm right down glad to hear it, miss.'

'But I had to live, somehow, and I had to keep my freedom, as well, so I got a job. There wasn't any money left, or anything,' she said, and wondered why her head wasn't so clear as it had been. There was a faint, curious buzzing somewhere, and Mrs. Snowdon didn't look quite as clear as she had done. Karen blinked and propped her eyes open, and her vision cleared. Mrs. Snowdon still sat staring.

'I got a beastly job. Usherette in a cinema.'

'What might that be, miss?'

From a long way off, the question came. Karen said, 'How funny, but I suppose you don't go to the pictures much. The usherettes are the girls who flash torches about and show you to your place. They don't get paid much.' She giggled, and started to shiver although the room was quite warm and she was sitting near the brightly burning coal fire.

'I'll pour you another cup of tea, I think,' Mrs. Snowdon said, and went to the cupboard and brought out a bottle, pouring some of it into the cup before she put the tea in. 'This'll do you good, miss.'

'It's got a funny taste,' Karen said, and the cup rattled in the saucer.

'Here, let me hold the saucer for you, miss.'

'Then I caught cold and got ill and the rent wasn't paid and the landlady wouldn't make

172

me any tea because she said it was a habit and I hadn't got any.'

'Yes, miss,' Mrs. Snowdon soothed, watching her closely.

'And then Molly came, and had me sent to her flat, and it's in a mews and Nick came up the stairs and got in the window. Oh, no, I'm telling it all wrong. Molly nursed me and Nick said I owed him a lot of money and I had to be nice to him when Molly wasn't there, to pay it back. The horse lost, you see, and although I didn't put any money up, I was the one who lost the money I didn't have. You do see, Mrs. Snowdon, don't you?'

'I don't think I do, miss, except that it seems a shocking thing for a young lady like you to have to mix with young gentlemen who know no better than to make such improper suggestions.'

'You aren't shocked, really, are you, Snowy?' Karen said with difficulty, slipping into Matthew's way of addressing Mrs. Snowdon because at that moment it was an easier word to manage. Her tongue seemed to be getting bigger, and filling her mouth, and her head was getting light. 'And so that I shouldn't have to do what he hadn't really suggested but I knew he meant, I came to ask Matthew to marry me now, so that I shouldn't have to go back to the flat because Molly isn't there and Nick is, and oh, it's all so beastly.'

173

She sat holding her head.

Mrs. Snowdon said, with satisfaction, 'That'll be the brandy. It soon does its work. Wards off any chill. You look done up, to me, miss, and I think it might be as well if I was to send one of the girls to get a guest-room prepared and as soon as the bed's aired, then in you'll get, and stay there till I get a doctor.'

Presently, after she had been dozing, Karen was aware that Mrs. Snowdon was coming back into the room, and was talking to her. She missed the actual words but caught the sense, and it seemed to her that Mrs. Snowdon was assuring her that although Mr. Pevensey was away, she knew that it would be all right, and that Karen was not to worry any more.

Mrs. Snowdon receded rapidly, then came forward at a great pace, and Karen remembered thinking dazedly, 'She doesn't really move that fast. It must be me!'

She caught the words that Mrs. Snowdon was saying, then, and the old woman's voice seemed abnormally clear, and inclined to boom.

'Mr. Pevensey has five wards, miss. The other four have all settled down nicely. Married off well. But you're the one that's a constant sore trial to him. Reckless, that's what he says you are.'

'But I did get married, Snowy, and I was very, very happy.'

'Reckless, miss. Many's the time that old master of mine has said to me, she doesn't take heed of to-morrow, that girl: Reckless . . . To-morrow . . .'

The words got all mixed up, and Karen heard herself murmuring 'Reckless to-morrow . . . reckless to-morrow . . . don't care . . . don't care . . .' and she started to laugh on a high cracked note.

She slept for two days. A doctor came and went. She was very hot and very cold by turns. There was the starched rustle of a nurse's uniform, and unpleasant liquids were forced down Karen's throat. The room was darkened, and a clock ticked with peculiar sweetness.

Karen, her throat abnormally large and sore, heard herself murmuring, 'Chris, Chris, don't let Nick . . .' and then a cool hand would take hers, and she slipped back, down into the darkness.

At another time she was crying for Blaize's photographs and the dressing-case he had given her, and begging someone to go and fetch them before Nick got at them. 'I don't want him to touch them . . . soil them . . .' she was crying.

Once she was in the farmhouse on the moor again, talking to Chris, and then she was crying out because she could see Chris at the train window, and the train was moving in the opposite direction, just as had really

175

happened that day, so long ago. What was it? Weeks? Months? Years? Finally, she called for Blaize, but only once. Chris was the name most on her lips, and Matthew Pevensey—back from his two-day trip to the sale, empty-handed and none too pleased with the waste of time and the annoyance of travelling—stood by the bedside, listening.

Mrs. Snowdon stood near at hand.

'Who is this Chris?' he asked her.

'I'm sure I don't know, sir. I told you all the young lady told me, and she hadn't mentioned anyone by the name of Chris. It couldn't be Nick, could it, sir?'

'It couldn't,' he said, shortly, and his mouth turned down at the corners in a way his housekeeper knew well.

When Karen was well enough to receive visitors, he permitted himself to be shown in to her.

She was deathly pale, and thin. Very weak, too. Her voice, strong, and attractively throaty, was nothing more than a husky whisper. Her eyes looked enormous, but her red-brown hair had lost its glorious richness, and its springiness. It lay in limp waves over the pillow, and there had been talk of cutting it off, but Matthew had held out against it until the last. He had won, but he felt he had been selfish. She looked so frail and spent.

'Well, my dear Karen,' he began, characteristically.

'... Matthew,' she whispered, and he missed the first word.

'You've come home, at last,' he said.

'Is it to be ... home?' she managed.

'If you want it,' he said, firmly, 'it's to be *home*.'

'I didn't want to marry ... anybody,' she said, a far-off look in her eyes.

He looked sharply at her. 'Because of Blaize?' he probed.

She shut her eyes.

He bent forward, to ask her who 'Chris' was, but the doctor, divining his intention, shook his head at him. Matthew subsided, with a scowl.

Karen looked at him again, and said, 'It's to be ... as you said, last time, Matthew?'

He nodded.

'No strings?'

'No strings, Karen, my dear. Just as we understood each other to mean it, when we last spoke of it,' he assured her.

She sighed. A ghost of a smile played round her pale mouth. 'Isn't it a funny thing? I always knew it would come to this. I planned what I meant to say to you. But I never got the chance. It was you who said it to me.'

CHAPTER FIFTEEN

Matthew had not long celebrated his sixtieth birthday. He remarked with a certain jocund note in his voice which vaguely irritated Karen, that for sixty years he had been groping, and now he had got what he was groping for, he wasn't sure that he wanted it, he had done so long without it.

Karen thought the remark was in somewhat bad taste, and said so. Matthew looked hurt, and Mrs. Snowdon who had been in the room when he had said it, looked reproachful.

'Please don't misunderstand, my dear Karen. I wasn't referring to having acquired a wife. I was referring to the model I had always yearned for.'

'Yes, I know you always wanted to paint me, but I didn't think you'd had any idea about that in your cradle.'

'Perhaps I should have said, then, that for the past *forty* years I had been wanting to paint you,' Matthew said, with precision and disapproval. He hated to be picked up when he was speaking rhetorically.

Karen, still painfully pulling herself back to health after her recent illness, was inclined to be literal, and a little pettish.

'But even that's silly,' she pointed out,

'because you didn't even know me then. I wasn't born then. Goodness, you've only seen a model in me for the last twenty years. That's a bit different from sixty, and besides, why make a fuss about a model? There must be hundreds about.'

He got up, and strode about the room, in exasperation. It was the dining-room, a room which Karen cordially disliked, because it was frankly period, and Spanish at that. Karen thought privately that it was the silliest idea to have each room a different period. She had felt it before, on many occasions. Each room had a different atmosphere, and this—facing south, with dusky pink washed walls and hideous old oil paintings also in keeping with the period, a severe monastic one—seemed to her the epitome of affectation. Matthew didn't know how she felt about it, and would probably have cared even less if he had, but the fact that it was in what he affectionately called the Spanish room, heightened the futility of their present argument.

He stopped striding and came to a full stop in front of her, staring sombrely down at her. Mrs. Snowdon came, too, and stood by him; a habit of hers. As if she shared something of her master's thoughts and inclinations through all these years of working so close to him, so alone with him.

'Karen, there are, indeed, many models.

Many red-heads, too. But a model has to be more than a mere pretty woman. More than a beautiful woman. She has to have something to excite the painter. A model may have a body which excites him. You have something more. You have a head. You *are* a head to me. A priceless, exotically beautiful head, on the face of which plays so many emotions, that the soul behind it has, for me, the study of years, and I have been denied years. I am possessing that head at the end of my life, when all my passion is spent. I don't even know if I have any left, with which to make use of that head.'

He glared down at her, as if it were her fault, and Mrs. Snowdon, with a funny little nod, echoed his look. Reproach. Reproach.

Karen shrugged her shoulders. 'A nice thing to say to the woman you're going to marry—just a head, eh? I'm not sure that I want to go through with it now. Have you considered my feelings, Matthew?'

'No, and I don't intend to,' he said. 'The marriage is purely one of convenience. That is obvious. You wouldn't have come to me if you hadn't been on your beam ends. I know you better than that. Very well, in exchange, you're getting your debts paid, the run of this house (and the run only, mind you: no interfering with Mrs. Snowdon—she still has *carte blanche*, as always, since she suits me) and what is more, you've got your freedom.

So long as you're here when I want you, you can do as you like for the rest of the time.'

'A head!' Karen said, bitterly. 'An exclusive head, though,' she said, grinning impishly up at him.

'No, my dear Karen, not exclusive. Just a head that particularly takes my fancy and electrifies my imagination, but very definitely not exclusive. Nor indispensable. So don't get ideas of that kind.'

'But you just said—'

'I am well aware of what I just said, Karen. Just let me repeat. No one, nothing, is either exclusive or indispensable in this uncertain and disappointing world. So don't go sticking a gun at my head on that score.'

'As if I would,' Karen murmured.

'That's just what you do do, if I know anything about you, and bear in mind that I know a lot. I've known you since you were born, and I'll say this, my girl. If I'd had the upbringing of you, as I wanted, you'd be a different woman to-day.'

Karen chuckled. 'No cigarettes, no drink, no horses, no gang, no wanderings, no fine clothes, no—' and she broke off suddenly and bit her lip. She had been going to say, 'no Chris', and the thought brought a shadow to her face.

'What were you going to say, child?' Matthew said, changing his censorious tone to one of gentleness.

181

'Never mind,' she answered, in sudden surliness.

Yet on the whole, she and Matthew were good enough friends. His general manner to her was one of good-humoured acceptance and pleasure, as a man watches the gambolling of a frolicsome puppy. She was that to him, and when she was well enough to be able to go to be fitted out for new clothes, she was also a lovely doll, to parade in her new things and let him watch the lighting effects on her hair, and on her face. At first she found it amusing, then it irked.

And then at last her marriage. Karen, to whom such things were sacred, and recalling her white bridal attire when she had married Blaize, was outraged because Matthew wanted her to have a full white wedding with a retinue of bridesmaids.

Matthew was frankly puzzled, and looked to Mrs. Snowdon to back him up, but the old woman stoutly refused.

'You can't do that, sir,' she expostulated, with that curious mixture of forthrightness and familiarity mixed with politeness which always excited Karen's amusement and admiration. 'It wouldn't answer at all, really, it wouldn't.'

'And why not, for heaven's sake?'

'Because Miss Karen's been married before. A woman's second marriage is always on the quiet side, begging your pardon, sir, for decency's sake.'

'There's nothing decent about this marriage,' Matthew snapped. 'She's a beauty and I want to show her off. I want everyone to see the subject of my series of portraits, and what better opportunity have I for it than this?'

Karen said, with finality. 'Afternoon frock at a registry office or nothing.'

'You're a fine one to talk of something or nothing—you haven't a leg to stand on,' Matthew fumed. He looked an odd scarecrow of a man, in his velvet jacket in which he sketched. When it came to the actual painting of a picture, he put on a white coat, a sort of butcher's coat (or, as he pleased to whimsically put it, a cricket umpire's coat) and wiped his brushes down it, to Mrs. Snowdon's annoyance. He allowed himself all sorts of fads and fancies, on the grounds that he didn't have to paint and never had had to. He had always been a wealthy man, inherited wealth.

He ruffled his sparse straight grey hair until it stood on end like dirty wisps of straw, and glared down at her. She was right, and he knew it.

'All right, all right,' he said. 'Have your little hole-and-corner wedding at a registry office, and think yourself lucky if I turn up.' That idea pleased him enormously and he laughed on and off at it all the afternoon. But

183

he had his way, and designed Karen's outfit himself, and upset the dressmakers more than once over the cut and the material. Yet Karen had to admit, when the finished outfit came, that it was a thing of beauty.

She took a pleasure in clothes, a pleasure which wasn't so much sensual as intelligent; to go out in anything but clothes which set off her beauty was at once an affront. She had forgotten already how she had felt when she had had to wear poor clothes and go to a job each day.

Matthew had, after all, insisted on white, and even in her present pale and thin state, she looked superb. There was a three-quarter length dress of brocade, the neckline and basque picked out in a pearl-encrusted design. The sleeves were three-quarter length, and the neck low-cut to allow of a magnificently worked pearl necklace. The hat was a bonnet-shape, also of the brocade, with knots of pearl flowers at each side. The back was cut away to allow for her hair to be coiled up to the top of her head. Matthew's master touch was in the gloves and shoes; they were handmade, in suede, a delicate shade of lavender.

'Why not emerald?' Karen said, excitedly turning over the things. 'These are so colourless.'

'Vandal,' Matthew said, succinctly. 'You will carry orchids and if you say you'd rather

184

have crimson roses, I shall take great pleasure in throttling you first.'

Karen had not seen Molly since she had left her flat, nor had she heard a word from Nick. Matthew had instructed his solicitors to wipe out the debt, the subject being too distasteful for him to permit of its being done otherwise. The gang had faded out of her life. She had played with the idea of telephoning to Molly, to thank her for all she had done, but shrank from the idea, on the grounds that Molly would want to know where she was now, and it would be difficult to keep the friendly tone which the need for thanks required and at the same time stop Molly's eager questioning. Worse, Molly would undoubtedly want to see her, whether at her flat, a teashop, or a visit to Matthew's house. Karen shuddered.

She hadn't been to see Chris's aunt for an entirely different reason, a reason which bothered her a great deal. Of late, she found herself thinking of Chris far too much. There was becoming a need of him which frightened her. She told herself she was being sentimental; that he could easily have looked her up if he had wanted to see her. And anyway, what was the use of a friendship with a fellow like Chris, who took himself off (as he had told her he was in the habit of doing) at the most sudden and surprising moment. She knew she was being irrational about the whole thing, according to her own codes.

At the holiday camp, she had been furiously angry next day to find he had really left. When she had returned to find him after her exhibition dance, the others said casually that he had gone in search of a drink and she had thought no more about it. But the note he had left for her, and which she received when she went back to bed that night, had a final ring about it, which had left no doubts. It was not that he had had the urge to go off again on his own which worried her, but the reason he could have had for going, without a word of good-bye to her. That, in itself, wasn't like Chris.

This reason, and the feeling that she couldn't bring herself to speak to him, or to see his photograph about without giving away her feelings on the subject, restrained her from going. Then her marriage to Matthew was another drawback. How could she go and see Mrs. Heath without telling her about it, and if she did, for what reason could she be said to be seeing Mrs. Heath? It was tacitly agreed between the two women, up till now, that their main link was Chris. Karen thought of Barbara, too, and decided not to see her again, either. When she thought seriously about the subject, it struck her as being a little silly, to say casually that since she had seen them she had been ill in one man's flat, and had decided to marry another, when all the while she had been taken to be a great friend of Chris.

There was a strong urge of rebellion in Karen just now, on top of all the other emotions. She had hated selling the house. In one way, it had been like parting with a limb, but quite staggeringly there was a great feeling of relief about finally letting it go, which she didn't understand. She thrashed out her feelings alone in the lovely sunny room over the Spanish room, which Matthew had allotted to her. Each night, before allowing herself to succumb to sleep, she tried to find the answer to the riddle.

Blaize had been to her, since his death, not only a precious memory, but an extremely hurtful one. A memory which had affected her sweepingly as the 'flu had done, leaving her weak and dizzy and ill. To combat it, she had done everything she could to make life a dizzy worrying affair which would tend to swamp everything else, even private thoughts. But she could never quite put Blaize out of her mind, nor could she obliterate that memory of him among the wreckage of the train.

That was another thing that bothered her a great deal. She rarely remembered the funeral, and that not very clearly. She seldom remembered the terrible days and nights spent in hospital, first hers and then Blaize's. Haziness had settled over it all, mixed with pain. Even the memory of his tortured existence until he died, and the time of his dying, were gradually receding into the mists. The train accident alone remained startlingly clear, and never seemed to cloud or show any signs of leaving her memory as a clear picture, an event that might have happened yesterday, it was so fresh.

She tried to remember Blaize on honeymoon with her, and to her intense grief, she couldn't. Couldn't even remember his face sometimes. On these occasions, she got out his photographs, the crazy snaps she took of him, and the ones he had taken of her. The places they had visited, the people they had seen, all those things connected with her brief marriage, she tried to recall, but they were fast held in some invisible grip that was gradually, imperceptibly almost, wrenching them away from her, until they were out of sight.

The night before her wedding to Matthew, she panicked. 'What's it all about?' she heard her own voice cry out, and in desperation she buried her face in the pillow and cried for hours. She knew she shouldn't give way to this weakness at any time, least of all the night before her wedding. After all, Matthew was giving her so much, she shouldn't take away from him the pleasure and pride in that one day.

He had planned so much. They were to have a small and well-planned reception with a lot of important people in the art world coming to a party afterwards. A dreary crowd, Karen considered, before whom she would have to pose pretty much as a film star would. But for Matthew, she clearly saw, it was the achievement of his life to take her as his wife. Whether she would fit into or disrupt his household, didn't matter to anyone outside. Whether they knew it was just a business arrangement, or thought she was truly married to him and would give him children—all that didn't matter, either. She saw clearly that that day was a big one for Matthew, and in gratitude she mustn't spoil it.

She went to sleep at last, and dreamed a curious dream. It was actually in the early hours of the dawn that she dropped off into that troubled slumber, and saw again the train accident. Blaize was lying there, as he had been that day, but instead of asking for a cigarette, he said, instead: 'Where's Chris?'

Chris, appearing miraculously, and seeming to be walking on air, as people do in dreams, stepped over the rubble and stood looking down at Blaize. Blaize took his hand, and reached (without apparently moving) and took Karen's, and put them together. 'Chris and Karen,' he said, and closed his eyes.

Karen woke up crying out aloud. She was wet with perspiration and shaking like a leaf. 'But that didn't happen at all,' she was shouting. 'It wasn't like that! It wasn't like that!'

There were heavy footfalls in the passage outside, and Mrs. Snowdon stumped in. 'Poor lamb, I heard you call out,' she said, soothingly, and pushed Karen down in bed again. ''Tisn't the first time you've cried out this night,' she said, shaking Karen's pillow, and re-covering her with the tossed and tumbled bedclothes.

'Isn't it?' Karen asked, guardedly, still shaking and cold. 'What did I say?'

'Oh, think nothing of it,' Mrs. Snowdon said. 'Reverse dreams they say, and this is your wedding morning, and if I were you, miss, I'd snatch a bit more sleep, for you look as if you can do with it.'

'I was dreaming of Blaize, you know, my husband,' Karen said, crying again.

'There, there, now,' Mrs. Snowdon murmured, and said something about making her a nice hot cup of tea, the old woman's panacea for all ills. Karen said she could do with a cup, and dabbed fiercely at her now swollen eyes.

At the door, Mrs. Snowdon turned, with a peculiar look on her old face. 'Blaize, was it you said? *Blaize!* Um.'

CHAPTER SIXTEEN

The registry office was a fashionable one in town, and the photographers were there in force because Matthew himself was a person well known enough to merit the photograph, and Karen, despite her difficult colouring, was extremely photogenic. Matthew, in impeccable morning clothes, looked faintly inane, Karen thought. She had the impulse to say to the small crowds gathered on each side of the front railings, 'This isn't really an exciting wedding at all,' but felt that she could not have convinced them.

There was a great friend of Matthew's, who was composing an opera, and was also a well known arranger. Karen disliked him, but for Matthew's sake had to be nice to him. As they stood at the reception it came over Karen that that would be the case with all Matthew's friends. When it came to the point, she found herself thoroughly disliking all of them. They were so much a part of Matthew's life, and she wondered whether she would ever fit in, or whether it would be, after all, as easy as Matthew said it would be for her to live her own life apart from his sittings.

There was a confused impression around her, at that reception, of people talking of things right above her head. They were all top-line professionals in the art world. There were one or two important stage people, playwrights, quite a few novelists and men of letters, but for the most part, they belonged to the world of pictures. Matthew, it seemed, was an important person to them. Karen looked at him with new eyes. She respected anyone who knew his job through and through, and she discovered that she respected anyone who could stay put long enough to do that.

She thought of Chris, and what it would have been like if he had been here. He would have poked delicious ridicule at all these people. He would have said that he could smell money, and that money had a vulgar smell. Chris had a strange, wild jealousy about his careering about, staying nowhere, doing nothing. He liked to feel that people were shocked at his shiftlessness, at his flinging aside the shackles of responsibility. He liked to feel that everyone considered him thoroughly selfish and unstable. Karen had found out that much in her few conversations with him.

She considered that the only point they had in common was their mutual love of flouting the decent, the stability of civilization, the honour of daily toil. It came to her then, as she stood there drinking champagne and giving pretty thanks for people's good wishes, that perhaps Chris had merely left her because she had started working. Perhaps he had thought she was going to stay on with the holiday camp people. It may well have been that he had heard someone mention that there was something in the air about her teaming up with Sally and O'Leary and working together through the winter, and this, of course, would have shocked Chris beyond words. The idea of a long-term winter scheme of employment was, she felt, an insult to him. He was very fond of talking about insulting people's intelligence. Karen didn't quite know what that meant or what it was intended to mean, and felt that perhaps it was after all, from Chris's point of view, just a lot of big talk. Hot air. Just the same she was convinced now that she had lost what little claim to his friendship she had had, because of her working, and he would have liked her less if he could have seen the efforts she made to keep that miserable job at the cinema.

They honeymooned, Matthew and Karen, conventionally, in the South of France. Karen chuckled when the taxi drew up outside the hotel. It was, as one would expect with Matthew, palatial. There was a creamy-white front, and striped awnings at each of the hundreds of windows, and a bewildering number of uniformed staff were about the place.

'What's the matter?' Matthew asked, solicitously. 'Don't you like it, my dear? Or have you been here before?'

'Oh, no,' Karen said, seriously. 'I was just thinking of something.'

He had a nettling habit of sometimes pressing the question to the point of exasperation, and at other times not taking a scrap of interest, and allowing the subject to drop. Karen wished he would be consistent, then she would know how to handle him. Then, characteristically she shrugged her shoulders, and wondered why she bothered her head with wanting to handle him. Just let him go his own way, even though she knew she would be bored to tears.

The time in the South of France wasn't so bad. There were tedious sittings in the mornings for three heads Matthew was doing of her, all at the same time. One against the background of the Mediterranean, with dense foliage etched in all round; one against the wall of a pink-washed villa some way out from the town, for which Karen had to wear peasant headdress; and a formal head, her hair piled high, and barbaric ear-rings hanging from her lobes. She hated them all.

In the afternoons she was free, but in the evenings there were tiresome dinners and parties, visits to the Casino, which Matthew surprisingly enjoyed, and drives in the new car he had bought for her.

She bought a lot of new clothes and consoled herself. Her bedroom was littered with boxes and clothes, and gave the maid a headache clearing up after Karen. Matthew's bedroom was painfully tidy in comparison.

Matthew gave her several pieces of good jewellery, for which she cared nothing and she bought herself one or two vivid junk pieces which meant a great deal to her.

'Why do you like them?' Matthew pressed. 'They don't suit you. They're vulgar in colour and design. They don't suit your personality.'

She shrugged. 'They're gay. Besides, the real jewellery you give me doesn't go with my taste in clothes.'

'That's true. My dear Karen, we'll have to do something about that.'

'No, Matthew!' Karen stormed. 'I let you design and choose my wedding outfit and the going-away things, but you said I could have a free rein with the rest of my wardrobe.'

'That's true,' he said, again, puzzled. 'I can't understand you, Karen. I want to get the real you on to canvas and it evades me. You pretend, you know, when you're sitting.' He leaned forward, eager and at the same time shockingly old and worldly-wise. 'Karen, my dear, let yourself go, next time, so that I can see that gloriously common streak in you that appreciates junk jewellery and over-smart clothes.'

She scowled, hating him for the moment. Too late, he saw he had pressed her too far. He stopped worrying her, and characteristically he cancelled the sittings and let her go off all day as she would. But he watched her.

Like a bird let out of a cage, she wandered a long way. She was away two days once, and came back tired out and happy, and incredibly dirty. She had been wearing beach kit; blue check jeans and a blue shirt with a yellow bandalero. They were stained and torn. Matthew raised inquiring eyes and wondered aloud if he dare ask, as her new husband, where she had been and what she had been up to.

'I hiked!' she said, triumphantly. 'It's rough country.'

'The sun's too hot for hiking,' he ventured, staring at her in unashamed fascination.

'I found this old straw hat,' she said, throwing down a frayed and none-too-clean object.

He winced, but asked her to put it on, thoughtfully.

She started to, then threw it down violently. 'No, Matthew, not another pose for a head! I won't! I won't!'

'I was only curious to see how the dirty old thing looked on you,' he murmured, hiding a smile. 'Hadn't you better get a bath?'

He loved watching her. He went down with her to the rocks when she bathed, and never took his eyes off her lovely bronze body in its white satin swim suit. He took her in his small sail craft. He wasn't a keen sailor, but he liked to watch the movement of the sails and Karen's glorious hair blowing red-brown against them. She had a way of sitting with her head thrown back and an air of getting—by sheer force of energy and will-power—every ounce out of what she was doing at the moment. And always, Matthew was there, watching, studying, sometimes touching her.

That was what she loathed most of all. His caressing hands on her face, her neck, her head. She knew he wasn't caressing her with affection, but with adoration for a work of art, as some men caress a fine piece of statuary, or gloat over a picture.

One day Karen gave Matthew the slip and took the car out to a little cove she had found, where there were deep rock pools and sheltered places, where she could be alone, gloriously alone, without having to go too far afield. The hotel put up excellent lunches and it annoyed her to have to go without them and put up with scrap food where she could, because of the need to get far enough away from Matthew. On this particular day, there was someone else sharing the cove. Her heart lurched, because at first she thought it was Chris. He had the same slim, yet strong build, the same devil-may-care style of clothes. He sauntered casually across the beach and dropped behind one of the rocks.

She went to look and found he had fallen asleep immediately. It wasn't Chris. Her heart sank, and she wandered back to her place. It was funny, this yearning for Chris, now at all times. She neither understood nor welcomed it.

Fuming, she went racing into the sea, without putting on her swim cap, and her hair fanned out around her like reddish-brown seaweed. She played with the idea of cutting it off and wondered what Matthew would say. It would ruin his three pictures. She knew they were only in abeyance, and must inevitably be finished.

She floated, and wondered what else she could do with the apparently limitless supply of money which Matthew gave her. It was funny. Not so long ago, she had needed money so badly. Now it was in abundance, and things were still not right. But here, there was little scope to spend money without people she knew. Wickedly, she played with the idea of sending for Sally, and striking up a friendship with the gang again. She wondered what Matthew would have to say to that. He had not forbidden her to see them, but it was tacitly agreed that with her marriage and his paying off of her debts, she was to cut herself off from that undesirable bunch of people.

The young man had got up and was standing at the water's edge watching her. Suddenly he ripped off his pants and jacket, and stood, a magnificent figure, in short blue trunks. He dived in and swam swiftly out to where she was. He had an engaging face, tanned to a dark olive and widely grinning. His black eyes danced.

'Hullo, mermaid!' He had a faint accent, a funny mixture of American impudence and Continental piquancy in his tone. She couldn't place it. 'Wanna play?'

'I'd love to,' she breathed.

Like children, they skirmished in the water. She was a very good swimmer. They raced, they played at porpoises, they dived underneath and chased each other. Finally they came out, and lay panting on the sands, drying out.

He sat up and leaned over her, then saw her wedding ring.

'Oh—oh!' he murmured, 'this is where I beat it.'

'No!' Karen cried. 'I mean, it doesn't matter at all.'

'You don't say!' he mocked.

'Honestly. My husband lets me do as I like. He doesn't care. He just paints his old pictures. And I'm so lonely.'

He laughed. 'Lady, I've heard that siren call before.'

She shrugged. 'All right. Clear off if you're scared. I just want someone to enjoy all this with. My husband ought to be with me but he doesn't know how to play. He'd think it silly.

Oh, and I'm bored, bored, bored!' She thumped her fist into the sand with the reiteration of the word, and flung herself down on her face.

'Do I go or stay?' the young man asked himself, with mock seriousness. 'Nope, I think I go. I've just gotten myself out of one mess! I stay out, I think.'

'Who wants a mess?' Karen burst out furiously. 'I just want someone to swim with, walk with, and *talk* with. You don't know what it's like to be married to an artist, and anyway, he's thirty-five whole years older than me, and he's trying to guide my footsteps! How about that?'

'Lady, you didn't have to marry him,' the young man said, mildly, but with a suspicion of laughter in his eyes. 'I know you,' he said, suddenly remembering. 'You're Karen Pevensey. I saw your picture in the papers not long ago. Honeymooning, eh, and you're bored! My, how some dames get all the jam and don't know when to stop crying for more.'

'I suppose you've seen my husband painting my head, too,' Karen said, viciously.

'I have, at that,' he agreed. 'My, he's some painter. Decent old boy, he looked,' and that was said with a curious ruminating air, with downcast eyes and a thoughtful frown. Looking up, suddenly, he laughed, 'But boy, how dull, as you say!'

He rolled over on his back and he and Karen laughed together, uproariously.

'Oh, it's good to laugh like that again. Matthew'd think I'd gone mad if I laughed like that with him.'

'He would?'

'He also thinks I'm mad, going off for two days by myself, hiking.'

'So would I, if you were my wife.'

'If I were your wife,' Karen retorted, 'I wouldn't have to look for anyone else to swim and walk with!' She scowled at the blue sea. 'Oh, I hate being grown-up. Why can't we stay school-age for ever and have fun, and not have to bother about things like money and responsibilities and being a good citizen.'

'Lady, you got something there, only let's skip the bit about school age.'

'My school days were fun,' Karen told him, seriously. 'Over here, you know, at Plessey.'

'Mine weren't,' he said. 'I helped my old man on a two-bit farm, near Challons-Gaieu. Boy, we were hard-up!'

'You're French?' she asked, in surprise.

'Sure,' he shrugged. 'Okay, I know, but I learnt English in America. Funny, huh?'

His name was Jean, and for the moment shelving the question of her married state, he enjoyed spending the long lazy days with her. He told Karen all about his life. It had been hard, not in the way that Chris had endured hardships, but hard from the beginning from

201

grinding poverty, lack of the education he craved, and hopeless when he wondered how he would ever realize his urge for foreign travel.

This Jean got eventually by boarding tramp steamers and working his passage. He had been all over the world. He was merry, kindly, yet utterly disillusioned. All he had left was the rather tired little dream that somewhere, somehow, he would find a girl like his mother; a girl who was utterly untouched and unambitious, with whom he could set up a small farm, and presumably work in the same grinding poverty with which he had begun. Farming in a poor way, seemed to be in the French peasant's blood.

'There's no such girl,' Karen told him, seriously. 'With the wireless everywhere, and newspapers, and everything, women have changed with the times. Everyone's smart, and wants a bit of life.'

'Nope, you're wrong, there, baby,' Jean said, lying on his back, his dark eyes for the moment serious, staring up at the blue sky of France. 'She's there all right. Right here,' he touched the place where his heart was. 'Say, I've seen everything, done everything. And yet I know that she's alive. I don't know how she's stayed like that, so pure, so good, but she is.'

He rolled over and stared into Karen's eyes. 'If I didn't know that, I wouldn't have anything left. Life wouldn't be worth two bits. Don't yer see? Baby, there isn't a fella breathing who hasn't got someone in his heart like that. That's why even the bad eggs like me aren't entirely bad. And why we can go on hoping.' He grinned engagingly. 'That's all we've got, see? Hope.'

Karen thought of Chris. Had he a dream woman in his heart? Was that what made him a wanderer? In that case, neither Barbara nor she herself could possibly mean a thing to him. She told Jean about Chris, but he offered no comment. He just listened.

'Ever been in love, Karen?' Jean asked, one day making tiny castles in the yellow sands with his lean brown hands, and then knocking them over again.

'Yes,' she said.

'What was the guy like?'

'Dark. Dark and handsome. An athlete.' She screwed her eyes tight closed, and panicked. Again she couldn't recall Blaize's face. It was Chris's face that came so readily to mind, with his laughing blue eyes and his tawny hair, all blown with the wind. Chris had light blue eyes, and they reminded Karen of the light quality of these Mediterranean waters. Youth and energy and sunlight and gaiety were all mixed up in the memory of Chris's eyes.

'A boxer, maybe?' Jean hazarded.

'Oh, no, no!' Karen was shocked. 'No,

Blaize was just naturally a fine figure of a man. He just played games for leisure. He was a professional man, had a partnership in a firm. He was kind and good and ...' and there the memory finished. She searched for words, and because she couldn't find any, the tears forced themselves through her closed lids. Had Blaize had a joyous sense of humour? Would he have understood her wildness? Had she ever shown him that side of her? She couldn't remember. She just called to mind a sedate courtship of two years, and a marriage of three weeks that was an idyll of bliss, chiefly because Blaize's personality was everywhere. But she hadn't seen him in private life, other than the honeymoon.

Her pictures of him were seriously going over the plans of the house, with the architect. Playing serious tennis and swimming seriously in the week-ends at house parties. Always smiling, courteous and friendly. But crazy? No, decidedly not. Imaginative? No, hardly. A young man, she now recalled, with a passion for moderation in all things. At the time she had thought it very fine. Now, she wondered.

'He was kind and good and ... the only man in my life,' she finished, with more determination than feeling.

'That's your story,' Jean allowed, frowning at a shell he had found.

'What d'you mean, Jean?'

'Oh, I don't mean a thing, I guess, except that I was kinda surprised. I thought you were going to say the guy you loved was this Chris fellow you were telling me about.'

She flushed. 'Certainly not!'

'Okay. Okay. I just asked the question. Only I guess I'm a bit in the dark as to where this paragon of all virtues fits in, seeing as you've got Chris in tow, and you're married to the old guy.'

She got up angrily. 'You've got a beastly trick of making everything seem mean and cheap, Jean! Blaize isn't . . . wasn't a paragon of all virtues.' She finished on a sob.

'Wasn't?' Jean picked on the word, getting up and staring down at her, his hands thrust deep in the pockets of his slacks.

She said, in a toneless voice, 'Wasn't. You see, he's dead.'

'I'm sorry, baby,' Jean said, genuinely contrite. 'I'm a heel. I ought to have my head punched.'

'Oh, you couldn't help it. You couldn't know.'

'Yes, I ought to have known,' Jean insisted. 'Why, the very way you were talking about the guy ought to have made me see. That's the way folks always try and remember things they've cared about in people who're dead and gone.'

CHAPTER SEVENTEEN

'Karen my dear,' Matthew said one day, coming into her room and watching her as she brushed her hair out in a flaming fan round her head. 'Would it be asking too much for my new wife to stay with me all day to-day?'

Karen flushed. 'Well, as a matter of fact—' she began, and bit her lip. As far as she knew, Matthew had no knowledge of Jean, nor did she intend to tell him. Jean was just a friend, but Matthew had an unhappy knack of dissecting other people's friendships and thereby tearing them to ribbons.

'Matthew, do you mind if we leave it until I've finished dressing?' Karen said, looking pointedly at the open communicating door. He never abused the unspoken pact between them that he should not go through the door until she herself had opened it.

'Certainly not,' he replied, courteously, 'only I asked your maid if you'd finished dressing, and she said you had. What's that thing you've got on?'

'It's a wrap,' she said, shortly.

'Well, in the ordinary way I wouldn't dream of venturing into my own wife's bedroom when she's in her wrap. However, as it looks uncommonly like the wrap I've seen you wear on the beach, and as the garment peeping from beneath it suggests nothing more intimate than a swim suit, I think I'll stay. I wanted to ask you to be present at a distinguished gathering of fellow artists to-day.'

Karen clenched her fists. 'It sounds like a command,' she said, trying to sound rational. 'All right, Matthew, what is it? Lunch? Dinner, or merely a soirée?'

'Lunch,' he said, 'and about an hour of sitting still afterwards while we all have a look at you and discuss you. And try to sound gracious, my dear, because you'll be able to run away and play with your little friend afterwards.'

Karen swung round, aghast. 'What d'you mean?'

'I was merely referring to the lean, dark, hungry-looking young man with whom I've seen you swim,' he murmured.

He wandered off, then. He always made terrific exits, Karen thought, bitterly.

She finished doing her hair, and slipped off to meet Jean, and stared at him. Matthew's description was very apt. He was lean and dark, and he was hungry-looking. Even when Jean laughed and played, he still had a hungry look about him, as if life had denied him the only thing that would ease him. Whether it was money, or a farm, or the girl he dreamed of, or perhaps all of those things, Karen couldn't decide.

After swimming they hired bicycles and went for a trip along the coast road. It was hot, and the breeze was welcome. Karen wore a vivid blue sweater over her swim suit, and brief white shorts. She looked like an advertisement for a health resort, so vivid, so vital, was she. Jean watched her with appreciation. He was also carefree. He liked being with a girl who was so good and wholesome to look at, and who didn't want to enveigle him into trouble. It was refreshing.

'Say, Karen, does the old guy really know you go out with other fellas?'

'He knows I go out with you,' Karen said. 'I told you, it doesn't matter a bit.'

'How can you say that?' He was properly shocked.

'Well, only to-day my husband said he wanted me to attend one of his luncheon parties, and when all his artist friends had chewed me over, and discussed me, I could go off with my boy-friend.'

'Well! D'you suppose he's screwy?'

'I doubt that,' Karen said, gravely.

'Well, what's he getting out of it, then?'

It was impossible for Karen to be angry with Jean. He was nothing more than a puzzled boy. If he had a wife, he wouldn't let any other fellow share her sweetness, even platonically. On that basis alone, he simply couldn't understand Matthew.

'You've seen him, Jean. You've seen him

painting. What would you say was in his mind when he was painting me?'

'Well,' Jean considered, 'he certainly looks all kinda boiled up about something, but I don't think it's you. You yourself, I mean. But *about* you, he's boiled up, maybe? I dunno. I just can't figure it out.'

'That's just what I mean, Jean, it's perfectly horrid. D'you know, he married me because he wanted my head.'

'Huh?'

'That's true. He'd tell you so himself. He's not interested in anything about me but my head. For the rest of his life he's going to do heads of me. Me laughing, me crying, me profile, me full face, me half-turned, me—'

'Whoa! Doesn't this guy ever paint anyone else?'

'Up till now, yes. But ever since I was a kid, he wanted to paint me, but my people wouldn't let him.'

'Wise folks you had. The guy's screwy,' Jean said again. 'Listen, honey, what did you have to marry him for, anyway? Aren't there enough young guys in the world who'd have you like a shot, without saying yes to that old sheebang?'

'I don't think you quite understand, Jean. I was in a devil of a mess for money. I'm a bit extravagant, you know.'

'I catch on quick,' Jean agreed, gravely. 'So the old guy said, "I love you, honey, and I'll die without you, so take my cellars full of gold, and make my old heart glad".'

'Don't be ridiculous, Jean. It wasn't like that at all. He doesn't love me. He looks on me as a tiresome child, his fifth godchild, and the only one of the bunch who didn't shut up and settle down and leave him in peace. No, he paid my debts and settled me in as his wife, provided I sat for him, left the housekeeping in the capable hands of Mrs. Snowdon (who's looked after him all his life) and if I'm a good girl and spend his money and come home early each night.'

Jean squinted at her. 'I shoulda reckoned you had more spirit, Karen, than to settle for a bum do like that.'

'You've got something there, pal,' Karen grinned at him. 'All I can say in my own defence is that I was ill and down-and-out. Otherwise, I would have said no as I've always done.'

'I guess that laughing picture of you looks pretty good,' Jean hazarded.

'Oh, we haven't got to that yet,' Karen laughed. 'We have three unfinished heads, all extremely serious, and then we graduate to a smile.'

'Are you kidding?' Jean gasped, stopping the bike and staring at her.

She stopped. 'What d'you mean?'

'Well, remember yesterday, we were out on the raft and you were laughing your head off.

Lights kept flashing from the shore and annoying me. Some wise guy must have been watching us through glasses, I figured, so when I swam back to get some popcorn I had a snoop round.'

'Go on, Jean.'

'I couldn't get a gander at the old guy, but there was his easel right enough, on the verandah outside his sitting-room. I got up the railings and I heard him talking on the phone. But I had a squint at it.'

'The picture?' Karen whispered.

'Sure enough. You. Laughing your head off, just like you were on the raft.'

'Spying on me!' she breathed, in cold fury. 'Oh, wait till I get back! I won't stay with him. I'll go back to London. I'll—'

'What would happen to you if you did that?' Jean asked.

'I don't know,' Karen said, slowly. Then she shrugged. 'Oh, yes, I do. I'd go back to my old friends, back horses, lose, and get into debt again, and have to come back to Matthew. And Matthew, curse him, knows it.'

She tackled Matthew about the picture when she got back. He said, mildly, 'It was meant to be a surprise. I've been working on it to show our guests to-day.'

'No, Matthew! I won't have it! I said I'd sit for you, but I didn't mean I'd put up with you spying on me to get me looking—well,

211

like—'

'To get a "shot" of you that you wouldn't dream of allowing me to see?' asked Matthew, calmly, and with a slight smile. 'Oh, I know that, my dear. But then, you see, you aren't in a position to quibble.'

She glared, but looked a little puzzled.

'You're getting all the advantages so far,' he said, gently. 'Money, the protection of my house and my name, and absolute freedom besides. Absolute freedom, I repeat. If I choose to study you while you're at play, no one can stop me painting what I see, even if it is unconscious. I share with the professional photographer the right to get what is known, I believe, as unrehearsed life studies. You are my wife.'

Karen felt like a prisoner receiving a life sentence. He would not let her see the picture until it was exhibited to their friends, and he also insisted that she wore a dress she particularly abhorred; a subdued and beautiful blueish-grey ninon, with a scarf collar which, at a given moment, she could drape over her head. Matthew demonstrated how he wished it to be done.

'More exhibiting,' Karen fumed.

'And I want your hair piled on top, so,' he showed her, taking a bunch of red-gold curls and fixing it to one side of the top of her head, 'and let me see, these ear-rings,' and he chose a very handsome pair of silver filigree which he had given her himself. They were so long, they almost touched her shoulders.

'I shall feel an ass, like a blooming Madonna,' Karen grumbled, crumpling the ninon in distaste. 'I was going to put on—'

'—the electric blue you bought yesterday,' Matthew smiled. 'I reserve the right to examine your shopping since it's my money being spent.'

'I wish some nice person would die and leave me a fortune, so I could shake myself free of your shackles,' Karen said, venomously, and at the same time, as she was well aware, a little childishly. Matthew was such a busybody, such a managing fellow, such a bully, and yet with it all, so utterly suave and well-mannered, that he left her feeling like a ridiculous child all the time.

He laughed a little at her retort, and smoothed her cheek. 'Such beauty can be forgiven anything,' he murmured, doting. Then, in a brisker tone, 'But to be candid, it wouldn't help you if you did acquire a fortune.'

'D'you suppose I'd spend it right away?' she jeered.

'Perhaps not,' he allowed, 'but you'd come back to me.'

'Why?'

'For protection. From yourself, and your stupidity.'

She swung away from him, unwilling for

213

him to see that his words had stung her to angry tears.

At the luncheon everyone talked animatedly, and smiled at her and said nice things to her. Her beauty stirred them in much the same way as it stirred Matthew. After lunch, he put her under the light, and out in the sunshine, and they discussed the shades in her hair, and the basic colours of her complexion.

'Rubens wouldn't have been impressed,' one sour little man said. The others cried him down.

'I suppose you think Murillo would have had the indecency to rave about her?' a great, bald man shouted, angrily.

'I say da Vinci would have made her a Madonna.'

'Franz Hals—' someone else said, and was promptly shouted down by several others who favoured the opinions and approaches of the moderns.

Karen sat and smiled vaguely at them all, infinitely bored. The little sour man came up to her.

'I apologize, Mrs. Pevensey, but for the moment—'

'—I was not a woman, but a model for a head,' she finished, with a little smile.

He was taken aback, and very ill at ease.

'That is so, I regret,' he stammered. Then, as an afterthought: 'Do you mind?'

Karen started to frame a polite negative, then something swept over her and filled her with repulsion. This crowd of senseless people, these fanatic followers of art, these friends of Matthew's, gaping at her, arguing about her, were one thing; but that one of them should be rude about her, suddenly discover she was alive and had feelings, and then ask her curiously if she minded, was too much.

She said, through her teeth: 'Mind? I don't understand you. I hate it! Do you hear me? I hate it! I hate it!'

Her voice was raised, and the others paused. Over the whole room settled a sharp silence, then the big man turned to Matthew and said, excitedly: 'Look, if you could only capture it old boy! Fury! Pure, unadulterated fury, with that glorious colouring!'

Matthew smiled, as the voices broke loose again, and looked over at Karen and the little man. 'I might indeed do worse, if Andrew would be there at the sittings, and say to Karen those same words which aroused such strong feelings in her!'

'I didn't know,' stammered the little man. 'I just asked her if she minded being stared at! I didn't realize your wife felt so strongly about it!'

'Oh, that!' Matthew said, disappointment flooding his face. He waved a deprecating hand, and turned their attention to the picture. After they had compared it with her, she was allowed to see it.

She stared at it, unbelieving, and connected it with their delighted and rather personal remarks.

Matthew must have been spying on her from the very first day she had met Jean. He had caught her in her laughter, with her head flung back, and her eyes full of merriment, a bawdiness, an earthiness, that she hadn't known was there. Jean had never said one word to her that could possibly have aroused her anger or indignation, yet Matthew had painted something in Karen's laughter which suggested that she was laughing at a smoking-room story.

She stared, trying to pin down what was there on the canvas. Nothing objectionable, but the healthy ribaldry, the colourful commonness of the barmaid, the milkmaid; the unrestrained laughter of the mob at something which is not humour but tickles the fancy. Karen was so angry at the sight of that picture that she had the impulse to tear it off the easel and crash her feet right through it.

Matthew, undoubtedly divining this intention, took her arm, and led her back a little, so that the others closed in on the picture. She scowled up at him, and he said, softly, 'You needn't stay, Karen, my dear. Run along, and have fun with your little

216

friend.'

She flung his arm off, and fought her way through the artists, to the door. Each had something complimentary or pleasant to say to her, and all of them took her anger as something which pleased them rather than worried them. She was, no doubt, Matthew's toy, as far as they were concerned, and they were all in on this; what he was going to make of his new possession.

She hurried up to her room and looked out. There was Jean, on the raft, dangling his legs in the sea. She fought off the desire to go and tell him what had happened, because she knew that in his heart he didn't really care. He felt, without saying so, or having to, that she had asked for all she got.

'I'll go back to London,' she decided, and started to pack. 'I won't stay here another minute to be humiliated like this.'

She tore off the blue-grey ninon, and flung it on the floor, so that each time she crossed the room in the business of gathering her things together, she trampled on it. She took with her the things she liked, the things she had bought and chosen herself, leaving behind rather pointedly the clothes of Matthew's choice and his jewellery.

She left him a note, too. A short one. 'I'm leaving you because I hate it all so much. I can manage very well without you.'

Matthew found it very much later in the

day, after she had left the hotel and got well away on the train.

He read it, and prowled round her room, reading all the signs as she had intended him to. But she had not intended him to smile, nor to put through a long-distance call to his bank manager, at his home.

'Karen's gone off in a huff,' he laughed. 'See that her account's kept replenished. You know how she can spend the stuff.'

There was a laugh at the other end. 'I get it, Pevensey, but I'm not to let her know, eh?'

CHAPTER EIGHTEEN

It was raining when Karen got back to London. She stood under the dripping glass roof outside the station and stared at the empty yard. All the taxis had gone.

She hadn't thought of what she was going to do. All through the journey she had been consumed with anger against Matthew, against his friends, and quite illogically against Jean, because she knew that everything that Jean had said was right.

Without putting it in so many words, Jean had intimated that she had made a bargain, a good bargain from her point of view, and that she should stick to it. Jean also intimated that her flashes of anger against Matthew were unreasonable.

Once, Karen had flared out at Jean: 'How would *you* like to be regarded as a sort of permanently acquired model, with no life in you, no thoughts of your own?'

Jean looked her over, with that mixture of impudence and lovableness which was so specially his, and chuckled: 'Baby, if I wanted out of life what you do, then I'd like it fine!'

Was she so empty-headed and clothes-mad as everyone seemed to think? She hadn't had much chance to prove otherwise, now she came to think of it. Home, before she had married Blaize, was a fashionable place, well run by a superb staff of servants; a jumping-off ground for parties and fun, but where nothing serious was ever discussed, and where the social graces were held to be the most important thing in life. Since Blaize had died, there had been ample opportunity, but little or no equipment, she considered, for her to show anything else.

If she had been trained for anything, she might have turned to her trade or profession in her grief, and flung herself into work, as many people did. As it was, there was nothing to fall back on but the old spending ways. And there was nothing from home to fall back on, either; no help, financial or otherwise. Her father died just after Blaize had died. Karen had felt no grief for him.

219

Her whole existence was taken up with her own tragedy. And all that was left of home was a very small sum, after the place had been sold to pay up the expensive façade which her father had built up. That, Karen decided bitterly, was where she got her own extravagant ways from.

She put up her hand to an incoming cab, and hesitated when the driver asked for the address. On a sudden impulse, she gave Mrs. Heath's. She had just enough left in her purse to pay for the cab, and when Mrs. Heath came to the door in surprise, Karen relinquished the momentary flash of anxiety as to where the next money was coming from, and smiled nicely.

'I've come to tea,' she said.

Mrs. Heath smiled. 'You're getting just like Chris, turning up suddenly and waiting for me to be delighted.'

She led the way into her sitting-room, where the french windows were opened onto the rain-drenched lawn. There were rustic seats dotted about, and a little round rustic table. A summerhouse stood against an overgrown rose-trellis which extended right across the garden, but for a little archway, beyond which glowed the fresh bright green of wet grass. It was all very wild and lovely, the roses a riot of red, pink and creamy-white. Karen stood and stared at it in rapture.

'Have you heard from Chris?' Karen asked.

'Never mind my nephew. I want to hear all about what you've been doing,' Mrs. Heath said, ringing for tea.

Karen shrugged. 'It's been a long time, hasn't it?'

'A very long time,' Mrs. Heath said, looking at Karen's blue suit and hat, very much in the style in which she had first seen her, and her pale pink kid sandals and handbag. The gloves were also pale pink, a soft suede, and exactly matched the pale pink cockatoo which sat on the top of the hat and draped its curled tail feathers right under Karen's chin. 'You look very nice and expensive, my dear.'

'Yes, but you'll be surprised to know that my cab fare was the last bean I had. Can I stay the night?' she asked, smiling impudently.

'Well, I don't know about that,' Mrs. Heath said.

'Oh, well, if you've other visitors, of course I take it back,' Karen said, still grinning.

She couldn't have said why she had come to Mrs. Heath's except that she was instinctively putting off to the last minute any visit to the gang. 'Perhaps Barbara can put me up,' she added.

'Where's your luggage?' Mrs Heath asked, suddenly.

'At the station,' Karen said, carelessly.

221

Then stared.

Mrs. Heath smiled. 'I mean your overnight bag, of course.'

'You said "luggage",' Karen said, wondering for a moment if Mrs. Heath connected this new outfit with Matthew. But of course if she suspected that Karen had married again, she would have asked about it at once.

'You look tanned, Karen. Have you been away?'

Karen hunched her shoulders crossly. With anyone else it would be merely small talk, all this. But with Mrs. Heath, it was undisguised curiosity. Karen felt that if only Chris's aunt would shut up and wait for confidences, she would feel tempted to tell her all about Matthew, if only to talk it out of her system. Then it might not feel so bad. But as always, Mrs. Heath rubbed her up the wrong way, and made her desire to keep her activities a secret, for no reason at all.

'I've had a wonderful time, with new people, lots of sunbathing and swimming and everything, but being me, I fell out with them and came back. So! If you don't mind, I'd rather not talk about it.'

'Oh. I see,' Mrs. Heath murmured.

The tea was wheeled in on a trolley.

'Well, come along, Karen, take your gloves off, and help yourself to some squashy cakes. You always liked them, I recall.'

Karen peeled off her gloves and saw with some amusement that Mrs. Heath eagerly scanned her left hand. It was bare. Karen smiled back at her look of faint surprise.

'Is anything wrong?' she asked, innocently.

'I thought you always wore your wedding ring, Karen.'

'I know a widow is supposed to, Mrs. Heath, but for me it has, as you know, unpleasant associations.' From force of habit, she always took Matthew's wedding ring and engagement ring off when she wasn't with him, and they now lay, in their ruched velvet cases, in her new handbag. She smiled again. 'I am a bit unorthodox in my ways, I suppose.'

'I'm afraid you are, Karen. Be careful, though. For some old-fashioned people like myself, you may prove to be too unorthodox for comfort.'

After tea, Karen sat and gossiped a little with Mrs. Heath about the girls she had known in the cinema, and about her illness. She permitted herself to mention that Matthew had been kind to her, and that his housekeeper had nursed her in his house, and that was why she hadn't gone out to work again.

Suavely, before Mrs. Heath could ask her whether she had left Matthew's house or not, she started speaking of what she had in mind to do now.

223

'You know, I used to think I was lazy as much as untrained, Mrs. Heath. Now, I'm not so sure. Although I didn't like the girls I was working with in that cinema, I liked the feeling of earning my own living. I'm seriously thinking of going back to work.'

Mrs. Heath stared a little, frankly surprised. 'Is that really necessary, Karen?'

'Oh, yes,' Karen said, coolly.

'But forgive me if I seem personal, with those clothes, you give the impression of being extremely prosperous.'

'Oh, those were the fruits of my honest labours since you saw me last,' Karen grinned. 'Now, with the kitty empty again, we have to seriously think about finance.'

Mrs. Heath leaned forward. 'Karen, I know you're pulling my leg. I'm used to it, because Chris does it, too. But candidly I don't like it. Suppose you tell me what's really been happening.'

Karen was nettled. She hated being asked outright to account for her movements, and although she was encroaching on Mrs. Heath's hospitality, she didn't feel that Chris's aunt was justified in demanding to know the facts. In any case, if she said she was married, Mrs. Heath wouldn't let her stay there, but would make her go back to her husband. In Karen's crowd, when hospitality was asked for, it was granted, and no questions asked. That was one of the things which appealed to Karen, in Sally's gang. They were generous, and since they did things in an unorthodox way themselves, they were, for the most part, without curiosity. Karen scowled.

'Oh, I expect I will tell you, when I'm in the mood, but for the moment I just haven't got the urge. Be a good soul and don't ask me.'

She got up, searching in her handbag for a cigarette. Mrs. Heath held out a small box to her. 'I don't smoke myself, but like to keep them here for visitors.'

They smiled at each other. 'You often, to my mind, Karen, need a thorough good spanking, and although I don't approve of half of what you do, I can't help liking you! And that, by the way, annoys me. I don't like liking people of whom I don't approve.'

'Are you sure that what you think, and what you do, is always right, Mrs. Heath?'

'No, Karen, but I abide by my thoughts and actions,' Mrs. Heath smiled, though there was a warning in the tone.

'Oh, well, I think I'll just go and collect my bag from the station in case it rains again,' Karen said, and hesitated.

'Oh, yes, and the banks are all closed,' Chris's aunt said, with a twitch of the lips, as she got two bank notes out of her purse. 'This ought to do until to-morrow morning.'

'That's kind of you,' Karen said,

mechanically, her brows knit in thought. 'Banks, yes, that's an idea. I'd forgotten . . .'

'Forgotten what?' Mrs. Heath asked softly.

Karen recovered herself. 'My bank account,' she said, imperturbably. 'It's had some money in it since I saw you last. I must investigate. There might be some left.' At the door she turned back. 'And please don't ask if I got it through horses, or I shall be really cross.'

Mrs. Heath watched her grimly, as Karen crossed the road to the cab rank. She looked very lovely in her new outfit, her lithe young figure swinging along with confidence and pleasure. Pleasure? Mrs. Heath asked herself what had caused it. Karen should, she considered, be feeling anything but confidence and pleasure at the moment.

Karen was thinking about the bank account. She had forgotten it. 'How could I be such a fool?' she kept asking herself. 'How could I be such a fool?' There was a certain figure left in there that she hadn't already spent. Her heart danced.

At the corner of the street she bumped into a man. A tall, lean, gay fellow, and as always, her heart bounced at the rakish mode of dress and the angle of the trilby.

'Karen!' There was incredulity in his voice. He swept her off her feet and swung her round. 'Karen, Karen!'

'Chris!' Her voice broke a little. She

226

couldn't believe it was really him. She searched his face, eagerness mixing a little with restraint when she recalled how he had left her last.

'God, I've missed you,' he said. 'Here, let's go and get some food or something. Where were you going, anyway?'

She giggled. 'Silly, isn't it, but I've just been to your aunt's and borrowed two pounds. I was going to get my bag from the station and stay the night with her.'

He roared with laughter. Unreasoning, joyous laughter. To him everything was a joke just now. 'That's a laugh. Has she got another room free, d'you know, because I haven't got a bed to-night, either?'

'I expect so,' she said, laughing idiotically, glad that he hadn't asked her why her bag was at the station.

He tucked her hand beneath his, and walked her along, nowhere in particular, while he talked.

'Wonder why I left you that time, Karen? Didn't mind, did you?' Without waiting for her denial, he said, 'I'm the world's worst ass. I got the idea in my head—oh, well, never mind. It's worked itself out of my head again, and all I could think of was you.' He looked down at her. 'Your eyes, your hair, the gaiety of you. You know, you're a bit of a vagabond, too.'

'Am I, Chris?'

'That time on the train—what happened to you? I got out at the next station, and went back, expecting you'd have got out of your train and waited, but I couldn't find you anywhere. What did you do?'

'I was just so stunned at seeing you that I sat like an idiot and did nothing, till the end of the line.' She remembered so poignantly the days that had followed seeing him on the train, and how she had been ill and alone and had had to go to Matthew eventually. As she had known she always would.

She didn't listen to Chris babbling now. She let him have his head, and walked in a daze by his side. Something had happened inside her since she met him a matter of minutes ago. Something had got released, something that had been held taut for far too long. She knew she ought to say, immediately, that she was now married to Matthew, and had merely left him in a temper, and would inevitably go back to him. But she couldn't. This was too rare, too precious, to spoil.

'You look wonderful, Karen,' he said, suddenly running his eye over her. But he didn't ask where she had got the new outfit. It never occurred to him to question her wardrobe. He had never seen her in other than wonderful clothes.

'I'm in the money again,' she laughed. 'No, don't start asking how. I'm being good, so don't spoil it.'

He was too happy to do anything but to take her at her word. 'I'm in the money, too, for once,' he told her, with happy pride. He was too practised a lover to spoil the magic of the moment by weary details of sweating in the factory up north to get that money. He let it go, lightly, just like that.

'We'll go and eat at a really nice place, for once,' he said, and found a little Italian restaurant where the food was good and intimately served. They sat in a corner, at a little table with a shaded light on it. Karen ate and laughed, while Chris talked. She had never heard him talk so much. All about his wanderings and the amusing people he had met.

He had a bottle of red wine brought. 'Karen, have you ever done a day's work in your life? A job, I mean?'

'Why?' she asked, guardedly, watching him pour it out.

'Well, remember the scheme I outlined to you, that day under the haystack?'

There was a little silence. He looked sharply up at her.

'Chris,' she murmured, 'isn't it horrible of me? I went to sleep while you were telling me. It was so hot, and I was so sleepy, and ... I just didn't hear a word.'

He stared, then let out a shout of laughter. 'Well I'm blowed! Of all the nerve!'

They laughed together. At this stage, it really was funny. The little Italian proprietor came up, and laughed with them. He thought they were newly-weds, or perhaps lovers about to be married. He brought them another bottle, a bottle of rare old wine, on the house, and drank with them.

'Karen,' Chris said, when they were alone again, 'it *is* a good scheme, honestly, and I'm as worked up about it now as I was then. But I can't tell it to you all over again here.'

She watched him, troubled. 'At your Aunt Margaret's, then?'

He pulled a face. 'Hardly.'

'Where, then?' Karen asked, wildly, intoxicated, not only with the wine, but with a new happiness that she had never experienced before, and while it lasted she wanted to suck it to the dregs.

'There's a friend of my father's,' Chris said, 'who lives by the sea, in an old cottage. I haven't been to see him in ages. He believes in letting other people have freedom. Karen, how about you and me going there? What d'you say? If only for a week, let's go away and have fun together.'

'I don't know that I ought to,' Karen murmured, fuming against a fate that had brought Chris back just a month or two too late. Fuming because Matthew had got his way after all these years because she was down and out, and hadn't a leg to stand on.

Rebellion seized her. She had the odd fancy that Matthew was there in France, finishing his queer honeymoon alone, and not only not caring, but secretly laughing at her, knowing full well that she'd go back to him when her money ran out, or when she needed protection from someone's unwelcome amorous attentions.

'I won't go back!' she fumed to herself. And to Chris, she said, 'Well, what will your aunt think?'

'Send her back the two quid you borrowed, Karen, with a nice little note. She won't care. She'll be jolly glad to see the back of you!'

'Perhaps you're right,' Karen said, obscurely.

CHAPTER NINETEEN

The friend of Chris's father was a man of some sixty-five years. Weatherbeaten, with a pair of twinkling eyes and a kindly expression which suggested that he knew the world was a pretty grim place, and people a pretty shiftless lot, but he liked being there, just the same, among them all. His name was Ruben Bly, and he had been born in the district and come back to it after years of seafaring.

Karen loved his cottage. He showed her over it quietly with an air of grave pride and satisfaction. Something of a stonemason and tiler, he had built it with his own hands. Slowly putting his heart into it. It was a weathered place, that cottage, mellowed by the battering of the tides and the elements. It stood on the shore of a cove. Sheer behind it was gaunt red-brown rock. All round it was ragged grass, and the little garden in front had been cultivated to take a sprinkling of each old-fashioned plant that the old man loved. It was at once colourful and gracious, mellow; a product of a bygone age, when there was no talk of manufactured goods and prefabricated houses. Ruben Bly and his generation found (and liked) things to be hard to come by. Then they were of value.

Chris said, standing behind her, his hands on her shoulders, and his lips barely touching her bright head. 'This brat, Uncle Ruben, is as big a scallywag and vagabond as your worthless favourite nephew.'

Ruben Bly looked at her, and taking his pipe from his mouth, he remarked: 'The lass looks as if she's been around.'

'What does that mean?' Karen demanded, in surprise.

'I think,' the old man said, 'that you've taken a few knocks, lass, one way and another, and,' he added, with a twinkle, 'I think you gave back as good as you got.'

'She does, oh, she does!' Chris cried, delightedly. 'She's a rare one, and I found her. On a moor, in a mist.'

'Chris!' Karen protested.

'That's the way to find a girl. Not in a dance-hall, all tricked out in a fancy dress. Not introduced at your aunt's tea-parties, sitting pretty and well-mannered, and saying the right things. But, lost, on a moor. Up against it, and still with her flag of courage flying high.'

Karen's eyes misted. Chris had a habit of touching her deeply. He was a vagabond, as he had said, but each day she found a little more in him to know and like. That was the way she found it, at the cottage in the cove. That was how she had begun to find it at the holiday camp last autumn, until he had gone away, and shattered all her new-found illusions about him.

The cottage was one of five, dotted at intervals round the arch of the cove. At each end of the cove itself was a long arm of toothy rocks, jutting out into the sea. You reached the cove by scrambling over either one of these, or by boat, or—more usually—by a tricky winding path down the cliffs. Each of the cottages had such a path down to its own back-door. Ruben had fixed a shaky railing to the edge of his, and put a gate at the top marked 'Private'. Karen was enchanted with it all.

'What do you do for a living? Fish?' she asked him one day.

'Fish,' he allowed, 'in a boat I built myself. Then I build a small boat now and then, as a special commission, you see, for say, a summer visitor, or one of the folk in the big houses on the cliffs. That's over and above my pensions, from the sea, and injuries in the wars.'

'Are you related to Chris in any way?'

'No, lass. Not by a long chalk. My brother was chauffeur to Chris's father, when his family had money. That's how it came about. The whole family used to come down here when they were young. Margaret, Chris's aunt, you know, she was a hoity-toity little madam as a girl. Used to plague the boys no end. But she liked the sea, and she used to get me to tell her things I'd seen abroad, and such. You know her?'

'I know her,' Karen said, laughing. 'I don't think she approves of me.'

'Think nothing of it, lass. Women are funny like that to each other. At each other's throats one minute, round each other's necks the next.' He shook his head in despair of the tricks of women in general, and Margaret Heath in particular.

Chris and Karen went fishing with him some nights, and sometimes just before the dawn. It was a new and exhilarating life, and she loved it.

In many ways Chris was like Jean. He romped in the water as Jean had loved to do.

234

But Karen didn't mention him. For one thing, Chris seemed to be uninquisitive about what she had been doing since he had seen her last. He seemed to take it for granted that she had just been around with Sally and the crowd, and Karen divined that because he so heartily disapproved of them, he preferred not to mention them at all.

Instead, he talked about the project he had had in mind when they had been at the holiday camp.

'There's a small village, miles from anywhere, that's absolutely made for opening up. It's over-crowded, and its inhabitants get fed up to the eyebrows with walking into town or waiting at the crossroads for the bus—a two hours' service.'

'Go on,' Karen said.

'Now, there's one shop only in the village. A dreary little general store, you know the type. The chap in there was telling me that he was too old and tired to do much about it, but if there was someone go-ahead, and young, to take a grip on the place—'

'Oh, just get a shop going,' Karen said, disappointed.

'Not a bit of it,' Chris said, indignantly. 'What we want to do is to put the place on the map. Now I've just got the idea. There's a large place in the centre of the village, an eyesore. A sort of shack, enormous. Don't know what it was, but it still isn't derelict, although no one's used it for ages. It's got living quarters attached, too. Now, what I thought was, we'd take that, and knock the front out and have glass put in, for windows, and show everything. Not just jumbled up, but in different sections, like a sort of store.'

'Won't that cut out the old man's trade?' Karen asked, doubtfully.

'No, we'd take him in. He's got the stock to start us off with. He lives next door.'

'Where *is* this village?' Karen asked, idly, lying flat on her back on the shingle and digging her hands in among the pebbles.

'It isn't too far out by car, from town,' Chris said, 'and it's called Derrybridge. Know it?'

'Derrybridge? Never heard of it.'

'It really has a bridge, a stone bridge, over the river Derry. Oh, Karen, if only I could get you really enthusiastic. The thing doesn't stop there, with the store, I mean. At the moment the villagers, a dreary bored lot, either lounge at street corners or on the doorsteps. There's nothing else to do except attend the church flower show and winter bazaar. The highlights of the year, unless they trek out to the crossroads and catch the bus, which is neither frequent nor cheap, into the nearest town.'

'Dull,' Karen commented.

'Now what I want to do is to give them a picture-house, and found a sports club. I want to set them all in work in my store, instead of scraping a living on the land around, where there's little work going, there's so many of 'em. And I'm going to start a bus service of my own, to bring people from outlying places into Derrybridge.'

'Wait a minute,' Karen laughed, sitting up. 'If wishes were horses—'

'That's not wishing,' he protested. 'I've got it all worked out. There's a big barn at the back of the living quarters, for the picture-house. I know a fellow who's a bit of an amateur projectionist. Met him on my travels. He'd love the chance of opening up his own picture-house.'

'Always supposing you can get the owner of the shack, the living quarters and the barn to sell them to you at a price you can afford,' Karen smiled, 'and supposing the villagers want a picture-house thrust upon them.'

He ignored that. 'I know the lads of the village would like a cricket club, and a football club too, if it can be managed. They've got a sort of green, where they practise on, but it's haphazard. Kit costs money, and it wants someone to organize the whole thing.'

Chris chewed his upper lip over that.

'Do you play cricket, Chris?'

It appeared that cricket was a passion of his youth, and that even now, though he didn't play, because of his wandering life, he still could never resist stopping to watch, whether the players were professionals or small boys with a ball and a bit of stick for bat and wicket.

'Oh, I suppose that settles it. The cricket club is as near fixed as makes no difference. But you haven't explained where you're going to get your bus service or its drivers.'

He grinned at the little triumphant note in her voice. 'Karen, my sweet, you were apparently asleep when I talked all this over (or part of it), last autumn, so of course, it's all new to you now. I, however, have had ever since then to consider it, and to do my talent scouting. I have a bus service—or at least, one unit of it, standing at present on a dump heap, its two front wheels missing, and a star-shaped crack on the windscreen. Apart from those trifles it's as good as new. I also know a chap who'd drive it, and his wife, who wants to make a bit on the side, said she'd conductor it for me, with a lot of pleasure.'

'Oh, an old junk-heap bus!' Karen was disappointed.

'Not at all! It was a very superior charabanc in its time, and therefore has quite nice upholstery. Of course, I suppose there'll be a few insects in it, owing to its front door being ripped off, but,' he brightened, 'that'll save us removing the door, for the passengers, won't it?'

'Well, I must say, Chris, you're a fine one

238

to weave fairy stories! I thought you said you didn't want to stay put?'

'Well, I don't. I'll just get the thing going, make my profit, and clear out when I'm tired, leaving the folks to carry on by themselves. They won't miss me, once I've shown them how.'

'And where do I fit into all this?' Karen wanted to know.

'Ever done a secretarial job? No, of course you haven't.' He sounded disappointed at the recollection that she had never been to work.

'I'll tell you a secret. I did have a secretarial job once, only without shorthand and typing, and I managed pretty well.'

'When? Why? What happened?' Chris wanted to know, getting up on one elbow and staring down at her.

'When? After you deserted me last autumn.' She gave him a sketchy account of the organizer's job. 'Why? Because I was hungry, having done a bit of running out myself, on Sally. What happened? My boss didn't like my hair and her husband did. So I was requested to move on.'

'Well I'm blowed!'

'Am I hired as your secretary, sir?'

'You're hired,' he nodded. He rolled over on his back again, and lay watching the gulls wheeling above them. Then he said, ecstatically, 'It'll be a fine thing for those people, Karen, in Derrybridge, I mean. The little dressmaker, for instance. She sews on an old crock that looks like an infernal machine, and she's way behind the times. How'd it be for her if we took her on and showed her how to use an electric machine, and put her wise to modern patterns? She'd make the things and we'd sell 'em to the inhabitants.'

'Fine, but would she like that? Wouldn't she clear off on her own after we trained her?'

'No, there'd be a sort of contract. Same as with the nearest farmer. He grumbles because he can't get rid of his stuff. He gets part of it taken, of course, but there's always quite a bit he could sell, that he can't calculate for. We'd take that, too, and the surplus dairy produce.'

'Who's the we? Just us two?' Karen wanted to know.

'And one or two chumps like us that I've picked up on my travels,' he grinned. 'I tell you who'd be keen, too. An old chap with a peg-leg. Lives in the village, and carves dolls and toys. No one wants to give him much for them at his backyard door, but in a shop on the green, well...'

There was a man who did carpentry in his spare time. Chris thought of engaging him to do the shop-fitting for them, and to make up the cinema, and after that, he considered he could use the man's energies by way of advertising for shelving to be put up cheap in people's homes, and wood porches and sheds and wooden repair work.

240

There was, too, he recalled, an electrician in the little manufacturing town up north, whose wife was ailing and wanted to get into the country, but he said it was no use unless you had a steady job waiting there. He didn't want to work far afield from her. 'I could send for him,' Chris said, contentedly.

'Suppose people get ideas and open up small shops for themselves, also in the village?' Karen objected.

'All to the good,' Chris said. 'Make the place thrive. Bring in folks from outside in the bus, and perhaps get one or two more buses. Oh, I see no end to the scheme.'

Karen was excited, too, and they talked ecstatically about it. Ruben Bly, from the cottage gate, watched them.

One day, Chris said, 'Karen, you know I'm not going to leave you now, don't you?'

She smiled into his eyes. 'That's what you say now, darling. I'll wait and see.' As always, she thought, with Chris, that his definition of being with her was merely friendship.

'But I'm not going to leave you again, ever. Don't you understand, Karen?'

'I'll believe it when I get tired of having you around, and find I can't get rid of you,' she chuckled.

He never pressed the point. Sometimes they lay, lazily, on the sands, his head in her lap, while she absently played with his tousled hair. Sometimes they swam, or strode briskly over the downs above the cliffs, or explored the dense woods in the hollows. A lovely time for both of them, a thoroughly restful time.

Sometimes Karen wondered where Matthew thought she was, and if he had contacted her bank to see if she had touched her account (on which she had been steadily drawing, without apparently exciting any concern on their behalf because of the obviously dwindling balance) and whether Matthew had thought of contacting Sally and the crowd. She couldn't remember whether there was any note of their addresses among her things in Matthew's house, but if there was, he would surely find it, in his searchings. Matthew was never above searching for what he wanted, she knew, if it was to his advantage.

Chris never attempted to kiss her. He walked with his arm casually round her waist on her shoulders, and called her endearing names in a carelessly tender fashion, but knew better than to go so far as to put his lips on hers. Although he believed what Sally had said, that Karen was ready for remarriage, he instinctively felt that he would lose her if he rushed things.

And so the happy days wore on through the summer, until they decided they couldn't trespass on Ruben Bly's hospitality any longer. They decided to write to Mrs. Heath and say they were going to descend on her.

Ruben said, 'I'm writing to her. I'll deliver the message for you,' and happily they left him to it.

At the end of his letter, recounting their happiness together, he put—to Mrs. Heath's horror—'When's the wedding?'

CHAPTER TWENTY

Chris went back to his aunt's alone. Karen said she had shopping to do.

'Why must you always be buying things?' he complained. 'I want you to come back with me to Aunt Margaret's and tell her about everything.'

'Why not let's just go down to Derrybridge and have a look at the place, and see how things work out first,' Karen objected. 'I mean, your aunt may think the whole thing a bit silly, but if we'd got it working, we could burst on her, in triumph. Two scallywags who've had a great idea and made it work.'

Chris wavered. 'Um, sounds attractive,' he grinned. 'On the other hand, Aunt Margaret's pretty sound in business, and she might have some ideas, and see some snags, too, that we hadn't thought up.'

Karen could see that he was adamant, so

she gave in. 'But I must buy some serviceable things first, Chris, and besides, you know what Mrs. Heath and I are when we get together. Much better you go and have a talk with her yourself. You'll keep it strictly to business, and it's doubtful whether we will!'

'I think there's a whole lot in that,' he told her, ruffling her hair affectionately. 'Well, go on, don't spend too much money, because I haven't got any yet, you know, to help out if you get broke.'

He arranged to meet her at the garden roof of a big store, where they could get a decent lunch at little roof-top tables, and talk.

Karen bought pleated skirts and vivid wool jumpers, one or two jackets, and a selection of small beret basques to tone. Then she succumbed to the lure of some soft walking shoes, and fine wool stockings, and firmly turned her back on pretty dresses.

In the store, she ran into Sally.

They stared at each other for a second, then they both grinned simultaneously.

'I ought to poke you in the eye for running out on me like that,' Sally said. 'Come on, let's get a drink. I'm parched. How you doing?'

'Oh, so-so,' Karen said.

'Don't be a liar,' Sally said, amiably. 'I happen to know you married Matt. Your picture was splashed somewhat in the newspapers.'

Karen was startled. 'Oh! I'd forgotten that!'

'Who're you kidding?' Sally said, from habit. 'I also happen to know that you ran out on Matt in the South of France, and came back alone.'

'How did you find that out?' Karen gasped.

Sally shrugged. 'I guessed you'd be at Matt's, so I thought I'd call and get matey. Matt was still in France, but Mrs. Snowdon opened up when she found I knew so much. She doesn't approve of me, you know.'

'I know,' Karen agreed.

'Molly's pretty wild that you ran out on them, too,' Sally said. 'Mrs. Snowdon seems to think you were of opinion that Nick was about to attack your maidenly virtue.'

'He was. What of it? I just went. By the way, I hope someone's acquainted you with the fact that Matthew paid Nick up in full, in cash?'

Sally nodded. 'Nick's hurt, because of the way it was done. He's never had letters from lawyers in his life. Made him feel like a criminal.'

'Well—' Karen smiled.

'Well, he isn't a criminal,' Sally said, imperturbably. 'He's just smart. Same as the rest of us. Same as you, too.'

Karen flushed. 'I've done with all that now, and anyway, have you ever known me to put anyone on a spot? Have I ever been dishonest?'

'Not half,' Sally said, laughing. 'What about Chris?'

'What d'you mean, what about Chris? And by the way, what made him leave me like that, at the holiday camp?'

Sally shrugged. 'Don't ask me! That's old history, anyhow. The point is, what about now? Does he know you're married to Matthew?' She craned over and looked at Karen's bare left hand. 'Perhaps I'm a bit particular, but that doesn't look particularly honest to me.'

That point was running through Mrs. Heath's mind at that moment. She was too wise to say anything outright against Karen, but she did feel that Chris ought to take more notice of such things for himself.

'Chris, you've been in my house almost two hours, and during that time you've done nothing but ramble on about a village that sounds as dead as mutton, in which I presume you mean to settle down, and try and liven the place up. Right?'

'Well, it's a harsh way of putting it,' he protested. 'I expect also to make quite a lot of money out of it, to say nothing of making the inhabitants happy, and getting a lot of fun out of it myself.'

'But it *will* take time,' Mrs. Heath pressed.

'Quite a time, Aunt Margaret.'

'Which will necessitate your staying in or

246

around one place for far longer than you've ever done before.'

'That's right,' Chris said, cheerfully.

'Something must have happened to you to make you change your whole way of living so suddenly.'

'You know me,' he said, quietly. 'If I'm sufficiently enthusiastic to want to do a thing, I do it, whatever the cost, or the time spent.'

'That's what I mean,' she said, though she hadn't got quite the answer she wanted.

'Can you think of anything to add to my scheme?'

She couldn't, and said so. The whole thing plainly bewildered her, and she couldn't see the point of it, or how Chris expected to make any money.

'Can you see any snags, then, Aunt Margaret?'

'Plenty. It seems to me you've got an idea as your only asset. You've got helpers in plenty, who strike me as being people you don't know very well, or hardly know at all, and that they're also people whose only interest in doing anything at all is to further their own ends.'

'That's why people work at all, isn't it?' he asked, quietly.

'Oh, I know you think I'm offering destruction only, and no construction whatever,' Mrs. Heath said, worriedly, 'but I can't see anything good in it. And I can't see

247

how Karen fits in.'

'She's going to be my secretary and helper.'

'Do you know whether she's ever worked before, Chris?'

'Of course. She told me she'd had a secretarial job, and the poor kid lost it because some silly old buffer got interested in her and his wife didn't like it.'

'Did she tell you she'd worked as a cinema usherette?'

Chris looked blank. 'No, I didn't know that. When was that?'

'After the other job. She got ill, and lost it.'

Chris said nothing, and let his aunt talk. He wondered why Karen hadn't told him all this, and supposed that as usual, she was reticent about her part of the story. A sort of defence, holding back information about herself.

'Just how old a friend is this Matthew Pevensey?' Mrs. Heath asked Chris. 'Do you know anything about him?'

'He's a sort of eccentric, I believe,' Chris said, unwillingly. 'Wealthy, and paints as a sideline. Quite good at it, so Karen says.'

'Oh, she *has* told you about him, then?'

'Aunt Margaret, I don't know what you're getting at, but on and off at odd times, Karen has told me quite a lot about her life, her very private life, and there has been no compulsion. If she doesn't tell me something, I realize it's because it seemed so small to her that she forgot, or that she didn't forget but thought it unessential.'

'Yes, but I sometimes wonder whether Karen is a fit judge of what is an essential point.'

'She isn't compelled to tell me, to tell either of us, anything at all about herself,' Chris said, angrily.

'Isn't she?' Mrs. Heath asked gently. 'Oh, perhaps I've got it all wrong. I rather thought, that is I gathered from what you've told me, that you seemed rather keen on her.'

'Well, what if I am?'

'Well, if you are, I suppose that means your intentions are honourable (if you can stand an old-fashioned phrase) and if they are, that means you naturally expect to know everything about her, if only as a basis for the future.'

Chris got up angrily. His aunt had caught him on the raw. He trusted Karen utterly, but sometimes he wished she wouldn't give the impression that she told him everything with disarming frankness, only to leave him to think over it and find that there were gaps in her life of which he knew nothing. He was too proud to ask her to fill in those gaps, and hoped that one day she would. Often, the conversation seemed to be veering that way, and then would imperceptibly but surely veer away again, and in the joyousness of her company, he didn't notice it until afterwards.

'Oh, well, if that's the way you feel about it all, I suppose it can't be helped, Chris. We'll talk about something else, shall we?'

She got out her cuttings album. 'Karen had a look at these when she was here last. You know, she often drops in to tea, and we have nice little chats. She quite liked the idea of my old book.'

'Incredible,' Chris growled. 'I think I'm growing out of it. The sort of thing I adored going through as a boy, but now I'm grown up I can't see why you waste so much time on it.'

'Don't be beastly, Chris. I've got a whole lot of new cuttings, and as I don't suppose you've looked at a single newspaper on your wanderings, you'd better get *au fait* now.'

'Oh, don't bother me, Aunt Margaret, I've too much on my mind to fritter about reading bits of local gossip.'

Mrs. Heath raised her eyebrows delicately. 'I listen to your interests. You might take an interest in mine.'

'Sorry, Aunt Margaret, but I simply couldn't. Not now. To-morrow, perhaps.'

'Well, will you stay to lunch?'

'Lord, no, I promised to meet Karen. She's been shopping.' He looked at the time. 'I must dash!'

He stooped to kiss her, and she moved forward. The cuttings book jerked from off her lap, and fell, shooting quite a number of loose cuttings all over the carpet.

'Oh, Chris, how clumsy of you. Do help me pick them up, there's a dear boy.'

He got down on the floor and bundled them together. She watched him anxiously. 'Careful, Chris, don't scrabble them up like that.'

He picked them up singly then, with exaggerated neatness, fully resigned to being late. His aunt, he considered, could be amazingly tiresome when she couldn't get her own way.

He had come to the last cutting, and was looking up at her to say something, when he caught the expression on her face. He looked down at the cutting, and knelt there, staring.

Chris said, at last, 'Karen and Matthew Pevensey, after their wedding. Is that what you wanted me to see?'

'Now, Chris, don't take it like that—'

'How else am I supposed to take it? You've been trying to belittle Karen in my eyes all the afternoon. You've wanted me to know this, haven't you? You knew she hadn't told me, and you weren't going to let me go until you saw that I did know. If you wanted me to know that badly, why didn't you have the courage to say so, right out, instead of this farce of the cuttings book?'

She had never seen him so angry before. If he was angry, it was with other people, never with her.

'I could hardly say that, Chris,' she said, mildly. 'Karen hasn't told me, either. It's the inference I put on the newspaper report. I wanted you to see it for what it was worth. It may be untrue, although reported weddings seldom are. However, since Karen wears no wedding ring, and since that in itself is odd, considering that photograph and the report underneath, I felt I wouldn't be honest if I hadn't let you know.'

'It's the way you did it,' he said, angrily. 'If you'd come right out and said, "Look, I don't know what it's all about, but Karen isn't wearing a ring, and I think she's married"—I could have understood that.'

'We all have our ways of doing things, Chris,' his aunt said. 'I'm too old to change my ways. But your welfare comes first with me. I do what I do for your sake.'

He passed a shaking hand over his head, and sat down again, studying the report. Mrs. Heath could see he was looking at the date of it. Thinking over it. Connecting it up with other things.

'Why didn't you ask Karen straight out, about it?' he demanded, at last.

'I did. At least, I gave her the opening to tell me of her own free will. She didn't take it. You know how she skips all round a subject if she doesn't want to give a straight answer.' She knew she had run a risk in saying that, and held her breath, but Chris

252

didn't answer.

After another interval, he said, 'I suppose when she came to see you, that day I met her in the street, she'd come straight back from the South of France.'

'That's what I deduced,' his aunt said, watching him closely. 'She said she'd go back to the station to fetch her overnight bag. I expect she had quite a lot of luggage with her.'

'I can put your mind at rest on that score. She had quite a lot of luggage. We took it all with us, down to the cove.'

'And she went with you, leaving her new husband still on his honeymoon, without even telling you!' Mrs. Heath ejaculated, scandalized, and for the moment showing it without a thought of the result.

Chris lay back in his chair, and gazed out of the window at the roses, now full-blown and falling, and the nodding fronds of the rose creepers, breaking away from the trellis.

'Let me see, you still see Barbara, don't you?'

A gleam came into Mrs. Heath's eyes. She dared not hope that her plans were going right, but it seemed there was still a chance.

'Yes, Chris. She still comes to tea, and she still asks after you. There's a really nice girl, and an honest one. Perhaps I should have said honourable.'

Chris smiled grimly to himself and got up.

'You know, Aunt Margaret,' he said, softly, 'you can say what you like. I don't care. I've just seen through all your plans, and I'm sorry that I can't oblige you. The fact is, I've got Karen under my skin.'

'Chris!'

'Does it surprise you? She's under my skin so much, that everything she does is right as far as I'm concerned. It doesn't even matter to me that she's married. I know what she feels about Matthew, and why she did it. There's always a good reason for everything that Karen does.'

'Chris, you're infatuated with her! You're out of your mind over that damned girl! Where do you think it's going to get you?'

'That's my worry, not yours. But get this, Aunt Margaret. I'm just going to stick by Karen, even if she never gets free. It doesn't matter to me. She's the only one I want, and I believe she feels the same about me. And just in case you start any more funny tricks like this, I don't think I'll come here any more.'

CHAPTER TWENTY-ONE

Matthew came back to town with an imperturbable expression that outraged Mrs. Snowdon.

The old woman took his hat and stick, and

watched the driver bring in the luggage with half attention, while she said to Matthew, with savage pleasure, 'She's not here, you know, sir.'

Matthew laughed easily. 'If you're referring to Karen, Snowy, I hardly expected she would be.'

He went into his study and locked himself in, but Mrs. Snowdon didn't let the matter rest there. As she poured his tea, she began again: 'What are you going to do, sir? Advertise for her?'

'Certainly not! And just what do you know about it?'

'That friend, Sally, has been here after her. And the hussy herself came, soon afterwards, and got some things from her room.'

'If you're referring to my wife, Snowy, kindly say "the mistress". She's a wild little thing. I've given her absolute freedom to come and go as she chooses. So let's have no more of it. And when she does come back, as I've no doubt she will, kindly act as if nothing at all unusual has happened.'

That outraged his housekeeper more than ever. She stumped away, muttering crossly to herself, and Matthew was more anxious over the possibility of bad feeling between Karen and his housekeeper, than any possible danger from Karen's friends.

Contrary to his expectations, it was not Karen who was shown into his study that day, but Chris's aunt. Mrs. Heath had telephoned first, to take the precaution of finding he was back, and at home, before venturing on her mission, which was a delicate one.

Matthew stood with his back to the fireplace, in his customary attitude, and Mrs. Heath took in the tall, slightly stooping, grey-haired man, with a feeling of intense dislike.

'You won't know my name,' she began, 'but I have a great deal of trouble caused me by your—er—wife, Karen.'

'Oh?' Matthew said, politely, and drew up a chair for her. His study armchairs were deep and comfortable, and she subsided gratefully. She didn't like men's rooms, and was a trifle put out by not having been shown into the drawing-room. Matthew gave her a cigarette, and lit it, and took one for himself.

'I knew Karen before she married you,' Mrs. Heath began. 'She was friendly with my nephew.'

'And who is your nephew?' Matthew asked, imperturbably.

'My nephew is Christopher Halliday. I don't suppose the name means very much to you.'

'On the contrary,' Matthew purred, thinking of 'Chris' which Karen had kept muttering over and over again, when she was ill. 'I believe I know whom you mean. Pray go on.'

Mrs. Heath felt ruffled. She had known from the first that it was going to be a difficult interview, but she hadn't realized that Matthew would be so urbane.

'Understand, Mr. Pevensey, I like Karen. She knows that. And frankly, I would have spoken to her myself about this matter, rather than come to you, but, well, frankly, one can't approach Karen by ordinary accepted conventional standards.'

'I agree with you most heartily,' Matthew said.

'You do?'

'I do. I've found the same trouble with her myself. Just how has she annoyed you, Mrs. Heath?'

Mrs. Heath flushed. Matthew was annoying her, too, in much the same way as Karen did, by putting her on the wrong foot.

'Karen keeps seeing my nephew, and she hadn't told him she was married. He's so infatuated with her, that even after I acquainted him with the fact, he still goes on seeing her.'

'Really?' Matthew seemed genuinely interested. 'Tell me, where are they now?'

'Don't you know where Karen is?' Mrs. Heath gasped.

'I haven't the faintest idea,' Matthew said, blandly. 'She left me on our honeymoon, you know.'

'And you take it so calmly?'

He spread his hands, and smiled. 'How else can I take it? Rage about the room, and send out detectives to find her? I could find her, I suppose, but that's no guarantee that she'd stay, even if they brought her back, you know. I have plenty of money, but I don't believe in throwing it away.'

'I'm afraid you're being facetious, Mr. Pevensey,' Mrs. Heath snorted.

'Aren't you, too, Mrs. Heath?' he smiled. 'Seriously now, what did you hope would come out of this very unusual visit of yours? Tell me, now.'

Tears stung her eyelids. She didn't want to show weakness before this man, but she was so enraged against Karen, for what she called her outrageous behaviour, and equally incensed against Matthew because he didn't seem to care. Marriage was not a thing to play at, she decided, but she had lost the initiative of the interview.

'There is a girl,' Mrs. Heath began, and told him about Barbara. Once on the subject of Barbara, she was on safe ground. Barbara was the sort of person she knew and liked and understood. Barbara would have made Chris an ideal wife, from Mrs. Heath's point of view, because the girl's feet were firmly planted on the ground. A man like Chris, Mrs. Heath felt, in her heart, needed a down-to-earth girl like Barbara. She would be

258

his one salvation.

Matthew listened, and the impish twinkle left his eyes. He watched her with the artist's eye, and thought he would like to paint her. The middle-aged woman, smart and well-dressed, keen in business, shrewd in her dealings with men and women. The sincerely selfish woman. That curious combination that one comes up against, at an average of about seven in ten. She was everywhere. But Matthew had never seen one of her kind who had that mixture of foolish courage that drove her to invade someone else's life in pursuit of her own ideals. Chris, Karen, Matthew himself, were to be given no peace until they surrendered themselves to her plan, which, it appeared to Matthew, was that he should take his wife decently into his household and keep her there, out of Chris's way, until Mrs. Heath could get Chris to marry Barbara and settle down to an existence under Mrs. Heath's maternal wing.

He shuddered delicately. He had no desire, himself, for the cosy married life. Karen was to him a beautiful toy, and as such he meant to keep her. He knew he could bring her back before she was ready, simply by cutting off her allowance at the bank. There was a risk that she would go back to her old friends first, and the horse-racing racket, if only out of cussedness. He didn't want her to do that.

He guessed that she was away somewhere

with Chris, and knowing Karen he guessed that her friendship with Chris would be as harmless as it was with Jean—a friendship he had watched with some amusement, and a surprising amount of tenderness. No one understood Matthew Pevensey, because he never permitted them to. His tenderness for Karen was kept hidden. He didn't show it now, as he turned to Mrs. Heath.

'You know, I thought, when you first came in, that you had in mind my welfare, and mine alone.'

'*Yours?*'

'Yes. The betrayed husband.'

She saw the amusement lying in his eyes again, and she snorted, indignantly. 'I think the whole thing is outrageous. Are you going to help me, Mr. Pevensey, or must I go further myself?'

'By all means don't do that,' he said, hurriedly. 'I will help you. By all means. But it must be my way.'

'Your way?' She sounded distrustful.

'I do not propose to go chasing after Karen, to bring her back. For one thing, I don't know where she is, and I never did like the idea of private detectives. No, what I *will* do, and with your help, is to go and see them both. My wife and your nephew.'

'How can you, Mr. Pevensey, if you don't know where Karen is?'

'Ah, my dear lady, but you know where

your nephew is.' He twinkled at her. 'You haven't said so, but I can see you do.'

'I don't *know* where he is, but I've got an idea he might be down in a village called Derrybridge. I don't even know where it is. He says himself that it's off the map. If you think you can locate that, you're welcome to go prancing after him. I should think my way would be more dignified: bring Karen back, and take her miles away.'

'There are only two places on this earth to which I could take my wife with any hope of keeping her there. To the far North, where I would dismiss the huskies and live in frozen isolation with her; or to the heart of Darkest Africa, where I would dismiss the bearers and lead a dreadful life keeping the place free from snakes and insects for her. In either case, it would be most unpleasant. Not only from the point of view of climate, but because Karen and I would bore each other to *death*!'

Mrs. Heath noticed that he spat the last word out in extreme exasperation. He was no longer twinkling at her and appeared to be getting tired of the conversation.

He got up, murmuring something about a gazetteer, on the shelf of a bookcase in the corner, on which was a globe. He appeared to totter a little, but got there, and stood gripping the edge of the bookcase, staring at the globe as if it was the only thing that held any interest for him.

Mrs. Heath watched him, then noticed that his eyes were closed.

'Is anything wrong, Mr. Pevensey?' she asked, wondering whether she should get up, or whether this tiresome man would say something cutting and make her look a complete fool.

He shook himself, and looked round at her, dazed a little, and rather tired. 'Wrong? Oh, no, no. I was just ... thinking.' He got the gazetteer, and came slowly back with it.

It took him a long time to find what he wanted, and during the course of it, he rang for his housekeeper, to ask for a glass of water and his pills. Then, after carefully taking a pill, he seemed better, and returned to his old acidular tone.

'It isn't very difficult to locate a village, if you go about it by the simple means,' he pointed out.

'Very likely,' Mrs. Heath retorted, 'but I don't happen to keep a gazetteer, or a globe.'

'Here is the place, and if you'll be good enough to state which day you can manage, I'll arrange for my chauffeur to pick you up. We'll go down together, and see these young people.'

'With what object?' Mrs. Heath asked, tartly.

'Well, that depends, doesn't it, on what your nephew is doing in a place like Derrybridge,' Matthew Pevensey reflected, adding, 'and what my wife is doing there—if she *is* there.'

'We shall look a pair of fools,' Mrs. Heath said, urgently. 'Chris is there on some hare-brained scheme of his. He's always getting them, but this one is a long-term one. That's what worries me.'

Matthew listened with increasing interest, to the details which Chris had put to his aunt. 'So the young man has ideas,' he said, at last. 'Does he want any money in this thing?'

'I forbid you to offer him any,' Mrs. Heath snapped.

'And why?'

'Don't you see? He'll want to settle there, and see the outcome of his schemes, and that means he'll want to marry Karen. Are you willing to divorce her?'

'That, I think, is my business—and hers.'

'No, it isn't,' she said, impatiently. 'If he has no money put into the scheme (I could put some up myself if I wanted to), then they'll both tire of it, and then, if you'd take Karen away, Chris'll come back to Barbara.'

'How sanguine you are,' he murmured. 'In my experience, human nature isn't so obliging. I might withhold money, which would do no good, in fact it would deprive a lot of people of pleasure and work, if this young man really carries out what he intends to do. I might bring Karen back, and make an enemy of her. No woman likes a man to go back on a bargain, and I made a bargain to leave her alone. (And I don't care if you do know it! We both knew what we were doing). And of course, you might get your nephew to come back to your house. But that you'll get your nephew to take this Barbara to the altar strikes me as being extremely improbable.'

Mrs. Heath fumed. 'I could manage it,' she muttered.

'But who would benefit?' he asked, idly.

'Oh, confound your logic, Mr. Pevensey. Young people don't know what they want, or what is good for them. You're assuming they do, and you're so wrong.'

·'No, Mrs. Heath. I assure you, I am not wrong. I try and guide the young, and help them. And when they get into nasty messes, I get them out—just for the fun of it. But I wouldn't sully my conscience by doing what you are doing. Perhaps that's because I am nearer death than you are.'

'Fiddlesticks! Then if that's all the help you're going to give, I'll take advantage of your offer of a drive down to Derrybridge. I can manage Thursday, if that'll do.'

'You waste no time,' murmured Matthew.

After she had gone, he reached for the telephone, and called up his solicitors.

'Is that you, Harold?' he said, tiredly.

The other man sounded surprised. 'Is that you, Matt? How are you, old fellow?'

'At times, fine. At other times, groggy.

264

This is one of the others.'

'Doing anything about it? Seen Gibbs?'

'Dr. Gibbs told me a lot of harsh things before I went away. In the South of France I saw a specialist.'

'And—?'

'And he told me to do what Gibbs told me to do.'

'What was that, old man?'

'Make that new Will right away.'

CHAPTER TWENTY-TWO

Chris lay on his stomach in the corner of a ragged field. Poppies flared everywhere, and Karen was making a ring of them to fix in her hair.

'Heavens, no,' he said, looking up at her, 'not red flowers in the coloured hair. It's awful!'

'What then? Pu-re white daisies?' she grinned.

'Leave it unadorned. Much the best,' he advised.

'Well, don't go to sleep again,' Karen said, 'I want to talk to you.'

'Haven't you talked enough for the two weeks we've been down here?' he said, severely.

'Perhaps, but I want to talk some more.

What are we going to do?'

'About us? Or about Derrybridge?'

'Both.'

He sat up and rested back on his elbows, a chew of coarse grass hanging from the corner of his mouth. He screwed up his eyes and looked over towards the point where the end of the village started. Over the grey stone bridge to where the huddle of houses began. Four streets of them, branching star-like in an uneven cross. In the centre was a moth-eaten patch, at one time the village green. In the middle stood the shack, that he had meant to do (and still was determined to do) so much with. If only the owner of it would say yes instead of no.

'Well, about Derrybridge, I hang on here until that old cut-throat gives up the shack. About us, well, that's another matter. I just don't know, Karen.'

'Do you want me to ask Matthew to divorce me?'

He looked sideways at her. 'I don't think that's a very bright remark, Karen. In the first place, it would look so darned silly, just after the honeymoon. In the second place, it would look so darned mean, getting him to marry you just to settle your debts, then wanting to be rid of him.'

'You make it sound horrid. Matthew doesn't care.'

'It *is* horrid, and as to the chap not caring

266

one way or the other about the woman he's taken the trouble to marry, well there's no sense in that remark.'

'All right, be horrid yourself, then.'

He sat chewing the grass and staring at the roof-tops of Derrybridge.

'If I'd known what was going to happen, Chris, that day I met Sally in the store, I wouldn't have been there when you came to lunch.'

'Well, what did you expect would happen, after Aunt Margaret had seen to it that I knew about your marriage, and you hadn't even told me first?'

'But you were so angry! You've never looked at me like that before!'

'Well, what'd you expect? Think I was going to say, Hallo, Karen, I just heard you'd married old Matthew Pevensey? Congratulations?'

'No, but I didn't think you'd be angry about it. You don't want to marry me yourself.'

'Who says I don't?'

She sat up, then, and stared into his eyes.

'Chris, when I said just now about getting Matthew to divorce me, I didn't mean so that you could marry me.'

'No? Then just what did you mean?'

'I meant, so that I could be free to be friends with you, because I thought you were worried about me having a husband who might make a nuisance of himself. If he divorced me, then I could be friends with whom I liked, and please myself, couldn't I? (I can now, of course, but I can't make you believe that). Anyway, it's all so silly. I don't see why we need do anything but please ourselves.'

'You know, Karen, you are a little beast,' Chris said. 'You want everything your way, don't you?'

'When you put it like that, it doesn't sound very nice,' she smiled. 'Why do you still go with me, if you think I'm so horrid?'

'Because I can't help myself,' he said, simply, and he wasn't smiling.

'I think it would be nicer for both of us if we were just friends together till we got sick of each other, then we could just part, and there the matter would end. Simple. Don't you?'

'Is that how you want it to be, Karen?'

She thought about it. 'Yes,' she said at last, with a troubled frown, 'I think that's how I want it to be.'

'All right. Having thrashed that out, I suppose we'd better leave it at that,' Chris said. 'Only I'm always expecting an irate husband to come storming down here, and that would not only be deuced awkward, but deuced infuriating, considering what I came down here to do.'

'I think the thought of Matthew storming

down here is a feat of the imagination,' Karen smiled. 'Touching the heights, that. I'd never have thought it of you.'

'You don't think it very probable? If you were my wife, I wouldn't give you the freedom that Matthew gives you.'

'You said that before, Chris. But then if you were my husband, you wouldn't . . .' she broke off, biting her lip.

'Wouldn't what, Karen?'

'You wouldn't have bound me to a farce of a marriage in the first place. You'd have lent me the money I wanted, or sent me packing about my business.'

'You despise the bloke for being kind in his own way?' Chris was incredulous.

'I despise cranks, I think,' Karen said, slowly. 'I prefer healthy people, who expect the normal things from marriage, or else leave marriage alone.'

'You're hard,' he murmured.

'No. No, I'm not. I wish . . . I wish very much that I could wipe out the memory of the past, so that I could contemplate a healthy, normal marriage again, with someone I cared for. I wish I could do that, supposing I were free.'

'I don't understand,' he said.

They left it at that, and went to sleep. Worriedly, Chris woke two hours later, to find that Karen was still beside him, and that everything was as it had been two hours ago, except that in his dream he had most realistically vanquished the formidable Mr. Shenks, who owned the shack, the living quarters and the barn at the back, and who was wily enough to realize that this young man who wanted to buy the derelict buildings for little or nothing, had something up his sleeve, and Mr. Shenks smelt business.

He was a thin, bent little man, bitter and inquisitive; shrewd in a certain way, miserly, and totally devoid of ideas that would catch the market. Because Chris had ideas, and wouldn't let him have them for nothing, he was deliberately blocking Chris's way to getting the wherewithal to work out those ideas of his.

Karen woke. 'What's the matter?' she asked, sleepily.

'Karen, it sounds silly, I know, but do you know of anything in old Shenks' life that he wouldn't want exposing? Or something he would like done and can't get done, that I could do for him?'

'So that you can have the buildings? Darling, there's only blackmail, I agree, since you won't stoop to murder.'

'I was serious,' he grumbled. 'Come on, let's go and find something to eat.'

They strolled into the village, stopping as always on the bridge, to watch the swift-flowing current beneath. On their first night here, a moonlit night, it had all seemed so full of promise. They had walked over the bridge, and imagined the first motorbus rumbling over it, and then those which would follow when Chris's business boomed. Now, everything was at a standstill, because of one man.

When they reached the centre of the village, Karen stopped and clutched Chris's arm. 'That car! That's—oh, it can't be.' She hurried forward and read the number plate. 'It is. Matthew's!'

It was outside the 'Royal Oak'. The potman came out with Matthew and Mrs. Heath, and pointed in the direction of the cottage where Chris was lodging. Then he saw them both and pointed at them instead.

'Aunt Margaret!' Chris fumed, going forward. 'Not looking for us by any chance?' he said, by way of welcome, and his face was grim.

'I was,' she began, with asperity, when Matthew broke in, smoothly. 'Karen, my dear, how are you? I trust you won't resent my presence here, but it wasn't really you I came to see. That was incidental.'

'What d'you mean, "incidental", Matthew?'

'Mrs. Heath is trying to interest me, financially, of course, in her nephew's project. Naturally I wanted to come down and hear about it first, before I thought of investing any money. Er, introduce us, my dear!'

Karen performed the introduction, less sullen now, but puzzled, and suspicious. Chris was frankly angry.

'I'm afraid you've had a journey for nothing, sir. My aunt had no business to talk about it to anyone else. I discussed it in private with her. It was meant to be private.'

'But my wife knows about it,' Matthew smiled. 'Do I understand you are taking in no strangers whatsoever?'

Chris thought of the bus driver and his wife, the electrician, and the host of other people, all strangers, whose help he would have to call upon. 'No,' he allowed.

'Very well, then. Another stranger won't hurt, particularly if he has any money to spare,' Matthew said, and promptly engaged the inn parlour for them to discuss the whole thing.

'How was it that you thought of my husband to approach, Mrs. Heath?' Karen asked, quietly.

'I went to see him, if you must know, about you and my nephew,' Mrs. Heath said, flushing angrily.

'You had no right to do that, Aunt Margaret,' Chris said. 'How could you do such a humiliating thing, and then come barging in on my business affairs?'

'Just a minute, young man. The business angle is my idea. It arose out of the other discussion. That I will dismiss here and now, as I dismissed it for Mrs. Heath. You know Karen is married to me, young man?'

'I do, sir.'

'And you still want to go on—er—with this odd association.'

'There's nothing between Karen and me—' Chris began, furiously.

'Oh, but I know!' Matthew said, lifting his eyebrows in a whimsical smile. 'In fact, I don't know why everyone should assume that I would think otherwise. You see, what your aunt finds so difficult to understand is, I happen to know that Karen has no mind to be unfaithful with anyone. She never has, and she never will. She likes these harmless little friendships with people, and I don't object to them at all. So that disposes of the need for your aunt's fruitless errand, in which, I imagine, she had in mind the putting right of everyone concerned. A noble desire, but one likely to stir up unpleasantness without knowing the facts.'

He smiled at Chris, he beamed at Karen, and he turned and gave a most knowing look at the infuriated Mrs. Heath, who was in two minds whether to get up and go, but was not at all certain how to get back to town without the aid of his car and chauffeur.

'On the other hand, during the course of our distressing conversation the other day, the most interesting facts came out about a project in which you are interested, young man. Now, then, is it money that's stopping you from turning this village upside down?'

'No, sir, it isn't money, and nothing's stopping me doing anything,' Chris said, a stony look on his face.

'Tell him, Chris, and perhaps he'll remove the obstacle,' Karen begged.

'No!' Chris said, furiously. 'He's the last man on earth I'd ask for help, and if everyone's said all they want to about me and the things that concern me only, I'll bid you all good-day.'

'Don't go like that, Chris, it's so silly,' Karen said. 'I think your aunt's been frightfully nosey, and Matt always rubs me up the wrong way with his facetious and almighty approach, but those are just trifles.'

'They aren't trifles!' Chris shouted.

'How dare you say I've been nosey, Karen,' his aunt fumed. 'I insist that you're behaving in the most reprehensible and questionable manner and I think it ought to be stopped! And if your husband had an ounce of guts, he *would* stop it!'

'Oh, well, if you're going to be rude about it,' Karen said, getting up, 'then I think Chris is right. Good-day to you.'

She followed Chris out, and though Matthew called to her, she wouldn't come back.

'Don't be cross with me, Chris,' she said,

hurrying after him. 'It wasn't my fault.'

'They want to know all about the scheme, and you were going to let him in on it,' Chris said, stonily.

'Well, he'd pay off old Shenks, and then we could get going. Matthew's like that. If he feels someone's being obstructive, he raises hell, no matter how much it costs.'

'I don't want his money,' Chris said again. 'I want nothing to do with him. I don't want to see or hear from him or of him. And if you don't mind, I'd like to be alone.'

'All right, if that's the way you feel about it,' Karen said, and swung off to the right and down a little lane. There was a random bench outside one of the houses and she sat on it, and got out a cigarette.

It was quiet. All the house windows were shut, although it was warm weather. In this village there were very few wireless sets, and those that were there, were poor, home-made things, used only for the news items. There was no blaring of tinned music on the streets, no screeches of brakes for there was no transport to speak of. It was all quiet, and deadening. Karen considered it, and asked herself if she really liked it. She could find no answer to that, except that she didn't actively dislike it. She was comfortable, in her green sweater and brown slacks, with no make-up, no jewellery, and her long curling red-brown hair tied back loosely with brown ribbon. At ease and more or less happy. What more could anyone ask?

Matthew looked down the street from the corner where the inn was. He was looking for her, and as he caught sight of her, he waved his stick. He seemed to be a long time covering the short distance between them, and he sank down on the seat beside her without speaking for a moment.

'Matt, is anything . . . wrong? You look . . . funny,' Karen said, hesitantly, searching his face, unable to decide whether his eyes were more sunken than usual, or his skin more parchment-like. Something was different but she couldn't put a finger on it.

'Might I ask just how you expect me to interpret the word "funny"?' he replied. 'Humorous, strange, or peculiar?'

'Oh, Matthew, you make me so wild!' she exploded. 'You always pick me up on everything I say! Well never mind—just skip it.'

'Karen, my dear, are you coming back to me?' he asked, ignoring her outburst.

'I suppose that means I must, doesn't it?'

'No. There's no compulsion. It was a question.'

'Oh, well, some day, though you don't really want me, do you? I mean you get along pretty well without me.'

'I did rather want to finish those three pictures of you . . . fairly soon,' he mused.

'Finish 'em from memory,' Karen said, wishing he wouldn't appeal to her sympathies in this way.

'It looks as though I shall have to,' he said, looking wistfully at her. 'Karen, you're happy.' It was an accusation. 'I see it in your eyes.'

'Well, perhaps I am. Is it so difficult to accept?'

'Are you in love with this young man?'

'Oh, mind your own business, Matthew!' she burst out. Then she laughed. 'That's a pretty silly thing to say to your own husband, isn't it?'

'A pretty silly thing,' he agreed, with a smile.

'But you know what I mean, Matt. I'm just happy, that's all. Chris and I speak the same language, and we work well together.'

'Well,' he said, looking down the deserted street, 'if a good many young couples expected that instead of futile passion, as a definition of being in love, there might be fewer unhappy marriages.' He got up. 'Good-bye, Karen. Keep happy, won't you?'

'Gracious, Matthew, how very final,' she laughed. 'I shall merely say "So-long", and thanks for squashing that horrid Mrs. Heath for me. I expect I shall turn up on your doorstep pretty soon, and ask for you to get me out of some mess or other, or keep some wolf out of my life, and you'll say, all stuffy and virtuous, "Very well, Karen, but I shall expect you to pose for me, at a fellow artists' gathering this afternoon".'

'I don't believe I shall,' he said, quietly, with a funny little smile lurking about the corners of his mouth. 'Karen, I'm going to kiss you, whether you like it or not.'

He bent, and kissed her on the mouth. She didn't flinch. It wasn't unpleasant, she found, nor was it pleasant. She just didn't feel anything beyond a faint flutter of uneasiness, because it was so unlike Matthew. He anxiously searched her eyes, and appeared content with what he saw. It occurred to her afterwards that he would have been very much hurt if she had attempted to stop him from that one small whim of his.

She watched him walk slowly back up the street, and soon after, the car crossed out of the green, on its way to the highway. She never saw Matthew again.

CHAPTER TWENTY-THREE

The news of Matthew's sudden death came to Chris and Karen at the end of a particularly stormy day, a day on which they had worked like niggers, getting details together, to form an accurate assessment of the scheme in the form of an account. They were going to show

278

it to old Shenks and offer to let him come in as a partner, if he wouldn't let them have the accommodation in any other way.

The little dressmaker had been difficult. Unexpectedly difficult. She was afraid of taking a chance, she said. It was, it appeared, an upheaval to think of working anywhere else than in her own front parlour, where she had worked for close on twenty years. In this, her old mother backed her up.

'New-fangled notions,' said the old woman.

'You see, it isn't as if I should be sure of getting trade, is it?' she asked, pathetically.

'You don't have to get trade,' Chris said, patiently. 'You'd be working for me, for the firm I'm going to run. I would pay you a wage each week, for working for me. Each new customer you got, through your work, I'd give you a commission on.'

'Commission?' the little woman asked, bewildered.

'New-fangled notions,' said her old mother.

'Mr. Halliday means he'd give you a small present of money for each new customer your work brought to the firm,' Karen explained.

'Accept a gift of money from a man? Oh, I couldn't, really. It wouldn't be decent,' the little woman protested.

'Not from a man, from your employer,' Karen explained. 'Everyone gets that, these days, in the towns, if they bring trade. It's usual. It's the custom. Not indecent at all.'

'Oh, in the towns, but this isn't a town.'

'We hope to make it one. A busy thriving one,' Chris barked, 'if no one stops us, by sheer stupidity.'

'Chris,' Karen said gently. 'Look, you'd like a lovely brand-new sewing machine to work on, wouldn't you? And new sets of patterns? You'd like to learn how to make up smart new fashions, instead of the same old ones you're used to? And look, the sewing machine isn't a treadle, it's worked by electricity. Goes by itself.'

'And don't you say "new-fangled notions"!' Chris barked at the old woman.

'She's deaf as a post,' the little dressmaker said.

'I think she's going to be less easy than we thought at first,' Karen sighed, as they left the cottage, to go and find the peg-legged man who carved the toys.

He had nothing to say, but his wife had a lot. 'I don't like all this, miss,' she began. 'You townsfolk are all talk and no do. Just supposing anything went wrong, where would we be? That's what I'd like to know?'

'Where d'you think you'd be?' Chris asked, with heavy sarcasm. 'Safe and sound in your own cottage, with wages in your pockets. I'm the one who's going to stand the racket, if there is any.'

The woman sniffed. 'Where'd my chap's

work all be, eh, tell me that! Shut up in your shop, that's where! We couldn't get at it, but you could. You'd flit overnight, and take it all with you—I've seen it done afore. No, we're keeping the stuff here, thank you very much, and we're going to sell in our back yard, same as we've always done.'

'Um,' Chris said. 'Change of wind all at once, eh?'

It was the same with the man who worked in wood. His carpenter's bench was littered with tools and scraps of wood, but he had no work. Yet he was unwilling to go further with his promises to work for Chris, and wouldn't say why.

'Doesn't your wife like the idea?' Chris demanded.

The man glanced at his wife, standing arms akimbo at the door, and said, hesitantly, 'Well, it's not exactly that, you see, sir.'

'Then what is it, then?'

'I'd rather not say. I just don't want to work for you, sir.'

Karen whispered to Chris, and he glared.

'Have you been talking to anyone about this?' he demanded of the carpenter and his wife.

'What if we have?' the woman said, sourly. 'It's a free country, isn't it?'

'To Shenks, I suppose!'

The couple eyed each other. Then the wife said, 'Well, and why not? He's a decent,

281

honest neighbour. We've known him for years. He's got none of these get-rich-quick ideas, and they don't get folks nowhere. He warned us, and we're grateful. That's all.'

'Ah. Well, I hope that Shenks warned you he's also standing in the way of my having his barns to open up, and I hope he warned you that when I do get accommodation, you two won't be wanted, so you'll have plenty of leisure to think over your friend's advice while other folks are making money working for me.'

The couple stared at him, and there was a suggestion of a smile in the woman's eyes, but they said nothing, and Chris and Karen went.

'That didn't do us much good, Chris,' Karen murmured.

'Oh, I lost my temper. They were all for the idea when I spoke to them about it at first. Since old Shenks has got at 'em—by the way, what made you think of that? I didn't know he talked with these people.'

Karen looked uncomfortable. 'Well, I went to his place to try and talk him round myself, yesterday, and they let out that he'd gone to see some of his tenants. Did you know he owns most of the cottages round the Green?'

'Oh! No, I didn't. Hell! That's done it.'

People living further afield, in houses which didn't belong to Shenks, were not quite so actively against Chris. Their attitude, however, was that they had heard that Chris was now in a position that he had no money to carry out his grand schemes. Shenks had done his work very well.

Chris left Karen at the cottage at which she was lodging and mooched on. His usual cheeriness had abated a little since Mrs. Heath had come down with Matthew some days ago. Explaining it to Karen, he had said that it had made him feel rather like a small boy tinkering with something too big for him, and some grown-up had come along, smiled at it in some amusement, and offered to buy him the proper thing instead.

Karen had tried to jolly him out of it, but she, too, felt that that fateful visit of Matthew and Chris's aunt, had done a lot to spoil their venture. A lot of the bright tinsel of it had gone, leaving it looking rather dreary and, as to-day, hopeless as well.

She came running after him. 'Chris, oh, Chris, look at this telegram.'

He took it and said, 'How long's this been there?'

'Most of the day. Mrs. Grey didn't know what to do with it. It never dawned on her to send after us with it.'

'It wouldn't,' he said, savagely, giving it back to her. 'Well, you can't do anything about it to-night, but I suppose you'll want to go back first thing in the morning.'

She nodded.

He looked curiously at her. She seemed
283

rather distressed, but only as one would when some male relative has passed away, and there are the usual distressing formulas to go through before it can all be decently put out of sight at the back of the memory. No real grief, as he had seen her show when she had told him, three years afterwards, about her first husband's death.

He wondered if she'd wear deep mourning, and what she'd look like. Whether she'd wear theatrical weeds, or just quiet black trimmed with white. He just couldn't cope with the idea at all.

'Want to walk a bit?' he asked her.

'Yes. Oh, yes, I want to talk, Chris.'

'Bit sudden. What was it, d'you suppose. Heart?'

'I don't know.' She recalled the incident when she had last seen him, and told Chris. 'He really did look ... well, funny, but you know Matthew. He picked me up about the word "funny", and I didn't get anything out of him. But he didn't seem his old vigorous self that day, somehow.'

'Fellow didn't look at all healthy to me,' Chris growled.

'Well, he didn't take any exercise, and he lived on very rich food and old wines,' Karen mused.

'Karen, do you want me to—well, I suppose I can't very well come up with you, or show myself, but it just struck me that you ought to have a man around, to do things, help you, or something.'

'Thank you, Chris, but I've got an idea that I shall just be required to go to the dressmaker's and get myself decently covered in black. Mrs. Snowdon and the solicitors will see to the rest, I expect. One solicitor was a boyhood friend of Matthew's. I remember him. I used to have to call him "Uncle Harold", in the days when I called Matthew "Uncle Matt." Odious custom to thrust on children, isn't it?'

Chris agreed, but Karen was glad of that ancient custom when she presented herself at the solicitor's office two days later.

'Why, Karen, come in, child,' he said, kindly.

'Is it all right to say, "Hallo, Uncle Harold"?' she said, uncertainly. He was much older, but much the same as she remembered him. Large, florid, twinkling, good-humoured. Not a bit like the accustomed idea of a solicitor, but rather like a fat, jolly publican.

'Just drop the Uncle, as you're a big girl now,' he smiled. She was much the same as in her photographs, and the picture Matt had finished of her, he noticed, except that black didn't sit so kindly on her as the gay riotous colours she herself preferred. The black looked rusty beside the vivid hues of her hair, and he felt that for any other reason than deep mourning, black was not in exactly good taste for her. It suggested to him the respectability of a barmaid in middle years, and he didn't like it. Perhaps it would have been better if the style of the outfit had been less smart in cut. He gave it up.

'I want to run over the details of the funeral with you first,' he said. It appeared that everyone who had attended Matthew's wedding were turning out in force to see him buried. If he hadn't been exactly popular, he was respected for his work, and his connections in the art world. Harold subtly suggested that it was an honour for these people to participate in Matthew's funeral.

Karen said, 'How ghoulish. Why don't they keep away?'

'You ought to be pleased,' he said.

Then he had a little talk with her. A 'pep' talk, Karen thought, with a smile, as she left the office. She didn't need it. She was saddened at the thought of Matthew's end. She remembered his one and only kiss, and realized that he must have known he was going to die pretty soon. She wished, illogically, that she had been less thoughtless where he was concerned, yet she knew that if he were alive, she would act in just the same way that she had.

She went back to the house, and wandered about, looking at everything, touching everything, and wondering why she felt no different about it all. She had thought that perhaps she would like it better now, if only out of respect to Matthew. But she didn't. She hated the curious differences in period and country, of each room; the pretentiousness of it, the slightly ridiculous air with which the place was clothed. She hoped that Matthew hadn't left the house to her. It would be an awful smack in the eye, knowing how she had hated it.

Mrs. Snowdon went about sniffing and red-eyed. The maids, mostly elderly, looked at her with thinly veiled reproach. She got the impression that they held her responsible, in some way, for their master's death. She was at once amused and shocked. For herself, all she wanted was for the funeral to be over, so that she could settle everything up and go back to Derrybridge and Chris.

It rained at the funeral, and there was a sort of reception (she couldn't think of a better word) when she got back, with Mrs. Snowdon discreetly serving, and everyone talking in unnaturally hushed voices, about the flowers, and about 'poor' Matthew. Karen was vaguely irritated by it all, and was glad when they went.

A few people stayed, evidently prompted by the solicitor, who was organizing the proceedings, and the staff were all ushered into the library, with Karen. Karen was placed in an armchair in the centre of the room, as the person of most importance, the others were all grouped around and behind her. Harold, at a table in front of her, read the will.

Matthew had left a great deal of property, even after death duties had been allowed for. Karen had always supposed him rich, but hadn't thought he was quite as rich as that. He came of wealthy connections, she understood. He had carved up his estate into beneficiaries for the servants (all extremely generous, Karen thought), and some legacies to close friends and some to charities, mostly connected with the art world.

And then came the surprise. The house, its contents and the residue of the estate, were left to Karen, on condition that she lived in it and nowhere else, and that she didn't re-marry. If, however, she wished to re-marry, there was nothing for her.

There was a startled little silence. The solicitor folded his papers with an air of finality, and the friends said good-bye and went, and the staff filed out. Karen sat there, a little dazed.

'Harold, is it true?' she whispered, as he came over and stopped in front of her.

'I'm afraid so, my dear.'

'How could Matthew be so beastly?'

He frowned. 'He wasn't, really, you know. He had your good at heart. You're to think it over, and let me know what you want to do.'

288

'Supposing I say I don't want to avail myself of it. What will happen to the house, and the money?'

'There are other instructions about it,' he said, after a slight pause.

She jumped to the conclusion that that meant they would sell the house and distribute the proceeds to charities.

'Matthew knew I couldn't get along without any money. He knew I'd tried. I got ill, with one beastly job I had. He only rescued me in time. How could he?'

'I know all that, Karen. But you don't have to do anything you don't want to, remember that. You either live in the house, as it is, and live like a wealthy woman, provided you don't re-marry, or . . . you can re-marry.'

'And be poor as a church mouse,' she said, thinking of Chris, who hadn't a bean. And, she recalled, who hadn't really asked her to marry him.

Panic flooded over her. She couldn't really leave it in abeyance, for Chris would be sure to ask her to marry him, if only to rescue her from that arbitrary will and its conditions. She hadn't give re-marriage a thought, and certainly not to Chris. Marriage again . . .

All its intimacies, its sweetnesses, its give and take, its pitfalls and sadnesses, flooded over her. She had had three weeks of it, three weeks only, with Blaize, and it had been perfect. Supposing the next time it wasn't perfect. How could it be perfect with Chris, with whom she fell in and out of trouble and argument?

And if she didn't marry Chris, and didn't take advantage of the will, what then? She remembered that filthy little room, in which she had lain ill, and she recalled with distaste the horrid little husband of her first employer. The memory of O'Leary popped up, and all that might have happened if she had stayed with Sally and the holiday camp people. She recalled Molly, and her tiresome husband Nick.

'No, no,' she heard herself saying. 'I can't.'

'Can't what, Karen?' Harold asked, gently, pulling on his gloves.

'I can't through all that again. There's no need to consider. You can transfer the deeds of the house to me, or whatever it is you have to do. I'll fall in with Matt's will ... I've no choice.'

CHAPTER TWENTY-FOUR

It was some two months later before Karen decided that she could bring herself to see Chris again.

It was going to be a cold autumn. Cold and wet. There was an early fall of leaves, and outside Matthew's house the quiet square had a carpet of them; limp, almost colourless, they lay. Nothing depressed Karen quite so much as a wet autumn, and she scowled out at the prospect and wondered what mean fate had made her so utterly dependent on schemes such as this, that tied her for ever to Matthew's ugly house, surrounded by the plane trees.

She roamed about the rooms, trying to make herself—if not actually like them—at least, accept them without loathing. But she could see it was not going to work.

She had kept the staff on. Any changes meant that she would have to get interested in the workings of the house in order to cope with the readjustments, and that was the last thing she wanted. So she kept the full staff on, so that things would go on just as before. She even kept on Matthew's pretentious car and his chauffeur.

One day she forced herself to go into his studio. She had not been in there since the day before they had left for their honeymoon, and it was with some curiosity that she went round the easels, uncovering timidly what she knew would turn out to be portraits of herself.

What did surprise her were the sketches. These were kept in a great portfolio standing by the dais. In them, Matthew had captured every possible mood of Karen's, and more. He had pried, unforgivingly, Karen considered. Prying coupled with his imagination, had produced in that sketch-book, vague pictures that had never been posed. Karen with Jean on the raft, and in the car (and they had never been in Matthew's car together), and striding up the hillside tracks. He must have studied them both unceasingly through his glasses, to get them so utterly true to life, because even the set of Jean's muscles in his back were so much like him, the way he strode with his head flung back and his chin slightly forward, and Karen had the uneasy feeling that on many occasions Matthew must have been walking behind them, sketchbook in hand.

Some of the heads were of Karen alone, in fantastic head-dresses she had never seen or dreamed of, and sometimes there were emotions on her face that she had never dreamed of, either. Fear—ghastly, irrational fear—and anger, low cunning, and virginal innocence. He had drawn them all in, with a few strokes of his brilliant pencil.

And then among them was a sketch that aroused hatred, dull throbbing hatred in Karen's heart. Somewhere Matthew must have found a photograph of Blaize. He had worked on it, and sketched Karen and Blaize together. Sometimes their full bodies, sitting or standing (and here Matthew's imagination hadn't been able to work, because never having seen Blaize alive, he hadn't captured his physical movements) but the face was Blaize's, and the expression the one in the photograph.

Karen squatted down in the studio and cried as bitterly over that sketch as she had the night in the farmhouse. And what shocked her most was that she was not crying *for* Blaize any more, but because Matthew had put prying hands into her box of memories, and selected ruthlessly and used them. He had no business to see, no business to do this at all. Almost as if he were saying, I can't possess Karen, so I won't let her possess Blaize. He's mine, too, from the artist's point of view just as she is mine from the artist's point of view. Only Karen knew that Matthew didn't reason like that.

After that, she wrote to Chris. She wanted him there. She hated the thought of spending another week in that house alone. It wasn't clear in her mind what she was going to do if and when Chris came. She could hardly ask him to stay with her alone, for propriety's sake, and she didn't want a house party, for that would be worse than being alone, since she wouldn't have the opportunity for quiet discussion with him. She wrote that she was miserable and bewildered, and hadn't felt like seeing him before, but now she wanted to see him badly.

Chris, of course, misconstrued. He came full of hope that she was now ready to become engaged and married to him. The first sight of her dashed that hope.

She looked rather ill, and certainly not in love with him. His heart sank.

'Chris, you've got to listen to me. I've got such a lot to tell you and it's so beastly. You'll never guess what's happened.'

Characteristically, she told him about the portfolio of sketches first, because that was closer to her, and fresher, than the matter of the Will. She had got used to the idea of that arrangement, but the sketches rankled still.

'The old blighter!' Chris ejaculated angrily. 'But why stay here? It's a frightful house, anyway. Why don't you sell it and come back to Derrybridge with me? I've got a lot to tell you, too.'

She brushed Derrybridge aside as of no importance, and that made him wonder. 'I can't sell the house. It isn't mine to sell.'

'What?'

'I've got the use of it, and the servants and everything, but I've got to leave it all as it is, and I've got to live in it all the time. I can spend the money, too, but those damned solicitors are behind me all the time, watching what I do, controlling the accounts.'

'Well, are you going to stand for that?'

She shrugged. 'What else can I do?'

'Are you crazy, Karen, or am I? Just chuck the whole thing. You don't want any more of this, do you? Good heavens, the poor old boy didn't last very long, and you're free, free as air. Karen, can't you see what I'm trying to say? Let me try and make you happy. You've had two marriages before. You don't know that another try won't work, do you?'

'Another try?' she repeated blankly. 'I hadn't thought of that.' She stared at him, emotions mixing furiously in her.

'Well, think about it now, darling,' he urged, forgetting all his previous caution in dealing with that highly delicate subject. 'We could be happy together, you and I. You know that. We part, then we always come together again. We can't help it. Look at the times I've left you, and had to come back. And you've looked as though you've cared.'

She got up and moved restively about the room. 'You don't understand, Chris,' she murmured, like a bewildered child. 'I just thought—well, I loved being with you and all that. I adored walking with you ...' She broke off, leaving it, because for her it was an impossible subject to explain. How could she say that although she had never resented the friendly touch of his arm round her waist, or the warmth in his hug of greeting, she still shrank from the thought of sharing an intimate married life with him? Or, indeed, with anyone?

'You see, the solicitors said that Matthew had given me two things to choose from. The house, and everything, and the money, or

295

nothing. I mean, if I chose the house, then I had to sign deeds and things, taking them over, and also to say I wouldn't marry again.'

'You signed?' Chris got up slowly, his brows knitting. 'You signed your life away for—for this old mausoleum and a bit of money? Are you out of your mind?'

'A bit of money! It was a lot, Chris, and besides, I hadn't a penny! What else could I do?'

'You could have come to me. You knew that,' he said, savagely. 'You could have come to me—if you'd wanted to.'

'But Chris, you don't understand ...' she began, piteously, but he brushed her protests to one side.

'Do you know what, Karen? I think you love money so much, you'd sell your soul for it. And to think I thought you'd want to *work* with me, make something fine out of nothing. Why, you don't know the meaning of the word "work".'

'Don't I?' she flung at him, stung to anger. 'Don't I? And what do you know about it, I'd like to know? Loafing about the country for years, because you had one set-back. Your girl let you down. Perhaps she knew what you were like!'

'You leave Barbara out of this!' he said, furiously, not really caring one way or the other about Barbara, but angry that Karen should have put her finger on the weak spot in his life. The time he ran away from reality because Barbara didn't stand by him.

'All right, I will! There's plenty of other things I can remember, to prove that you've no right to taunt me about work. For instance, look at you now, loafing about at Derrybridge because one old man is stuck in your way. You had your chance to deal with him, when Matthew offered to buy him out for you, but you were too pig-headed to take it!'

'And I was right,' he told her, savagely. 'You'll be surprised to know that I've got the buildings I wanted—my way! How about that?'

'Did you, Chris?' Interest caught her, and her anger swiftly abated, but his didn't.

'I did! I happened to be tailing him home one night, waiting my chance to catch him up and talk him round, blast him! A couple of louts ran out of the hedge and attacked him, and being the fool I am, I went to his rescue, instead of leaving the old swine to get his deserts.'

'And so he rewarded you?'

'And so he agreed that my price was about right for the buildings,' he corrected, 'and he let me have them, because he had wads of cash on him from market, and I happened to preserve it for him. How some people set a store on money,' he finished, bitterly.

'It's useful, as I'm sure you must see,' she

murmured.

'And what have I got the buildings for now, I'd like to know.' He stared morosely into her eyes. 'I was going to build up something, for us. You and I. And because I didn't tell you so, in so many words, you have to dash in and sign your future away, because you're so darned scared of being without money. Oh, well, perhaps I could never have provided enough cash for you, at that,' he finished, with the suspicion of a break in his voice, and before she could think of anything to say, he strode out of the room.

She let him go. There was nothing more to say or do. If she had been free to marry him, it would have been far worse, because she would still have had to refuse him.

She thought of Derrybridge, and that great ugly building which, for want of a better name, they called a shack. At one time it had been part barn, part stable, with drivers' living quarters above. Strongly built, so that even now, with the high windows broken from neglect, the structure was still quite strong. Built to the back of it was a nice little house. They had been over it together, and made plans. The barn at the end of the plot of land opened on to a side lane, which could have been used as the public way into the cinema, and still give them complete privacy. Perfect, for want of a little attention, time and money. Money.

That hateful word. Karen pressed her face against the double glass of the window, and stared out into the formal square. Winter would clamp down on them, and she would be alone in this house. She thought of having wild parties with the gang, but they would break things, and she supposed there'd be trouble with Harold, who had already hinted that she owed it to Matthew to revere his house, because he had loved it that way.

The next week, and the week after, she suppressed the desire to go down to Derrybridge. She stuck it out until a month after Chris's visit, and finally gave in. Rodgers didn't like the idea of a drive through the slushy lanes with the car, but when she curtly informed him that they'd probably be making the journey quite a lot, he caved in suddenly, and said it would be a nice change. She found the servants a trifle resentful in their attitude to her, although there wasn't enough resentment to be able to put her finger on it and stamp it out.

Derrybridge looked more ugly than ever, now the trees were bare. It was a bitterly cold day in November. One or two children, inadequately clad, were playing with a bit of wood and a ball, on the starved grass of the Green; no women stood at doors in the accustomed way, and no one was outside the public house, on the little bench, as she had been accustomed to seeing. The whole place had a forlorn look.

The children left their play and came up to the car. Rodgers would have chased them off, but Karen recognized one of them as Peg-leg's child.

'My dad said you weren't coming no more,' the boy offered.

'That's where your dad was wrong,' Karen said. 'Is he in?'

Peg-leg was, and his wife wasn't. Karen didn't know his real name. Everyone knew him by that unflattering nick-name, and he didn't seem to mind.

'Still want to work for us?' she smiled, as the child took her into the bare little kitchen.

He shrugged. 'Where's the work to do? The gentleman went off and left everything.'

Karen looked troubled. 'When was this?'

Peg-leg reckoned up. It must have been the same day that Chris came to Matthew's house; that same disastrous day that he flung himself out with his 'all-is-lost' air. Karen laughed.

'Oh, then! I know about that. He wasn't very pleased. The thing looked like falling through. Since then we've got money to put in the project. It's all different now. Didn't he tell you?' Her heart beat faintly as she looked at Peg-leg and strove to make it all sound casual. She was so afraid that Chris might, in his anger and frustration, have flung the keys back at Shenks and told him to sell the buildings to anyone who'd buy them. That would be just like Chris. Karen was glad Peg-leg's wife wasn't there.

'No, that he didn't,' Peg-leg said, stolidly. 'He just stood and stared at the shack, and he said, angry-like, it's all over and done with. And something about putting your trust in someone and finding you couldn't trust no one.'

'I don't blame him,' Karen said. 'We've been let down again and again, but it's all right now. Look, can you get together the other people that Mr. Halliday wanted to work with him? I suggest we talk it out.' She looked round the little kitchen. 'We might go to the shack. It's the place where we shall be working, anyway.'

'Aye, I can get 'em,' Peg-leg said, staring at her.

'All of them,' Karen said, firmly, 'even Miss Prynn.'

'She won't leave her mother,' Peg-leg said.

'Ah, but I want her to,' Karen smiled. 'Her mother keeps saying "new-fangled notions", and that puts us all off.'

Peg-leg permitted a faint smile to flicker round his mouth. He knew old Mrs. Prynn's views as well as anyone.

Karen went back to the car, and got out a notebook and fountain-pen. 'You'd better engage rooms for us to-night at the inn, Rodgers. I shall want you, and the car, to-morrow, and possibly the next day.'

She watched Rodgers go into the inn, with distaste written all over his face. She hoped he wouldn't antagonize everyone.

Without thinking, she went to the door of the building and turned the handle. It stuck. Of course, Chris would have the keys.

She stood thinking. What right had she to do this? She had expected opposition from Peg-leg, but he was singularly trusting. He hadn't questioned her right, since she had asserted that she had the money to go on. Perhaps the sight of the car and Rodgers, had clinched the matter.

'He said you'd come back,' someone said.

She turned round, and saw the little wizened figure of Shenks. The man who had caused them so much heart-ache and frustration from the first. The man who had curbed even their violent enthusiasm, because he formed a solid and formidable block in their path.

'And he said to give you these,' the little man said, with a knowing grin. He held up the bunch of keys, for the main building, the living quarters and the barn. All there, left, presumably, by Chris, in his bitter humour, that day!

She took them. 'What else did he say?' she asked, tartly, but with a tug at her heart.

'He said, she's welcome to the lot. Quarrelled, maybe, eh?' he hazarded, his little eyes bright with curiosity.

'On the contrary,' she said, coolly. 'We have many irons in the fire. This is just one of them.'

'And he's off on business, elsewhere?' Shenks purred.

'That's right.' Karen let herself into the shack, and Shenks followed her. 'Why did they always call this the Shack?' she asked, irritably.

He shrugged. 'Hard to find another name for it.'

'Well, from now on, its going to be called Halliday's Store,' she said, firmly.

Peg-leg looked round the door.

'Come on in,' Karen called. 'Got 'em all?'

He nodded. He had the carpenter, the blacksmith, a little man who did locks and odd jobs, and was also a glazier. Little Miss Prynn, with her mother hobbling on two sticks. One or two other people whom Chris thought needed jobs badly enough to do anything, and a woman who had been engaged to clean up when wanted.

'Where's the grocer?'

'He can't leave his store just now,' Peg-leg said.

'You'd better fetch him. Tell him to shut up shop.'

Peg-leg fetched him.

'Take your mother back, Miss Prynn. If you want to work for me, you leave your mother out of discussions,' Karen said, firmly.

The little dressmaker burst into tears, but did as she was asked, with much argument from the old woman.

'Someone set a fire going, or fetch a stove,' Karen commanded, and stared at Shenks.

'You want for me to go?' he grinned.

Karen considered him. The others were watching her. This was a decision, she knew, that would affect her life and Chris's in a most far-reaching manner. Every instinct in her urged her to make him go, and stay away. But a sixth sense struck a warning note.

'No,' she said, at length. 'You'd better stay.'

'Stay?' His face dropped for a second, before he could bring the habitual grin back. He hadn't expected that.

'Yes, Mr. Shenks, stay,' Karen said, firmly. 'I think I'd rather have you with me than against me.'

CHAPTER TWENTY-FIVE

Chris dropped in suddenly to see Karen in the Spring. He took her completely by surprise. She had been preparing to go down to Derrybridge. The car was actually at the door.

He said, awkwardly, 'Hallo, Karen. Hope I'm not stopping you from going out?'

She said, equally awkwardly, 'Well, I was, Chris, but it doesn't matter.'

That was the fore-runner of several visits. Strange visits, during which they sat and talked formally, and looked yearningly at each other, neither giving way on a single point. The strangest part of those visits was that Chris never once mentioned Derry-bridge, and Karen always found it so hard to suddenly bring it into the conversation herself.

He talked about his aunt, and the people he saw on his wanderings. Once he went back to the northern factory, and really started to work it up again, but a yearning to get free again, stopped him. The man said he didn't want to see him again. He felt he would never stay put. It was the same with other people. They seemed to like him, and wanted his services. He had personality, a flair for working with people and bringing out the best in them. He had plenty of ideas, too. But that restlessness of his was dangerous; it spread.

'Well, what are you going to do with your life, Chris?'

'What are you going to do with yours?' he countered.

She smiled, wearily. 'You won't believe me, but I don't think I mind very much. I

305

miss you very much, but I know you wouldn't stay, or if you did, I'd never be really easy, because I'd think you secretly chafed at having to stay.'

'You really miss me, Karen?' he asked, hungrily.

'As a friend,' she said, swiftly, and the light died out of his eyes.

He came again in the Summer, and the Autumn, and she realized that he was allotting himself a visit to her, once a quarter. She mentioned this to him once.

'That's right,' he said. 'I take back a picture of you, and each one's different. You wore a white linen suit, last Spring. And a silly white hat, like a bonnet. You had a green muslin on in the Summer. I liked that.' He stared at the businesslike shirt blouse she now wore, and the trim navy suit. 'What's that get-up for?'

'You don't like it?'

'Looks as if you're a business woman, but knowing you, well, that's just silly.'

'Just silly,' she agreed. 'Chris, ever go down to Derrybridge?' she said, casually.

'No,' he replied, roughly. 'Do you?'

'Occasionally,' she said, watching him, hoping he'd show some interest.

'What's it look like?' he forced himself to say.

'Why don't you go and see for yourself?' she said, softly.

He stared at her, then laughed. 'So you can take me down, sitting behind your fancy chauffeur, and tempt me to start up my poor little project with your ill-gotten gains? No, thanks, Karen. If I ever went back to Derrybridge to work that out, it'd be on my own terms.'

She felt a pang of anxiety. What would happen if he did go down on his own, out of curiosity, and saw the row of shops with 'Halliday's Store' over them? Would he be angry that she had started the bus service on her own? Got the village started on her own, with the money from Matthew, settled in the local bank as the Store account? And what would he say if he knew that Shenks was a partner? She had needed a man, and a shrewd man, to help her cope. With Shenks against her, she had known at the outset that it would have been impossible. With him in the firm with her, she had flagrantly made use of him, and discovered that his peculiar sense of humour caused him to like being pushed around by a business woman. He liked it. She even got on reasonably well with him, now.

The following Spring brought a visitor to Karen, who made a volcano out of her little mole-hill. He was a hard-bitten man, with a sparseness of words that made dealing with him no pleasure. He wanted to build a factory, for some unknown reason, on the fringe of Derrybridge.

'But why? It's only a village.'

'No, ma'am. It was a village. You've made it a town. I want to make capital out of the town.'

Karen took him to see Shenks, and Shenks was all for it. When Karen wanted to call Chris back, Shenks told her in effect that she could do as she liked about that, but the fact was, the whole thing had now got beyond them.

'I don't see,' Karen said. 'Why has it?'

Shenks sat back and half closed his eyes. There was a man called Philmore, who owned the land to the north of the village, and leased the houses. Two farmers and Shenks himself owned the rest of the land, and they also leased the houses. The village was part of the local Urban District.

Shenks said, in words of one syllable, as to a child, that if this factory owner came in, bought the land, built his factory and started up, other things would happen. He would build houses for his workers. They would want more shops. More buses. The thing would get big. They would become a town-size village, and need a council of their own. The thing would get beyond a woman's hands, Shenks repeated.

'Why do you want to come and build your factory here?' she asked the other man.

'It's the clay,' he said, briefly.

It appeared that it was a special kind of

308

local clay—a kind that he needed—and he needed it badly.

'How did you know it was here?' Karen asked, in wonderment, and looked at Shenks. Shenks was playing with a pencil, and said nothing.

'You told him,' she said, almost beside herself with fury. 'You fetched him down from—wherever he lives—and let him in on this. Why? You don't own the land he wants.'

'I didn't,' Shenks murmured.

'But you do now!' Karen whispered, horrified. 'You'd no business to do all this without consulting me.'

'You're not quite clear about this,' Shenks said. 'I'm only your partner so far as the store's concerned. The store and the bus service. I did this on the side. Nothing to do with you.'

'Well, you've got that wrong,' Karen said. 'It was our idea, Chris and me. It was a dead village when we came and put the people in work. We wanted a flourishing village, that's what it is, and that's what it's going to stay as. Our idea, remember? You just cashed in on it.'

'You can't patent an idea, miss,' the factory owner said. 'I'm going to cash in on it, too.'

'And Halliday flung in the towel, anyway,' Shenks said, rubbing his hands to denote that the argument was closed.

Karen flung out of the office, and glared

back up at it. She had had frosted glass windows put in the lower half of each window, so that the top floor of what had once been the shack, was now of a uniform tidiness. One half of the windows belonged to the inner office and the typist's room; the other windows were those of the work-rooms, where Miss Prynn and her two girls worked at turning out modern clothes for the store. One of the girls had blossomed out as a milliner.

The store looked nice. It had been painted a bright, fresh green. The old general store had been incorporated in it, and the carpenter, who had nurtured a fever for putting up new woodwork structures, had made good use of everything that came to his hand. The new building made the inn look older and shabbier than before, so they had painted it red.

She grinned a little, as she recalled the rash of painting that that had brought out. Everyone wanted to paint their little houses. Recklessly, Karen had supplied them with free paint, of as many bright colours as she could find, and also had window boxes put in for them. Outside the village, the other side of the bridge, she had had put up—to the vicar's disgust—a yellow board, which said, 'This is Derrybridge, the Garden Village', and had had the pleasure of seeing his disgust turn to amused admiration.

'You're indomitable, young woman,' he had said. 'To do so much, with such poor material.'

'If you mean the people, well, they were a miserable bunch at first,' Karen had admitted. 'But don't forget, I had plenty of money behind me.'

He had said nothing to that. She had swelled his fund for doing up the church, and endowed the various clubs he had been trying to run. In Chris's absence, she had been distracted about the cricket club, and discovered the vicar was as keen a cricketer as Chris, but always, in Derrybridge, it had been the question of money.

'Well, who cares, we've got plenty,' Karen had said, and equipped them with kit, and made them a present of a little clubhouse. Derrybridge. That name of bright hopes for her and Chris, until . . .

Chris walked in from the highway, where he had hitch-hiked on a lorry. He was dirty and travel-stained, and glared resentfully at her trim navy and white business dress.

From her, he looked round the place, twinkling with gawdy paint and gay with flowers, in the spring sunshine. 'This is Derrybridge, the Garden Village,' he quoted, bitterly, and thrust a crumpled newspaper at her. 'You're news, my girl.'

It was a national daily, and the article, though not front-page news, was at least on a

311

prominent position inside. It told all about what had been done to the village, and mentioned a Mrs. Pevensey as the money behind it, but the article led the public to think that the brains and the big noise in the venture was a Mr. Shenks.

Karen nearly exploded. 'Chris, you fool, you fool! You always turn up when I've been dying for you, and it's too late. Look, there he goes, the little blighter!'

She watched Shenks leaving the store, with the factory owner. 'The little devil, he told me nothing of this. I haven't even seen the papers this morning!'

'Who's with him?' Chris asked, in a still voice.

'A man he got down to build a factory on his land. He's going to make this a town, Shenks is, and he says I and the idea don't count any more. It's all his.'

Chris went over to Shenks and knocked him down.

'Chris! You didn't have to do that!' Karen cried.

The factory owner, who was Chris's height, said, 'Why don't you pick a man your own size?'

Chris said, 'All right, I will, at once.'

Karen sat on the bench outside the pub and watched them fighting. A crowd gathered, and formed a nice ring, but before it had had time to get settled, the fight was over. Chris

312

walked off, dusting himself. His nose was bleeding. Karen recalled the fight in the farmhouse, and watched him with mixed emotions. The crowd closed in on Shenks and the factory owner, and the local policeman took charge. He was also one or two other things in the village, and recognized Chris as the man who had started the prosperity, and took no notice of him.

'Where are you going, Chris?'

He looked at Karen. 'Where d'you think?'

'Off again, I suppose, after that spectacular bit of work. You wouldn't, of course, like to see what I've done with your idea, while you've been sulking all over the British Isles? You wouldn't like to come up to the office and look at the books, I suppose, just to see how much money I've put in, how much I've made, and what those two propose to rob me of?'

Chris nodded. 'All right.'

He followed her through the store, looking round at everything as he went, and up the carpenter's new wooden stairs to the offices. A girl who used to run errands half-heartedly for the store-keeper, was now the typist. She sat proudly and a trifle self-consciously at her new desk, in a navy frock Miss Prynn had made for her. She also answered the telephone.

Chris smiled sourly. He followed Karen into the inner office, and permitted her to

313

show him the company's books and he stopped looking sour.

The girl outside poked her head in presently, and said she was going to lunch. The crowd below had long since gone. Shenks had walked home. Someone had helped the factory owner over to the doctor's, to be patched up.

Karen, staring out of the window, over the top of the frosted glass, said, 'Shenks is right. It isn't a village any longer. It's a community.'

Chris didn't answer.

She turned to look at him, and found him behind her. He pulled her roughly into his arms, and pressed his lips down hard on hers.

When he at last let her go, he said, thickly, 'I don't care what the damned place is. I don't care about anything, Karen, except that I can't go on living without you.'

CHAPTER TWENTY-SIX

Chris was all for selling out their interest and getting away from the place, but Karen wouldn't have it.

'No, darling,' she said, over their steak pie and chips in the inn parlour, 'I've put too much work and thought into it all. I've spent too much energy chivvying people to get going. I've put a bit of my life into this, and—'

'—and what? Don't say you want to stay here for ever and ever?' Chris asked, appalled.

'No, darling,' she smiled. 'You know, I don't think either of us are fitted to do that. But I'm damned if I've got what it takes to let old Shenks get away with anything. I *know* he's used the partnership funds for this deal, and he's going to do me out of my profit.'

'You still love money so much.'

'No. No, I don't, that's the funny part of it. I've had so much to do with money this last two years, Chris, watching it to see what happened to it, playing with it, making and losing, that I don't think I'd care if I never saw the stuff again. No, it's the principle of the thing. I was forced to take Shenks in with me because I couldn't afford to make an enemy of him. I know they're right about anyone being able to cash in on the original idea. You can't stop that. But he's been using my money, and he's not going to get away with it.'

'Oh, well, if that's all,' Chris said, 'all we have to do is to get a solicitor bloke to take a look at the books and the bank accounts, and get him to cough up our share.'

'Solicitors! Harold, of course, I'd forgotten him,' Karen said. 'He'd be the bloke, he's been handling all the document side of the business all through.'

'Good girl,' Chris approved. 'I had a horrid feeling you might have been trying to do everything yourself.'

'Chris, you *are* pleased with what I've done, aren't you? Even though you don't care about Derrybridge any more?'

He was silent.

'Chris?' she pleaded.

'I don't think I can put into words, my pride, my pride in you, when I realized just what you had been up to,' he said, at last. 'I was hurt, a bit, to think I'd visited you all those times and you'd never let me in on it. But I don't suppose I gave you much opportunity, come to think of it.'

'I wanted so badly for you to say, let's go down and have a look at the place again. But you never did.'

'What are we going to do, Karen?'

'Heaven knows,' she said. 'I wonder if Harold could help us. D'you suppose there's any way out of such a Will?'

Chris shrugged. 'If there were, I should think he'd have told you, long before this.'

Karen telephoned Harold to say they were coming to see him. 'We're in trouble, financially, and you've got to be ruthless, Harold!'

He laughed. 'I was going to write to you next week, and ask you to come. There's

316

something I want to say to you, young woman.'

But although they saw him before then, he made them wait until the following week before he would tell Karen what it was he had wanted her for.

'I suppose we've got to be content with that, as you're going to make Shenks pay up everything. It's as well that you think you can, Harold, seeing as it's Matthew's money I've been flinging about.'

Harold's eyes twinkled, but he said nothing.

The following week, she and Chris were shown into his room, and he said without preamble: 'What's to-day, Karen?'

'I don't know. I never know dates,' she complained, looking at Chris.

'Strictly speaking, Mr. Halliday shouldn't be in on this interview, but in the circumstances, I think it doesn't matter. To-day is the second anniversary of Matthew's death.'

Karen whitened. Chris gripped her hand.

'I was instructed on that day to read a letter to you, Karen, from Matt. It's sealed.'

'Do you know what's in it, Harold?' Karen whispered.

'Of course I do. I helped him to compile it in decent English. But that's by the way.'

He read it out. It was very long, and though the English was undoubtedly Harold's legal style, the lecturing was Matthew's.

317

Karen slumped a little during the reading of it, but Chris looked first alert, then interested, and finally she caught a little of his excitement.

'Then that means Karen's free?' he broke in.

'Wait till Harold's finished reading,' Karen said.

'But good lord, it'll go on for ever by the sound of it,' Chris exploded. 'Does it mean, sir, that Karen's free?'

Harold smiled. 'I might have known I wouldn't be allowed to read it through to the end. I could insist, you know! But I'll put you out of your misery, both of you. It does. Karen is released from the obligations she has undertaken.' He pursed his lips to hide a tiny smile. 'You'll realize of course, that Matt took it for granted that Karen would do as she did. This is a cogent point. If she hadn't, then she'd have had the proceeds of the house and the money just the same.'

A long drawn breath escaped Karen. Tied to the house for two years, for nothing! A flicker of anger against Matthew overcame her. That sense of humour of his, and that love of showing people!

'Don't be angry, Karen,' Harold said, watching her. 'Matthew wanted to help you, to guide you. He thought he could do it better after his death than before. His idea was that you should chafe against the imprisonment of it all, as you did. He hoped you'd try and speculate with the money (as you have, in a sense) but he set a limit on the amount you could spend. If you'd overspent, you'd have had to make money to keep the place going, as that was part of the terms of the Will. He thought you wouldn't get into serious trouble in those two years, especially as you didn't know the time limit, and that if you'd had a thin time during that period, you'd have been cured, and ready to marry Chris.'

'Did he know?'

Harold smiled at Karen. 'It wasn't very difficult to read the signs. Even I knew.'

She flushed and avoided Chris's eye.

Harold said, 'When Matt knew he was dying, he said to me, "What d'you think'll happen when the young man finds she's mortgaged her future?" I said, "If I were him, I'd clear out". Matt said, "That's what I thought. So that leaves her with the village or horses to gamble with. What'll it be?" I ventured to suggest that it would be the village first, horses next. Was I right?'

'I've forgotten about racing,' Karen said, thoughtfully. 'Derrybridge got under my skin. But what puzzles me is, if Matt tried to stop me gambling, what was he doing, for heaven's sake?'

'At Matt's age,' Harold said, 'anyone can be forgiven a little flutter.'

'Well, then, we don't want to hear any

319

more, do we?' Chris said, impatient to be off.

'You're going to hear it to the end, both of you,' Harold said. 'But what are you in such a hurry for?'

'Well, no one has asked me what I've got to live on. It's all been, so far, about Karen's fortune. I just wanted to get Karen into a quiet corner and tell her about my wealth.' He couldn't help grinning a little, at Karen's expression.

'You? Wealth?' she gasped. 'Chris, it isn't the time for joking.'

'It's no joke. I was so darned fed-up with the whole thing, when I went abroad, that I spent my last bit from the factory on a bunch of sweepstake tickets. One of 'em got the jackpot.'

Harold flinched at the word 'jackpot', and permitted himself to lean back for a second and ruminate on these young people, who without caution or a thought for the next hour or two, flung their last few possessions into the gamble of the moment, and pulled it off.

'I suppose,' he broke in on their excitement, 'it isn't any use my mentioning any safe investments for all this money? Such things wouldn't interest either of you?'

The rest of Matthew's letter was read without interruption, though he didn't think they heard much of it. They sat looking into each other's eyes, as though they were alone.

He didn't dare wonder what new mad schemes they were planning, once they were free from Matthew's carefully woven bonds. He could only hope that Matthew's final words might sink in somewhere, and produce a good effect at a time when they were most needed.

'Gambling is the resource of the weak. Work is not only a necessity, but a duty. And life is a duty, too. Those who gamble away their future, often find they have lost. So, my beautiful Karen, remember, those who are careless about to-morrow, do not deserve to-day '

Photoset, printed and bound in Great Britain by REDWOOD PRESS LIMITED, Melksham, Wiltshire

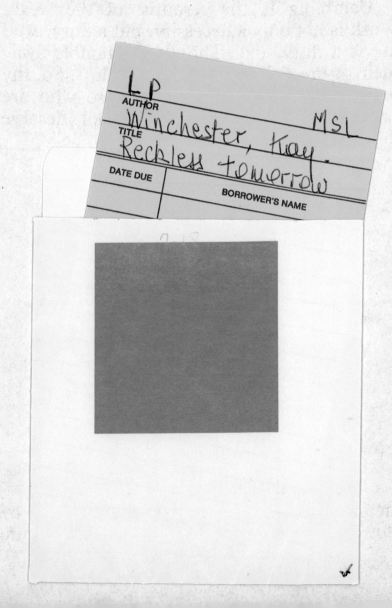